Unspeakable Magic

IRIS BEAGLEHOLE

For all my wonderful readers. Thank you for coming with me on this Myrtlewood journey so far. I couldn't have done it without you, and don't worry, there are plenty more adventures to come. You are all part of the magic, and I only hope that my stories continue to amuse and inspire you!

Blessed be
xx
Iris

One

A snowflake drifted down, between the purple trees.

"Look," said Rosemary, pointing to the perfect rosette pattern formed by the crystalised water. "Do you think it's snowing in Myrtlewood?"

Athena squinted at the snowflake. "It's an aberration," she said. "It shouldn't be snowing. Not in this region of the fae realm."

Their red hair fluttered around them in what should have been a breeze, only the air was strangely too thick and thin at the same time. The trees were not the colour trees should be, everything was far too purple, and even Athena looked different – elongated somehow with pointy ears. The whole place felt surreal. They were standing in a clearing near the castle of West Eloria, watching as fae servers set up an array of spectacular decorations.

Rosemary felt a chill that had nothing to do with the solitary

1

snowflake. She rubbed her forearms to warm them. "It's strange to be here without being on some kind of dangerous quest."

The only time she'd been to the fae realm before was to rescue her wayward daughter, and Rosemary had a slightly queasy feeling being back, though perhaps that was just the change in atmosphere.

Athena nodded. "Strange but nice." She appeared to be glowing.

Rosemary might not feel at home here, but Athena often said she did, and that being here felt relaxing and lovely. She felt a stab of fear that Athena might not want to return with her. To Rosemary, being in the fae realm only felt peculiar, and she longed to be home in Thorn Manor by the fire with a nice cup of tea and perhaps a cat on her lap, though at least the wedding was a welcome distraction from the dread surrounding her upcoming fortieth birthday which she was trying not to think about, especially as she'd been seeing an ageless vampire for the last several months.

Several fae dressed in gold moved to the tree in front of them and began sending up glowing sparkling lights.

"There you are," said Dain, strolling over to greet them wearing a dark purple embroidered suit.

"I can't believe this is all happening," said Athena. "And so fast."

Dain gave her a quizzical look. "It's been over a year and a day here."

Athena rolled her eyes. "Sure, but it's only been a few weeks in the earth realm and I'm still adjusting."

Rosemary shot her daughter an uneasy glance. They'd been

through so much recently, Athena's sort-of-ex-boyfriend-turned-foster-brother marrying her cousin was possibly a little much on top of everything else. However, almost everyone was relieved that Queen Áine didn't get her first wish of Athena marrying Cedar.

Fae customs were a little bit off, if you asked Rosemary, but no one seemed to be asking at the moment.

"Almost done," said Una, coming out from the side entrance of the enormous mushroom castle. She too was wearing fae finery, a deep green dress that looked to be made of leaves. Only Rosemary and Athena were wearing normal human clothes, having just arrived in the realm.

Una carried a tray of what looked like lemonade, though Rosemary was suspicious about consuming anything here so she hadn't dare try it. Being human here made her particularly vulnerable, whereas Athena and Una at least had their solid fae ancestry to keep them safe.

"I feel woozy," said Rosemary. "I think I need to sit down."

Una's mouth tightened in concern. "Come over here," she said, leading Rosemary to a small tree stump table with mushroom stools.

"Are you okay, Mum?" Athena asked, patting Rosemary on the shoulder.

"This place just doesn't agree with me," said Rosemary. "But I don't mean to be a drag. I'll be fine."

"I might have just the thing for you," said Una. She rummaged in her leafy green leather handbag and produced a small purple bottle.

"I feel like I'm in Wonderland," said Rosemary. "Will this make me grow or shrink?"

Una laughed. "Neither," she said. "It's a formula I've been working on to help humans adjust here. It was great when Ashwyn came to visit before Samhain."

Rosemary looked sceptically at the bottle, but decided if it was good enough for Una's gentle human sister she could probably handle it. "How will it help?"

"It kind of imbues you with fae magic, but in a subtle way, so your body adjusts to this place and you can even eat the food."

Rosemary grimaced. "Really?"

"Just do it, Mum. You're going to love the food here. Besides, you should be enjoying yourself. It would certainly help the rest of us."

"Sure, but I'm just adjusting to the idea of being 'enfaed'."

"It's subtle magic," said Una. "Basically like homeopathy. It should just very gently send signals to your body, energetically. Nothing too extreme!"

Rosemary sighed, opened the bottle, and put a tentative dropper-full under her tongue as Una instructed.

She felt an immediate tingle, along with a wave of anxiety, but as it subsided, her body relaxed. "Oh, nice. I'm actually starting to feel quite good."

Athena beamed at her. "I told you this place was cool."

Rosemary stretched out her arms with a sense of energy and mild euphoria. "I suppose I can get used to this."

"Excellent," said Una. "And thanks for being a guinea pig. We are going to have a bunch more humans coming through for the wedding and we'll need to be prepared in case they struggle to adjust."

Rosemary made a face and Athena laughed.

"What?" Una asked.

"Mum's just reacting to the idea of being a guinea pig," said Athena. "But don't worry. She'll adjust."

"I'd better go and check on things in the grand hall," said Dain. "See you soon!"

He skipped off and Rosemary sighed again, though this time it wasn't a resigned sigh, or a frustrated one. She was genuinely feeling quite relaxed as she watched the purple leaves dancing gently on the trees and the industrious fae decorating everything in sight. "Perhaps we can just have a nice quiet time, for the next little while," she said.

Athena laughed again. "Don't forget that the winter solstice is coming up soon."

Normally, Rosemary would have groaned, but in that moment she felt a lovely peacefulness – tranquillity that she didn't want to sacrifice for the sake of a good moan. Instead she laughed at the preposterousness of everything magical in their lives, and so did Una and Athena, and for a few minutes, all that could be heard around the clearing was the sound of their laughter.

Two

Athena wrapped her cloak around her shoulders. She was wearing a cornflower blue gown picked out for her by the Queen herself, and a matching silk cloak, but it wasn't quite warm enough. There was a definite chill in the air, though she'd seen no more stray snowflakes. She stood on the lower balcony of the fae castle out over the surrounding grounds, elaborately decorated with glowing lights.

Athena heard the sound of someone approaching. She was hoping to see Elise, but it was Ashwyn, instead. It had been ten days since Samhain and Athena had tried to text and call to no avail. Elise had had such a rough time, being possessed by the ghost of a poor murdered girl, but she'd been released of that burden, and the last time Athena had seen her at the cemetery on Samhain night she'd seemed herself again. Athena had tried to give her space. She knew Fleur and Elise had been sent an invite to the wedding and was hoping they'd make it.

Athena sighed and turned back out towards the deep violet forests. Technically, Elise was still her girlfriend. They'd never officially broken up, but perhaps everything she'd gone through had changed things between them.

"The service is about to start," said Ashwyn gently. "Apparently the Queen wants you to sit with her."

"Why do you think fae weddings are traditionally at night?" Athena asked as they made their way inside.

"Believe me, I'm not the one to ask about anything fae," Ashwyn said with a laugh.

Hundreds of guests had assembled in the enchanted gardens surrounding the castle of West Eloria. It was a fantastic sight. The whole area was decorated elaborately, with thousands of tiny sparkling lights that hovered in the air above them.

Athena made her way awkwardly outside, noticing a murmur running through the assembled fae at the entrance. It was strange to be a princess here when she hardly knew what that meant.

As she walked, she noticed some familiar faces in the crowd, including her former nemesis, Beryl, who sat next to two of her sisters and smiled weakly at Athena.

They'd never be friends, exactly, but perhaps after Samhain they were no longer enemies. It shouldn't have been a surprise to see her at the wedding, after all. Beryl had been close to Finnigan even before he'd redeemed himself.

Queen Áine sat on what was more of a throne than a chair, set off to one side to get the best view of the ceremony. Athena took her seat next to her grandmother. Dain sat on the other side. And the crowd hushed as the fae celebrant began to speak.

It was strange to see Finnigan there, in his golden suit, so much more grown up than Athena had known him to be. There was a lot of history between them, which had made things complicated at times, but she was happy for him. He'd found a place to belong and a home here, with Cedar, who wasn't all that bad as long as Athena didn't have to be the one marrying him. She even shed a tear during the exchange of vows as the two lovebirds beamed at each other, vowing not only their love and care, personally, but for the whole region of West Eloria and the fae realm.

Queen Áine nodded approval at that part, and soon the formal ceremony was over and the guests milled around the gardens, eating exquisite finger food and dancing to the pan pipes played by wood sprites. Athena noticed Sherry standing with Neve, Little Mei, and a heavily pregnant Nesta.

She was grateful that Una's potion had been so successful at helping them adjust to the fae realm. Thea and Clio rushed up to Athena, giggling and grabbing hold of her hands, and begging her to spin them around in the air. The other foundling children quickly joined in, and Athena spent a good half hour playing with them amid joyful shrieks and laughter, until she needed a little break to catch her breath. She suggested they embark on a treasure hunt in the gardens. As they skipped and sprinted off Athena hoped her father was right in his assurances that the whole area had been child-proofed.

She brushed a stray strand of hair behind her ear and looked out towards the gardens where the children were now playing with some gentle fae creatures, floating, ethereal in shades of pink and green, perhaps some kind of forest sprites.

Rosemary joined her wearing a silver gown and holding an

enormous plate of canapes. "You were right, the food here is amazing."

"I think the waiters are supposed to be the ones holding those," said Athena with a giggle.

"No, I asked for this one especially," Rosemary said proudly. "It has two of each thing!"

"Good thinking," said Athena, amused. "You won't miss out on trying anything."

"Exactly – ooh you have to taste this pink thing. I have no idea what it is, but it reminds me of carnival rides. I wonder if I can replicate it in chocolate form."

Athena giggled, but her laughter was cut short by a disturbance. She turned to see the crowd parting as a woman dressed in baggy ripped jeans and a hoodie broke through. Her hair was inky black and it took Athena a moment to recognise her. "Fleur?"

Elise's mother rushed over to her and Rosemary, fighting off the guards that tried to restrain her.

"Stop," Athena said. "Leave her."

The guards reluctantly followed her orders, standing back warily.

"She's gone," said Fleur. "I've looked everywhere...but it was no use."

"What do you mean?" Rosemary asked.

"Elise," said Athena, fighting the realisation that was sinking in.

Fleur nodded as tears pooled down her face. They guided her over to the table where Rosemary had sat earlier and coaxed her to tell them what was going on.

Fleur hadn't been there on Samhain. She didn't know Elise had been restored to her former self.

"She didn't come home that night?" Athena asked, cold dread taking over her insides.

Fleur shook her head. "Since Elise had gone missing I'd gone across the country to track down her father, wondering if he knew anything about where she was. He was always a scoundrel. I thought he might have had a hand in her disappearance..."

Athena merely shook her head in horror. It had been days. Weeks. Where had Elise gone?

"I got home to find the wedding invitation," Fleur continued. "And that's when I realised you didn't know. I went to your house, but you were gone. I asked everyone about Elise and pieced together the puzzle as much as I could. It was the cemetery..."

"Samhain night," said Athena. "That's when I last saw her, but I was sure she was going home with the others. She seemed... fine."

Fleur shook her head. "I went there. It felt awful – the atmosphere of the graveyard. But I kept going until I reached the tree."

"The yew tree," said Rosemary.

Fleur nodded. "That's where I found this." She held up a note. It was hastily scrawled in Elise's handwriting.

I know you don't understand, but this is something I have to do. To carve my own destiny. I love you. Goodbye.

. . .

It felt as if the entire world was spinning into an inconceivable void.

Athena sank to the ground. "Elise is gone." Her words didn't sound like her own.

She felt Rosemary's hand on her shoulder.

Her heart squeezed tight as if it were in a vice.

"Where did you find it?" Athena asked motioning to the note, but she felt in her soul that she already knew the answer.

"I found it in the yew tree," said Fleur. "It was sticking out, as though the tree had...swallowed it, had swallowed...her!"

"No!" said Athena. "She can't..."

But it was too late.

She had.

"Elise must have slipped through before the gateway fully closed," said Rosemary. "But that means she's gone to the Underworld."

Athena couldn't breathe, or maybe she no longer wanted to. In that moment, everything went black.

Three

"Athena!" Rosemary felt her gut drop as her daughter fell to the ground.

"What is it? What happened?" Dain cried, running over to where Rosemary and a small group were gathered around their daughter.

Una felt Athena's pulse and then placed a hand on her forehead. "She's okay. It's some kind of magic-induced shock, I think. When Fleur told her about Elise, her powers must have short-circuited."

"Oh no," said Rosemary.

Fleur looked down, as if guilty.

"Actually, that probably saved a whole lot of lives," said Dain. "Athena is so powerful. Imagine if all that burst out, uncontrolled. But what do you mean about Elise?"

Rosemary narrowed her eyes at Dain.

"Did you just nonchalantly accuse our daughter of almost killing everyone by accident and then change the subject?"

Dain shrugged. "I'm just saying it's lucky she's like one of those power boards with the little button that pops out instead of going supernova on us."

Rosemary shook her head in disbelief. Come to think of it, Dain had always possessed a child-like wonder when it came to simple electrical gadgets. "The signs were there all along that you were a lost fae prince, weren't they?"

He furrowed his brow as if trying to work out whether she was insulting him.

Just then, Fleur crumpled forward in distress. Rosemary reached for her. "It's not your fault," she said as Fleur sobbed on her shoulder. "Tell Dain what you found."

Moments later, Dain and Queen Áine had been filled in on the details and it was decided that they'd transport Athena back to the earth realm to recover in the world she knew best.

Rosemary's relief eased the tension in her shoulders as they carried Athena back through the portal.

She still worried about Athena, but felt instinctually that all the girl needed was a rest at home and some good cups of tea – at least physically. The emotional side was far more complicated.

She looked down at her gown, and then back at the worried faces of Finnigan and Cedar. It was a shame that a happy occasion had to be cut short.

She'd actually begun to quite enjoy herself at the wedding until the shock with Athena, but she'd much rather be at home at a time like this, rather than in a strange and unusual fairy land.

Rosemary stepped towards the portal, following Dain and the

enchanted stretcher bearing Athena, when something caught her wrist. She turned to see Queen Áine, glowing and resplendent and slightly unnerving as always.

"Uhh, yes?" said Rosemary, still unsure what the appropriate way to greet her daughter's royal fae grandma was.

"There's an ancient prophecy," the Queen said in a low whisper. "I've been thinking about this for the past few days. It keeps surfacing in my mind and I'm sure it's relevant to the situation at hand."

Rosemary's gut tightened. She'd had enough chaos for one lifetime – an ancient prophecy was the last thing she needed – but she had a sinking feeling that this was important, and that like it or not, she had to know about it.

Queen Áine continued. "It tells of a fae-witch who will hold the key to unravelling the mysteries of the past and the fate of the future. My sister, whom you know as the Morrigan, is sure it's about her, but I've been reflecting on it lately and I wonder if it could be..."

"Athena?" Rosemary asked.

Queen Áine nodded. "That is what I'm coming to suspect. She wields so much power for one so young."

Rosemary's heart began to thud wildly in her chest. An ancient prophecy sounded ominous and dangerous. "What else does the prophecy say?"

The queen waived her delicate hand through the air vaguely. "That is the unfortunate thing."

"Don't tell me, it's so ancient that no one remembers what it says and the details have been lost to time?" Rosemary had to brace herself not to roll her eyes like a teenager.

14

"Not exactly," said Queen Áine. "Rather, it is so old that very many stories and songs have been told and sung about it. There is no consensus on the details."

"Great. So there might as well be no prophecy at all," said Rosemary impatiently. She wanted to follow after Athena and forget all about creepy ancient foretellings.

"It is no light matter, Rosemary Thorn," said another voice, interrupting the conversation and making Rosemary jump.

"Elspeth?"

The ancient druid priestess had been among the wedding guests and was now approaching behind the fae queen, her wise eyes boring into Rosemary, contrasting sharply with her ageless face. She wore a gown that looked to be made of moss and bark, delicately woven so that she could blend in both in a forest and at a ball, or a fae wedding as the case may be, but her staring made Rosemary uncomfortable.

Rosemary shook her head. "I'm sorry, but I don't know what to make of any of this."

Elspeth cleared her throat and then said quietly, "There will come a time when the very fabric of the world is unravelling, and she must rise – she who is both fae and witch, light and dark, open and strong. She will face the paradox and save all realms from destruction."

A tingle ran through Rosemary, which shimmered right to her core, resonating in a haunting way. It was a recognition of something deep and ancient and viscerally true.

She took a deep breath and slowly exhaled. "How can we help? How can we prepare her?"

"We can only do so much," said Queen Áine, patting Rosemary gently on her arm. "She must do the rest herself. We can only carry our children so far, the rest they must walk alone."

Rosemary shook her head as the queen and druid priestess receded into the distance, which meant she was already moving through the portal, without even realising she'd made it there. She wasn't sure whether it had floated closer to her, or whether she'd stepped away in shock at the revelations, but it was too late to go back now. The world around had shifted and she was standing in Finn's creek, with Dain looking at her, somewhat impatiently – at least until he saw the expression on her face.

"What is it?" he asked.

"You don't want to know."

Four

Rosemary put the kettle on for tea. As the water boiled, she looked out of the kitchen window across the garden to see snowflakes beginning to fall.

Winter's coming.

Her mind flashed back to the solitary snowflake that they'd seen gliding through the air in the fae realm, so out of place. Perhaps there was more interconnectedness between the two worlds than she'd realised.

She finished making the tea and began carrying the tray back to the living room when she heard a muffled groan. "Athena?"

Athena was lying on the sofa by the fire. The idea of taking her upstairs had seemed too hard, and Rosemary wanted to keep an eye on her. So they'd set her up near the fireplace. Dain was sitting next to her on the couch, reading a newspaper - something he said he'd taken to doing recently to keep up with current events. Newspapers seemed strangely old-fashioned and the irony did not escape Rosemary, who couldn't ever remember him doing such a thing back in the days when they were together. He put down the paper and reached over to place a hand on Athena's shoulder. "It's alright, love. You're safe."

"What's happening? I was having the strangest dream," said Athena, looking from one parent to another. "But...you're still dressed for the wedding. It did happen." Athena groaned again. This time it was the sound of grief. "Elise is gone, isn't she?" Tears ran down her face.

"That's what we fear," said Rosemary. "But who knows what's really happened? It could be..."

"No, Mum. Fleur found a note in the yew tree. Elise wrote that note."

"What if it's a trick?" said Dain. "Somebody might be trying to catch you out, you know? Playing power games on the royal fae. Maybe they've got Elise locked up somewhere."

Rosemary gave Dain a look. "As if it would be better for her to be kidnapped by nefarious forces!"

"I don't know, just keep an open mind is all I'm saying," said Dain.

"Dad!" said Athena.

Dain raised his arms in surrender.

Athena tried to push herself up off the couch.

"Wait. Take it easy, love," said Rosemary.

Athena collapsed back down.

"You've had a shock. You need to rest," Rosemary continued.

"I can't rest," Athena yelled. "I need to find Elise. Fleur's been out of her mind and I had no idea anything was even wrong. This is my fault."

"How was it your fault?" asked Dain. "You weren't the one who ran off to the Underworld of your own free will."

Rosemary and Athena looked at each other. It was an uncomfortable reminder of another such note that Athena left for her mother when she had run off to the fae realm.

"Do you think she's really gone of her own free will?" Athena asked, looking miserable. "She left me..."

"She left all of us," Fleur said from the doorway. "It's not your fault – don't take it upon yourself."

"Oh there you are," said Rosemary. She had sent Fleur upstairs to have a shower and lent her some clothes. The poor woman shouldn't be alone at a time like this. Not after the last ten days of horror that she had been through alone. "You can stay here as long as you like."

"I don't want to trouble you," said Fleur.

"No," said Athena, "please stay. We need to stick together. We need to figure out how to help Elise. We've got to do whatever we can. Anything..."

"Thank you," said Fleur, sounding as if she were biting back tears.

Rosemary passed her a cup of tea with an extra dollop of Marjie's special remedy. She was missing Marjie at that particular moment. Her friend who was always so warm and nurturing and stern at times, but in a good way. Marjie had been living with them in Thorn Manor since her husband, Herb's, shocking death, but they seemed to pass each other like ships in the night, living their own separate lives.

Just then, there was a bustling sound and Marjie burst into the room holding two cake boxes as if Rosemary's thoughts had summoned her. Marjie had been at the wedding reception too. But of course, knowing what was going on, she must have thought to stop in at her tea shop for baked treats before coming home.

She dropped the boxes on the nearest table, wrapping Rosemary and then Fleur in warm hugs. Then she descended on Athena, perching on the edge of the couch and placing her palm against the girl's forehead.

"Deary, deary me," said Marjie. "We've had quite a shock. But don't you worry, my dear. It will all work out, you'll see."

Athena wiped back tears. "How can you say that? We don't know."

"No. You're right," said Marjie sternly. "We don't know. But that's what we need right now. We need to think thoughts that will get us through the night and tomorrow and the next and we must do what we can to get our girl back home safe and sound where she belongs."

Everyone in the room nodded solemnly, and the corner of Rosemary's mouth twitched, despite the circumstances. Marjie was so warm and nurturing and stern at exactly the right times.

"We'll leave you to rest, dear," said Marjie to Athena, after placing a warm pasty, and a cream and jam scone on a plate next to her cup of tea. "We'll all clear out and let you have a little nap."

"Alright, but just a little one," Athena said, her energy clearly waning. "And then we'll figure out how to get Elise back."

Rosemary nodded and ushered her friends out, including

Dain, who was reluctant to leave his daughter. Rosemary appreciated his new parental instincts. They were certainly something he had been developing over the past few months – or perhaps years – considering the way time had apparently stretched while he'd been in the fae realm. Oddly enough, Finnigan was a good influence on the equally wayward Dain.

Back in the kitchen, Fleur cupped her face and moaned. "It's hopeless, isn't it?" She raised her arms in the air as if reaching for the impossible. "Hopeless…it's like every pathway is a dead end."

"There, there," said Marjie as she patted Fleur on the shoulder.

"What do we know about the Underworld?" Rosemary asked.

"Not a great deal," said Marjie.

"That's right." Dain shook his head. "It's a mysterious place. Of course, there are many tales of Tír na nÓg and Mag Mell, the land of honey under the sea."

"That's a little bit too much to grasp all at once," said Rosemary.

"But the Underworld, by its very nature, is mysterious," said Marjie, putting her hands on her hips. "Don't fancy trying to navigate there myself. But…"

"But what?" said Athena from the doorway.

Rosemary turned to her. "You're supposed to be resting, love."

"I can't," Athena argued. "I really can't. I tried to close my eyes. And all I can see is Elise's face."

Fleur went to her and hugged her. The two stood together, consoling each other for a moment.

"Now look here," said Marjie. "Just because we don't know, that doesn't mean that there aren't ways and means. It just means we'll have to find them. If I were you, I'd go straight to Agatha Twigg."

"The historian?" said Fleur.

"That's right."

"She's not always a great deal of help," said Rosemary.

"And perhaps she won't be now either," said Marjie. "But I'm sure she'll know a thing or two. And there may be documented accounts of people making it there. If there's one thing Agatha is good at, it's separating facts from fiction."

"The problem with the Underworld is that there are so many different accounts of it," said Dain. "Even among the fae...so that's what you need to figure out. Which ones are true and false."

"Do you think we could get there through the fae realm?" Athena asked.

He shook his head. "That myth is definitely not true. In the past, I think a lot of humans have confused the two realms, partly because they knew so little about the fae realm itself. But we know that it's an entirely different place."

Athena choked back a sob.

"But there are other realms, too," said Marjie. "The realm of dreams, for instance. Legend has it that dreams can be a doorway to anywhere."

"Sure, it might be possible, if you can access it," said Dain. "Though that's a pretty big hypothetical. Lucid dreaming is one thing I might have dabbled with a little in the past, but you need somebody incredibly skilled to navigate *that* place. You think the fae realm is strange and unpredictable, the Dreamrealm is more

22

like a chaotic buffet of surreal surprises, and not always the good kind."

Athena shook her head. "We need more than just dreams. Dreams make no sense and we absolutely need sense right now. We need a plan. We need reality."

"We'll get there," said Rosemary. "I promise, I'll help. I'll do whatever I can."

Athena turned towards the window, the dusky light. "It's snowing," she said in a soft, high voice, almost like a child. She turned to Rosemary and looked her in the eye. "That snowflake in the fae realm, do you think it could have been Elise that sent it?"

Rosemary was baffled for a moment. The thought hadn't occurred to her and it seemed totally unlikely. But perhaps that was what Athena needed right at that moment, some kind of sign.

"It's possible," she said. It wasn't a lie, but it wasn't exactly the whole truth either. She wrapped her arm around her daughter's shoulder and they stared out at the falling snow.

"Maybe," said Athena, "wherever Elise is, it's wintery there too and she's sending us a message."

Rosemary smiled. It was a nice thought. Of course, the winter solstice was approaching and the weather wasn't entirely ill-fitting of the season. Though the snow did seem a little early. She squeezed her daughter's shoulder. "We'll get organised and we'll do whatever we can."

"Thanks, Mum," Athena said, sniffling. "I appreciate it."

Later that night, when everyone was tucked up in bed and the house was silent, Rosemary lay awake. She'd given Athena the last of Ursula's sleeping draught, which had blessedly helped her to fall asleep straight away. Rosemary wished she had more on hand. A chilly loneliness haunted her. Dain was a night owl and was probably still awake in bed, reading, in the guest room where he sometimes stayed. Perhaps he would be in the mood for a brandy nightcap, but it wasn't a drink Rosemary was craving.

She reached for her phone on the nightstand and sent a message to Burk.

Can't sleep. Nightmare of a day. Long story. Come over?

She put her phone down, turned over, and buried her face in her pillow in an attempt to stem the unexpected tide of emotions that came flooding in. It had been a terrible day and she was terrified for Elise, and for Athena. What if the girl was lost and never coming back? After all, the Underworld was the realm of the dead.

If she was honest with herself, she'd also been avoiding Burk, yet again. Her impending birthday definitely had something to do with it, but she wasn't ready to unpack that can of worms. Not yet.

It was only moments before a soft tapping sounded on her window.

With a wave of Rosemary's hand, it opened and an incredibly handsome vampire climbed into the room.

"Sneaking around like teenagers again, are we?" he said in his silky voice.

"If only," said Rosemary. "No. Scratch that. Being a teenager was awful."

24

"Care to tell me about your nightmare day?" he asked, taking a step closer to the bed.

"Maybe in a bit," said Rosemary. "But first, I'd prefer if you'd take my mind off it, completely."

In the blink of an eye, Burk closed the distance between them, and all disturbing thoughts melted away.

Five

Athena awoke, stretching into the morning light, and for a moment she could almost believe that it had all been a nightmare, but the truth lingered on the back of her tongue like a stubborn bitter taste.

Her friends had sent messages and tried to call, but Athena couldn't face them. Seeing them, or even talking to them, would make her feel even more guilty than she already did. Elise had gone, and Athena had done nothing to save her. The note might have sounded like it was of her own free will, but Elise had only just been freed from possession and couldn't possibly have been in her right mind. Furthermore, Athena feared the Morrigan herself might have taken her, claiming her mistakenly as a dark Underworldly thing, rather than as the bright, beautiful, rainbow creature she truly was.

Rosemary had summoned the Morrigan mistakenly in the past, and also on purpose at Samhain, but both times had brought great risk. Besides, if a goddess had taken Elise she might not be keen to hand her back easily, and ruffling the feathers of a powerful deity didn't seem like a wise course of action.

The whole situation seemed hopeless, but Athena couldn't indulge in wallowing. She had to *do* something. She pushed herself out of bed and dressed in jeans and a short leather jacket which she'd chosen for its good pockets.

She scanned her room, including her secret hidden library and her shelves of potions and charms.

What will I need?

The surge of energy that had driven her out of bed abated and she was left feeling heavy and hopeless.

I have no idea...

She had the urge to throw herself back into bed, but resisted. Wallowing in self-pity wasn't going to get her anywhere. Instead, she made her way slowly downstairs, carefully navigating the perils of her own mind. She couldn't help but feel guilty. What had she done to drive Elise away? What could she have done differently?

It's not your fault, Dain's voice cut into her mind.

Athena blushed slightly. She didn't realise she'd been thinking so loudly or unguardedly that her thoughts had cut through to her father's mind.

Sorry.

"No," said Dain, approaching the bottom of the stairs. "Don't be sorry. Have pancakes." He held up a plate stacked high with them.

Athena couldn't help but laugh a little.

"Come on." He led her through to the kitchen table where Fleur and Rosemary already sat.

27

Fleur's hair was a deep navy colour, much darker than her usual electric blue, but not as black as the day before. She was pushing syrupy pancakes around her plate but stood up when she saw Athena and gave her a big hug.

"Alright, let's—" Athena started.

"Breakfast," Dain cut in insistently, serving Athena a large portion of pancakes, onto which he sprinkled sugar and squeezed lemon. "You'll need your strength if you're going to be useful."

Athena nodded and accepted tea from Rosemary as well, before attempting to eat, though her stomach felt like a solid brick of fear. She was just lifting a second forkful to her mouth when there was a knock at the door.

Athena turned her head and started to rise, but Dain stopped her. "I mean it. Eat. And don't think about getting up until you've had a proper meal."

Athena sighed and rolled her eyes but did as she was told.

Moments later, Rosemary returned to the room. Detective Neve followed closely behind her, looking flustered as she greeted them briskly.

"I take it this is a work related visit?" said Rosemary.

"Do you know anything about what happened to Elise?" Athena asked at the same time.

"Yes it is a work call, and I'm afraid I don't know much about the Elise situation yet – though I'm here to take formal statements from you about the last time you saw her."

Athena lowered her gaze back to her barely-eaten breakfast. "Oh, I see." She tried to take another bite, mostly because Dain was staring at her. *Why did he have to pick now of all times to be a concerned parent?*

I heard that.

Athena narrowed her eyes.

"And there's something else," said Neve. "I got a call last night about a mysterious death."

Everyone in the room looked at her in alarm.

"Not Elise!" said Fleur.

Neve shook her head. "It's probably unrelated, but I thought you should know since..."

"It's magical?" said Rosemary.

Neve nodded. "We might require your consultancy services. But it's probably best I talk to you and Dain alone."

"No," said Athena. "Please just tell us what's going on."

Neve looked around at all of them. "I suppose you're of age," she said to Athena. "And maybe the expertise of everyone in this room could be of help...if your parents don't mind, that is."

Athena looked from Rosemary to Dain, expecting resistance, but apparently their parenting interests lay primarily in feeding her this morning. Dain simply shrugged, Rosemary nodded, and Athena breathed a small sigh of relief. She didn't have the energy to waste on picking fights with her parents, and perhaps they felt the same way at this point.

"Late last night," said Neve, pacing the floor, "after we got home from the wedding, I got a phone call. A man had been discovered dead in his cabin. Apparently, some neighbours noticed a lack of smoke in his chimney and decided to check up since it was a cold night with the first snowfall..."

"Anyone we know?" Rosemary asked.

Neve shook her head. "Probably not. Mr. Thompson was a reclusive hermit who lived on the outskirts of the village. He was an old man, so at first we thought he might have died of natural causes, especially given the cold night, but when we went to investigate we found him frozen solid in his bed, with a snowflake on his forehead."

Athena and Rosemary looked at each other.

"What?" Neve asked.

"It's probably nothing," said Rosemary. "But we saw a snowflake in the fae realm, floating in the air."

Dain shook his head. "In West Eloria? Impossible."

"It did seem out of place," said Athena, her mind racing. "Maybe..."

Rosemary shook her head. There was no point in jumping to speculations about Elise. Not yet.

"Was there anything else strange at the scene?" Dain asked.

Neve nodded. "His pet raven was there, on the windowsill, still alive but trapped in ice that was covering its claws."

"A raven reminds me of the Morrigan," said Rosemary.

Athena shook her head. "No, it was his pet. Besides, the Morrigan isn't a winter goddess and she'd hardly want to attack the raven, would she?"

Rosemary shrugged. "Who knows? She's not exactly predictable."

Fleur shook her head. "I don't understand, are you saying there's a connection to Elise?"

"Probably not," said Neve. "But we won't discount the possibility. Though Elise left a note, it's possible she was abducted, and whoever did that may also be involved in other sinister activities."

Athena shuddered. "You're saying someone might have forced her to write that note?"

Rosemary put down her cup of tea. "Maybe they're trying to send us on a wild goose chase to the Underworld as a distraction."

"That's what I said before," Dain muttered. "But no one ever listens to me."

Athena raised an eyebrow at her father and then turned her attention back to Neve. "I agree about not discounting possibilities, but I don't think the note was a trick. I'm not sure why, but it just feels...intuitively...like Elise wrote it all of her own accord."

Fleur let out a sob. "She left us. I don't understand it either, but I think you're right, Athena."

Rosemary and the detective looked at each other sceptically before Neve turned her attention back to Fleur. "I'll take your formal statement now, if that's okay?"

Fleur nodded. "I'm sorry I didn't come in earlier...I was frantic and I didn't think the police could help."

"It's okay," said Neve. "We'll do whatever we can."

She led Fleur to the living room, leaving Athena alone with her parents.

Rosemary sighed and Athena cleared her throat. "I meant what I said about Elise writing that note and going of her own accord," she said. "But that doesn't mean she isn't involved."

"Love," said Rosemary, approaching and putting her hand on Athena's shoulder. "I know you want to make a connection between the snowflakes and Elise, but it may just be a coincidence."

"But it would be a sign," Athena said. "That she's..."

The tears came, hot and fast, and Athena felt her mother's arms wrapping around her.

"We have to believe she's alive," said Rosemary. "Even if she doesn't have the power to send us messages through the snow. Besides, the last thing we want is to implicate her in that poor man's death."

Athena sighed. "Maybe it was an accident. Maybe she was trying to come back...or send me a message and it went wrong."

"We just don't know," said Rosemary, and Athena had to concede that she was right. She needed to believe that Elise was alive and maybe that was distorting her perception of reality so that everything seemed connected. She shook herself. *I have to think clearly.*

That's the spirit, said Dain.

Out of my head!

She pulled back and looked at her mother. "You're right, we don't know. But we're going to find out."

Six

That afternoon, Marjie announced she'd arranged for them to see Agatha Twigg at her house the next morning. In the meantime, they spent the day scouring Granny Thorn's magical library, trying to find anything that might be useful.

As Dain and Marjie had said, there were many different accounts of the Underworld, but it was hard to figure out what might be a reputable source. Athena was supposed to be back at school, but Rosemary had called to let them know that she wouldn't be able to make it in for a while. She wasn't in a fit state and probably wouldn't be until Elise was back safe and sound. Rosemary crossed her fingers and silently wished for the girl's safe return.

It was mid-morning when Rosemary and Athena arrived at the old Twigg farm. Agatha had said they were not to come until after 10 a.m., as she liked to have a good sleep in. Fleur and Dain had chosen to come with them.

Rosemary had only ever seen Agatha Twigg in town before, so it felt oddly personal to be going to her house. Rosemary got the impression that Agatha was quite a guarded character.

They parked in front of the small farm cottage and made their way up through the overgrown blackberry brambles and rose bushes, which were now covered in a dusting of snow that strangely hadn't seemed to kill off the late blooms. Rosemary briefly wondered if that was a Myrtlewood thing, or if there was something particularly magical about the snow.

She made a note to ask about it sometime and knocked on the bright green front door, which had a small brass goblin knocker. The goblin face moved, making Rosemary jump away in fear of being bitten.

"Who's there?" the knocker said in a voice that sounded like Agatha's.

"Rosemary Thorn, coming to see you," Rosemary replied.

"Oh, yes," Agatha said, and the door opened to reveal a very tiny woman.

Rosemary recognised Ms Marla Twigg, the librarian from the school, instantly, especially since Myrtlewood Academy had been based inside her house for a term. She vaguely recalled her first name was Marla.

"Ms Thorns." She nodded to them and then to Fleur and Dain. "My aunt's right through this way. You'll be having tea?"

Rosemary shook her head, but Athena put a hand on her shoulder and said, "Always accept tea, it's important."

"Okay, thank you," Rosemary said, and Marla led them inside.

The house seemed to be much larger on the inside than it

appeared, with many passageways branching off in different directions. They were led towards a large oak door.

"She's in there," said Marla Twigg, and then added, "I'll be right back with your tea."

She disappeared down the hallway.

Rosemary and Athena looked at each other.

"Do we knock?" Athena said.

"It's only polite," Rosemary replied.

Athena raised her fist to knock on the door. However, it swung open before she had the chance. Nobody was standing behind it. They looked around tentatively.

"Now I know why Ms Twigg always complained about the school library being so small," Athena muttered.

The library they found themselves in was enormous, with dozens of shelves and rows of books.

"Through here," a scratchy voice called out, and they followed the sound, weaving through the rows of shelves until they reached a more open space.

A large mahogany desk stood in front of a bay window, and Agatha sat behind it, wearing spectacles which she peered over at the visitors in a curious way as if they were animals in a zoo.

"Right, then," she said. "Take a seat." Though there were none. With a wave of her hand, four wooden chairs appeared, although they were not particularly comfortable. Rosemary got the impression that Agatha was not expecting them to stay for very long – just a quick sit-down and a cup of tea.

They took their seats and Marla reappeared, bringing tea. She began to pour it without asking what they wanted. Rosemary was surprised to find that the tea she received was exactly as she liked it and wondered if Marla had some kind of second sense for tea, like Marjie did.

As soon as the tea was poured, Marla left the room, leaving them alone with Agatha. "Now, tell me, what is it you want from me?" Agatha said.

"We need to know about the Underworld," Athena said before launching into the story about Elise disappearing, muddling it somewhat with snowflakes and the unexpected death of the hermit in the woods.

Fleur sat at her side, nodding pensively as Athena went through the whole story.

"Now, now, one thing at a time," Agatha said.

"Start with the Underworld," Rosemary said. "We need to know what is actually true about it, compared to all the stuff that's made up."

Agatha stared at her, giving her a long hard look. "You want to go there, don't you? You want to put on your hiking boots and stroll into the Underworld and bring your friend back. You know that's just not possible."

Athena squirmed in her seat. "We need to get her back."

Agatha laughed, not in amusement or even cruelly. It was a hollow laugh as if it all just seemed particularly unlikely. "Very little is known about the Underworld," she said. "It's not like your realm"—she waved to Dain—"where people can come and go through portals if they find the means. There is no door to the Underworld. No route. There is no portal that can get you there."

Athena sighed in defeat.

"That's not to say it's impossible," Agatha said cautiously.

"You just said it was," Rosemary pointed out.

"It can't be impossible," Athena said. "Elise must have gotten there somehow on Samhain."

"Ah," Agatha said, raising a finger. "That is the opportunity. That is when the veil between our world and the Underworld is the thinnest."

"But we can't wait for almost a year!" Fleur said, aghast, her face even paler.

Agatha shook her head. "Pity. That would have been by far the easiest."

"Do you think we could ask the Morrigan?" Rosemary said.

Agatha visibly shuddered. "I daren't if I were you."

"It's not like we haven't asked her for things before, though," Athena said. "And she's sometimes been helpful."

"There is always a price to pay with the Morrigan," Agatha said. "And I dare say you're paying it right now."

A chill ran down Rosemary's spine. "You're saying that when we asked her for help on Samhain, she took Elise in response?"

Agatha shrugged. "I'm not saying that she plucked the girl from this realm and dragged her forth. But it's fated thing, like the concept of karma. There must be a balancing. Perhaps if the Morrigan wasn't called upon to help, then the girl would never have gotten the idea in her head to go to the Underworld. Besides, who even gave her a piece of paper to write that note?"

"How do you know what happened that night?" said Dain. "We didn't tell you about that."

"Everyone knows already. It's the word about town."

Rosemary's eyes narrowed suspiciously. "Are there any books?" she asked, finally realising there was no point in trying to challenge an old crone like Agatha. It would get her nowhere.

Agatha waved her arms about, gesturing to the library around. "There are many books, as you've no doubt discovered in your own house. Books are just as full of speculation as the town gossip. Which ones tell us anything useful, or even true? I'm not even an expert on this particular field."

Athena's shoulders slumped forward.

"But," Agatha continued, "Benjamin Thorax is, and he lives not too far from here. I could take you to him."

"Really?" Rosemary said, hope in her voice. "You'd do that?"

"As long as we leave soon, I should have the time."

Rosemary and Athena shot each other a glance. What did Agatha have apart from time? She was often just hanging about the pub. Perhaps that was her priority.

"All right, then. Let's go," Rosemary said. They piled into the Rolls Royce. Agatha wanted to drive, but Rosemary placated her with the passenger seat instead.

"Lucky it's roomy back here," said Marjie, propping herself behind Rosemary.

Dain happily took the middle seat, insisting it had the best view, while Fleur and Athena managed to share a seatbelt.

"You really should get this lovely old vehicle expanded," Agatha muttered in a disapproving tone as she looked at the four passengers packed into the back seat like sardines. "I suppose Galdie never bothered because she didn't want to be troubled with too many passengers."

Rosemary shrugged and started the car. Agatha directed them down the long and windy road, through pine trees and over at least two hills.

"You said it wasn't far," Athena said.

"No, he's virtually my neighbour," Agatha said.

Rosemary shook her head.

Ten minutes later, they pulled up outside a small cottage, more rustic-looking than Agatha's. It was more like a hut, and Rosemary was reminded of the other man found in his cabin only days ago.

She shivered, feeling a chill of discomfort. "Perhaps I should go in first," Rosemary said.

Athena shook her head. "Don't be silly, Mum."

They got out of the car and approached the cottage.

Agatha knocked on the door. There was no response, and after several more attempts at knocking, she turned around. "Perhaps he's not home."

"Go back to the car," Rosemary said to Athena, who tried to protest, but Rosemary gave her an insistent look.

"Oh, fine," Athena said.

"What?" Agatha said.

"I think we should check on him just in case."

"Rosemary Thorn," Agatha said. "Are you suggesting we invade this poor man's house when he's probably out for a walk in the woods?"

The skin on Rosemary's neck prickled. "We told you about that suspicious death? What if it wasn't just the one?"

"Oh, very well," Agatha grumbled. She tapped the door with her finger and it flew open. "Benjamin," Agatha called out. "We're coming in whether you like it or not." She stomped into the cottage, which, unlike Agatha's house was just as small on the inside as it seemed from outside. It was almost entirely one room, with a small bedroom and bathroom off to one side, which looked

39

as if it had once been an old outhouse and had only more recently been connected to the rest of the dwelling.

The room was cluttered and chaotic. Paper was strewn about. Rosemary and Dain looked at each other.

"Here he is," said Agatha. "You were right, and you may not want to get any closer."

Rosemary sidled forward and peered over the desk. Lying straight as an arrow on the floor was an old, bearded man, wearing spectacles that looked to be shattered but on closer inspection were actually covered in ice.

"He's frozen solid," said Dain after attempting to feel for a pulse.

"Just like the other guy," Rosemary said as Fleur went outside, looking even more pale, saying she was going to call the police.

"Look at this." Dain pointed to the desk. "All sorts of notes about the Cailleach and the Holly King."

"I'm sure I've heard of them," said Rosemary.

Agatha shot her a withering look. "Winter solstice mythos. Perhaps you should have done your research – this poor corpse clearly was doing *his*. I'd have thought you'd take more responsibility, considering how you and your family have brought about such interesting seasonal festivals..."

Rosemary ignored the blame Agatha seemed to be placing on her and pored over the desk, finding something scrawled on old parchment that looked a lot like poetry:

Cloaked in winter's mantle, the Cailleach wields her icy staff, painting the land in frost and snow.

From Samhain's final whisper to Beltane's first sigh, her reign covers the world in a blanket of white.

She, the winter crone, weaves tales of life and death, mirroring the eternal dance of the seasons.

The Holly King, crowned in frost-bitten leaves, rules the realm of long nights and short days.

In a ancient cycle of battle with his brother, the Oak King, the Holly King emerges victorious when the sun bows low in the sky.

Clothed in winter's dark splendour, he paints the world in hues of holly and ice.

"Do you think that's what's causing the deaths?" Rosemary asked. "Maybe one of these mythological figures?"

Agatha shook her head. "I can't think why they would bother."

"Maybe he uncovered some kind of secret," said Dain. "And they didn't want it to get it out."

Agatha waved her hand dismissively. "Gods don't concern themselves with that kind of mortal drama. It would bore them to death. And when you're immortal, you don't tolerate being bored very well."

"What's this?" said Rosemary, picking up an old book that looked to be scrawled by hand.

"Don't touch it," Agatha said. "It's evidence."

"Sorry, I forgot." Rosemary put the book back down and wiped her hands on her jeans, although it didn't quite make sense to do so. "I just saw something about the realm of dreams." She pointed to the book. She didn't touch it again, though she doubted her fingerprints would muddy the already baffling state of the evidence, somehow.

"The realm of dreams," Agatha said with a faraway look. "Yes, that is one possibility. Although it's not something to take lightly."

"That's what I said," said Dain. "The Dreamrealm is dangerous."

"Come on," Rosemary said. "Let's get out of here. I don't think we're going to find anything, at least not today. We shouldn't be disturbing a crime scene."

They went back to the car to find a sullen teenager pouting with her arms folded. "What happened?" she asked, looking at the gaunt expressions.

"Let's just say I'm glad you stayed in the car," said Rosemary.

"Another one? Really?" She looked almost hopeful.

Rosemary shook her head. "I don't think it's Elise, love."

"Definitely not," said Fleur. "My daughter wouldn't do that. Whoever killed those men did it intentionally, although why, I'm not sure I'll ever understand."

Athena sighed. "Well, that's just great."

"We've got some kind of frosty murderer on our hands," said Rosemary.

"And no more clues on Elise," Fleur added in an anguished tone. Athena wrapped an arm around her shoulder to console her.

"How about we go to the pub, then?" said Agatha. "I've got a few ideas marinating that I just might share with you. Besides, I could do with a tipple."

Seven

The pub was crowded for a weeknight, but Rosemary managed to find a table in the corner. Dain had gone off to follow up on some other business and Rosemary felt strangely bereft without his jovial company. Athena and Fleur certainly weren't going to lighten the mood and she had a tempestuous historian to contend with.

"I'll have two double sherries," said Agatha. "And the beef pie as well."

Rosemary and Athena looked at each other, bemused.

"Actually, I'm famished," Fleur said.

"Maybe we should all eat," Rosemary suggested.

Rosemary placed their orders with Sherry at the bar and returned to the table.

"So what is it you wanted to tell us?" Athena asked Agatha.

"I'm still marinating on that," said Agatha drily. "I may need a sip of sherry first."

Fortunately, the drinks arrived a moment later, with a worried-looking Sherry bearing a tray laden with her namesake. She'd expressed her sympathies about Elise with Fleur and Athena before leaving them in peace.

Agatha took a swig of sherry and launched into a spiel. "The winter solstice is important. Think about it this way. The solstices are notable because time is said to stand still for five days."

Fleur looked at her bleakly, through bleary tear-puffed eyes. "Why is that important, exactly?"

"Look," said Agatha. "It's not going to be easy to get to the Underworld in the first place, but even if you can find a way there, getting in and out again is going to be a problem – if you intend to return."

"I think we intend to return!" said Rosemary.

Agatha shrugged. "Yes, well, the problem is the sheer force of time. It can crush your physical body."

"What?" said Athena. "You're saying time has the power to crush us?"

"Aye," said Agatha. "Time is a force, you see. We move through it, we move with it, and it moves upon us. The Underworld has a different take on time, you might say."

By then, Agatha had finished her sherries and requested two more. Rosemary went up to the bar to order them and bumped into a very handsome vampire who kissed her on the cheek.

"Hello, stranger," said Rosemary.

Burk smiled at her. "I hear you've been hanging out with Dain."

"Athena, mostly...don't get jealous."

He gave her a smouldering look and she wondered why she

hadn't made any plans with him recently, until her creeping insecurity about ageing while he stayed forever young reminded her.

"Rosemary?" Burk said.

"Yes?"

"I have to go away for a few weeks – it's work related and rather urgent. I'll be heading across continental Europe and rather busy."

"Oh..." Rosemary deflated slightly. "That's fine. I hope you have fun."

Rosemary turned away. She didn't know what to make of the interaction, or the fact that Burk would be out of the country for some undecided time period, though her insecurities had a lot of ideas about the situation.

She began to return to the table only to notice that Athena was no longer sitting where she had been.

"Not this again," she mumbled. It was a bit like déjà vu. On their first visit to the pub, Athena had gone missing with none other than Finnigan.

This time, however, she spotted her teen sitting at another table nearby with some familiar faces that Rosemary couldn't quite place. She began walking towards them and as she reached the table she recognised it was the Travellers who'd helped them at Samhain.

The dark haired young woman, who Rosemary recalled was named Ursula, smiled at her.

"I was just telling them what's going on," said Athena.

Rosemary shot her a serious look. After all, they shouldn't be revealing any details about the murders.

"What?" said Athena. "I was just telling them about Elise and how we need to get to the Underworld."

"We were sorry to hear about that," said Ursula. "The police asked us for a statement as we saw her that night, but unfortunately we had nothing of use to tell them."

Rowan invited Rosemary to join them. She looked across the room to see Agatha was busy tucking into her pie. "Okay, I will, thanks. But I can't stay long or our dinner will get cold."

She sat down next to the purple-haired girl whose name she couldn't remember until Athena referred to her as Hazel.

"I'm afraid we weren't much help with the police," said Ursula.

"Nothing is at the moment," said Athena. "Don't be too hard on yourselves."

"But Athena just mentioned something about the realm of dreams?" said Ursula, her eyes lighting up with recognition.

"You know about it?" Rosemary asked.

"Not personally," she replied. "But I know someone who does. Back in New Zealand, my cousin has a friend who's apparently a Dreamweaver. I don't completely understand it myself, but apparently Dreamweavers are very rare. They can navigate the Dreamrealm."

"That's exactly what we need," said Rosemary. "Provided the stories are true and you can access all the other realms from there."

"Dream magic is potent," said Hazel. "You've got to be careful meddling with that kind of thing."

"But if we had a guide, though," said Athena hopefully. "It might work out. It's definitely worth investigating."

Rosemary nodded. "How can we find out more?"

"Why don't we visit you tomorrow?" Ursula said. "By the evening we might have a little more information. I can't even remember what time it is in New Zealand right now, but my cousin usually responds to messages within the day."

"That would be excellent. Come for dinner," said Athena.

Rosemary and Athena thanked them and returned to their table.

"Ah, finally back with my sherry," said Agatha.

Rosemary's own dinner of fish and chips was only slightly warm, but she was starving and dug in anyway. Athena hardly touched her chicken salad, just pushing the pieces around the plate until Rosemary and Dain both gave her serious glances and she made an effort to have a few bites.

"Do you have anything else to tell us?" Rosemary asked Agatha as she finished her pie.

Agatha rubbed her chin as if deep in thought. "The winter solstice...I don't believe in coincidence. There must be some connection."

"Are you implying my daughter is behind those deaths?" Fleur asked sharply.

"No," Agatha said sternly. "Well, she might be, but the magic of the season is important at any rate. You should learn whatever you can, especially about the Holly King and the Cailleach."

"Fine," said Rosemary. "We'll do our homework."

If Agatha knew anything else of use she didn't appear to be willing to share. But as Rosemary munched on her dinner she had a satisfying notion to ponder. At least they had a lead on the realm of dreams.

Eight

It was only a quarter past four and the sun was starting to set. Athena had been poring over old magical reference books, looking for more information on the gods that might be responsible for winter magic. It was good to have a distraction from thinking about Elise, and Rosemary clearly didn't have the attention span for the task. She kept getting up to make cups of tea and then got distracted with new chocolate ideas or making food in general. Right now she was starting on dinner instead of staring for a moment longer at dusty old books.

Athena didn't mind. She preferred to read in peace. So far she'd found a lot of descriptions much like the one in her school mythology text book, which happened to be written by Agatha Twigg:

· · ·

The Oak King and The Holly King

As chronicled in the annals of the Celtic Pantheon, the Oak King and the Holly King represent the duality of nature, the undulating ebb and flow of the seasons, depicted as two halves of the same divine essence.

Adorned in emerald hues, the Oak King is the embodiment of the waxing year. From the moment of the winter solstice, he reigns supreme as the days grow longer and the warmth returns.

This deity, garbed in the robust strength of summer's vitality, orchestrates the song of life, ensuring nature's canvas is painted in verdant splendour.

The Oak King's period of dominance, symbolic of growth, abundance, and the zenith of light, resonates within the sacred woodland groves, his essence intertwined with the very life force of the trees.

The Holly King, the sovereign of the waning year, assumes his throne at the zenith of the summer solstice. As the light begins to fade, he casts a spell of transformation upon the land, garbing it in the frosted cloak of winter.

Cloaked in the deep green of holly, flecked with vibrant berries like droplets of blood, he represents the strength found in endurance and the wisdom of surrender.

His reign is a time for reflection and introspection, a testament to the cycle of decline and rebirth. The Holly King's influence is not one of death but of preparation, a time of gathering one's strength for the renewal promised by the coming spring.

Together, the Oak King and the Holly King, in their eternal cyclical struggle, depict the perpetual balance of light and dark, warmth and cold, growth and retreat. They serve as a powerful reminder of nature's rhythm, the cycle of life and death, and the promise of rebirth.

According to this description, all things should be in balance, but something clearly wasn't. Athena chewed her pencil as she thought about it. Could it be that the Cailleach had tipped the scales in favour of winter? The crone goddess was said to embody winter's harshness, her icy touch transforming the land over the colder months of the year. Perhaps it wasn't even the gods at all.

She sighed and looked out the window to see a purplish-green house truck with stained glass windows pulling up outside.

Her heart raced in anticipation. She closed the text book, no longer interested in distractions.

This was the closest they had come so far to figuring out how to reach Elise.

Ursula had made no promises, but the fact that she'd shown up at all was a hopeful sign. If she hadn't been able to reach her cousin or had no news for them, she would have just texted to say so.

"They're here!" Athena called to Rosemary, who was busy tending to the roast vegetables in the kitchen.

"Dinner won't be done for a little while," said Rosemary. "But I suppose that doesn't matter."

"This is...exciting," Fleur said as they waited with bated breath. "It's strange, I've hardly felt any emotions other than fear and despair lately. It makes a nice change."

Athena reached for her and gave her hand a squeeze.

The house truck stopped. Athena ran outside and hugged Ursula as soon as she stepped out of the door.

"Thank you so much for coming," said Athena as she hugged Hazel and Rowan in turn. "You're welcome to take a bath while you're here and use the facilities in general. Like last time."

"Excellent," said Hazel. She was already carrying a duffle bag into the house.

"Thanks for inviting us over again," said Rowan. "The truck is nice, but it's also good to have a few larger scale home comforts occasionally."

Athena was eager to find out what the Travellers had to say, but her mother called her in to help with dinner.

"What did they tell you?" Rosemary asked, adding a vinaigrette to the fennel and radish salad.

"Nothing yet," said Athena, impatiently grabbing cutlery for the table. "But I have a good feeling about all this."

Rosemary smiled.

Just then, Dain wandered into the kitchen, having let himself into the house.

"I see you've arrived just in time for dinner," said Rosemary.

"Impeccable timing, as always," said Dain. "Speaking of time ticking on – don't you have a big birthday to celebrate next week?"

Rosemary groaned. "Don't remind me."

"Oh that's right," said Athena. "I've been so distracted by all the chaos that I almost forgot. How do you want to celebrate?"

"Perhaps by crawling into a cave for a few months of peace?" Rosemary suggested.

"Don't be silly," said Athena with a teasing grin. "Just because you're ancient, it doesn't mean you don't have plenty of life left to live."

"Forty is young, these days," said Dain. "Anyway, I never pegged you as one of those vain, youth-obsessed people."

"I'm not really," said Rosemary defensively. "I just have a whole lot of emotional baggage that I'm unprepared to deal with, especially on my birthday. Can't we just pretend it's already passed?"

"No way," said Athena. "You're not getting out of this one."

It wasn't long before the table was set and everyone had assembled for dinner.

"So, what's the news?" Fleur asked eagerly, as soon as they'd all sat down at the table.

"Apparently, my cousin has some kind of dream magic," Ursula said. "She said she's a dream witch. I don't know what it means. She's been in touch her friend, Awa, the Dreamweaver, who's happy to help."

"That's great!" Athena beamed.

"I like the sound of that," said Dain. "But she better know what she's doing with my girls."

Rosemary glared at him. "For the last time, we are not your girls."

"It's worth a try, though," said Dain. "I haven't seen that vampire around much lately."

Athena looked at her mother suspiciously. What was going on with Perseus Burk? She made a note to interrogate Rosemary later given that she was notorious for dodging relationship-related things.

"At any rate, the Dreamweaver situation is worth investigating," said Ursula, getting the conversation back on track.

Athena beamed at her. "Thank you so much."

"Happy to help," said Ursula. "I just hope I'm not leading you into a whole lot of danger."

Nine

By the end of the week, Rosemary was back in the chocolate shop. Papa Jack had been holding the fort for a few days while the Thorns dealt with the rather gnarly issues plaguing their lives. Rosemary couldn't leave him burdened with all the responsibility for too long, even though Papa Jack did have help from his son.

One of Rosemary's favourite things to do was design and create fabulous window displays. These usually worked a treat and brought in a lot of customers, barring Samhain when the shop had been cursed to drive them away despite Rosemary's adorable chocolate pumpkins on display.

For Yule and the winter solstice, she'd created dozens of large snowflakes from white peppermint chocolate which she strung from the top of the window display. Below that, she'd crafted a sleigh with reindeer. It was laden with little truffles shaped into presents. Sitting atop the sleigh, rather than Santa Claus, was the

Holly King, jovial in his green and red cloak. She had also constructed boughs of holly, an enormous yule log, and an array of decorated pine trees, which Athena now refused to call Christmas trees.

Rosemary had been working on these pieces in her spare time at home for several days. She'd spent all morning setting up in the shop. It was wonderful to see it all come together.

"It looks fabulous," said Papa Jack as he entered the shop.

"What are you doing here? I was trying to give you the day off," said Rosemary.

"And I've had a brilliant day," replied Papa Jack with a jolly chuckle. "But I thought I'd pop in to check on you, not the store. How are you holding up?"

Rosemary shrugged. "I'm worried about Athena of course, and Elise, and Fleur. It hasn't been an easy time."

"When is it ever an easy time?" replied Papa Jack. "But the challenges are all part of the joy, if you ask me."

"I'm not sure I'd call it joy," said Rosemary.

"Well, then let's call it character building," said Papa Jack.

"I must have plenty of character by now. Maybe we could sell it in the shop."

"Character building chocolates! I like that," said Papa Jack. "Although maybe it would make people cheat and not do the actual work they've come to this planet to do."

Rosemary laughed. "Sometimes I wonder about that – what is it I'm here to do?"

"Some people say it's for the gods to determine, but I think it's up to us," replied Papa Jack.

"I agree," said Rosemary. "Well...I determine that we'll get through this latest drama in one piece. We might not be able to avoid challenges, but I think we have a reasonable success rate of overcoming them."

"Let's have a hot chocolate and drink to that," said Papa Jack.

They sat down with a jug of his specially prepared hot chocolate. Rosemary filled him in on everything that had happened over the past few days.

"The winter is a time of dreaming," said Papa Jack.

"Really?"

"It's a peaceful time of year when everything slows down. The leaves have fallen, the earth is still and cold, and animals go into hibernation. And from what I've been reading, the winter solstice is associated with the Underworld. So perhaps what Agatha says has some truth to it."

Rosemary sighed. "Does that mean it's all our fault that Elise has gone missing? We called on the Morrigan for help, which always comes with a price. Besides, the Thorn family magic is tied into the seasonal festivals becoming so much more pronounced in Myrtlewood over the past year or so."

"Fault and blame are not useful here," replied Papa Jack. "You need to think clearly, Rosemary. You've done none of this on purpose, let alone with malicious intentions."

Rosemary nodded. Of course, magic enacted with malicious intent would only bring bad energy threefold. That was part of magic 101 that Rosemary tried not to think too much about because it made things seem too overwhelming.

"A little birdie tells me it's your birthday coming up soon," said Papa Jack.

Rosemary groaned. "Only a few more days to go, and I dread that Athena is trying to plan some kind of surprise party."

Papa Jack chuckled again. "Celebrate it! Your age is your wisdom. You've done a lot on all your years on this planet."

Rosemary shrugged. "For so many of them I feel like I just toiled away, barely accomplishing anything, barely surviving."

"Look around you," said Papa Jack, just as Marjie entered the chocolate shop. "Look at everything you've created. You're a strong, brilliant, and capable woman."

"That's right," said Marjie. "Stand in your power, Rosemary."

Rosemary took a deep breath and exhaled slowly. "You're both right. That's what I needed to do to access the Thorn magic in the first place. And it's always the answer, isn't it?"

"The truth is usually uncomfortably simple," said Marjie sagely.

"And what is your truth right now in this moment, Rosemary?" asked Papa Jack.

"The truth is, I'm about to turn forty and I'm not sure I've even fully gotten used to being thirty properly," replied Rosemary. The corner of her mouth twitched. "But you know what? I'm going to enjoy it."

"That's the spirit," said Marjie. "Society might tell us women that we're only valuable for our youth and good looks. But we're a whole lot more than just gorgeous." She winked.

Papa Jack shrugged. "Youth is overrated anyway. I was a fool when I was young. I'm much happier now."

Rosemary laughed. "Isn't that the truth?"

"So we're celebrating, then," said Marjie, pouring herself a cup of hot chocolate and raising her glass. "To aging, if not gracefully, then at least with plenty of style!"

"And a great deal of laughter, too," said Papa Jack.

"I'll drink to that," said Rosemary, taking a deep gulp of Papa Jack's mood-boosting hot chocolate. "You know what? This birthday situation has really stirred up my insecurities, I'll be the first to admit to that, but I'm not going to let them ruin my fun. Forty is going to be excellent."

"Why, yes it is!" said Marjie. "It's a good thing too. Athena has all but called off your party."

"I had my suspicions," said Rosemary. "I thought Athena might be planning something, although with everything that's been going on lately, I doubt she'd be in the mood for celebrating."

"That's not the reason she called it off though," said Marjie. "She just didn't want you to have a bad time if you really didn't want a surprise party."

"I don't think I do," replied Rosemary. "Surprises aren't always fun."

"Maybe something else would be better too," said Marjie. "Let's have a think about what you'd really like to do for your birthday. I have an idea that just might be perfect, come to think of it."

Rosemary raised an eyebrow. "As long as it doesn't involve too many people, I'll let you surprise me."

Marjie grinned. "I'll call Athena straight away and we'll sort this out."

Ten

There was something magical about the season, even though Athena had not been in much of a state to enjoy it. Snow covered the ground all over Myrtlewood, and the town was decorated in wreaths of holly and red-and-white candles that were enchanted to never go out or set fire to anything.

All of the things Athena loved about Christmas in the mundane world were even more magical in a town with centuries of celebrations of the seasons. They'd decided to go into the centre of Myrtlewood to pick out a tree at the Yule tree sale, which was happening that weekend. Rosemary had suggested this might take Athena's mind off things.

She was just getting dressed in her warm coat that she'd bought with winter in mind. It was a deep red velvet with white fur lining the collar and cuffs.

She checked her reflection in the mirror only to see a message scrawled on the glass.

I love you, it said, as if someone had breathed steam onto the surface and written it with their finger.

"Mum!" Athena called out. "Have you been leaving me notes?"

Rosemary came into the room. "That wasn't me," she said.

A chill ran across Athena, giving her goosebumps. Somebody had been in her room. Then the penny dropped. "But it must be Elise," she said, filling with a sudden wave of agonising hope.

"We don't know that for sure," said Rosemary. "It could be a trick. Or it could even have been your father."

"No, I know it's her," said Athena, convinced. "She's still alive."

"I believe that," said Rosemary.

"She's trying to communicate with me." Athena wiped the message off the mirror and scrawled back, *I love you too.*

Her mind raced with possibilities of all the things she could write. *Where are you? Are you safe? Come home. We're coming to get you.*

She settled on the last one, but though she stared at the mirror for minutes on end, hoping for another message, nothing happened.

"Come on, love," said Rosemary. "If it is really Elise, she might have responded by the time we get back."

"I don't want to miss it," said Athena reluctantly.

"For all you know, your attention on the mirror might be stopping Elise from being able to interact. You know, a watched pot never boils."

"Okay, fine. But when we come back, don't be surprised if I stay up all night staring just in case another message comes."

Rosemary pulled Athena into a hug. "All right, let's go," she said.

Athena stuffed a compact mirror into her pocket before they left, just in case.

The village was busy, buzzing with excitement. Many people had already bought trees and there were dozens of families carrying them down the streets of Myrtlewood.

As they walked through the town, Athena couldn't shake the feeling that Elise was trying to reach out to her. She kept glancing at the mirror in her pocket, hoping for another message. But the mirror remained clear.

Athena and Rosemary found a large pine big enough to make a statement in the Myrtlewood lounge.

"Do you want to take it home now or will it be delivery?" asked Ferg, peering over a clipboard while wearing a brown corduroy suit. Nobody would have guessed that he was also the Myrtlewood mayor.

He seemed to be keeping up with many of his odd jobs around the town while also being an official, and he didn't seem to mind the fact that people came to him with all their troubles. In fact, he seemed to like being unhelpful and officious in response. He was really flourishing, having taken over from the corrupt Mr. June.

"Delivery would be great, thanks," Rosemary said.

"And where would you like it delivered?" asked Ferg.

"To our house," said Athena. "Where else would it be, Ferg?"

Ferg cleared his throat. "My official title is Your Majestic Excellency," he said. "I prefer to be addressed that way."

Rosemary and Athena looked at each other, bemused. "All

right then, Your Majestic Excellency," said Rosemary, putting on a posh voice. "Please have it delivered to Thorn Manor."

"And the address?" said Ferg, pointing to his clipboard.

"You know where it is," said Athena.

"Address, Ms Thorn."

Rosemary took the clipboard from Ferg and scrawled "Thorn Manor," in the address line, next to her name.

"Very well," said Ferg. "I'll have my people call you to arrange the details."

Rosemary and Athena walked away somewhat puzzled. They were often puzzled in their interactions with *His Majestic Excellency*, the now mayor of Myrtlewood.

"Still, he seems to be thriving in that role," said Athena.

"You're right. I've never seen him so happy."

"I'm just glad he's not corrupt like his predecessor," said Athena. "I suspect he's even good at it – all the paperwork and admin."

"He's good at being a pain, I suppose," said Rosemary. "That job would be my worst nightmare now. I'm glad you didn't make me sign up to be deputy mayor after that nightmare of a campaign."

"Luckily, there isn't really a position for deputy," Athena agreed. "But for what it's worth, I think you'd be great. And speaking of great things...your birthday."

Rosemary laughed. "Not this again."

"Marjie and I have a plan and it doesn't involve too many people."

"And it's not going to make a mess of the house?" said Rosemary.

Athena shook her head. "No, but it does involve a fancy dress."

Rosemary pursed her lips. "I do quite like fancy dresses. All right, I'm in. As long as it's not going to be too exhausting for either of us."

"Of course not," said Athena. "We need to save our strength."

"All right, I'm in."

By the time they returned to Thorn Manor, Athena was desperate to check her bedroom mirror. There was no message.

She blew on the glass, but even the message she'd left had disappeared, giving her hope.

Perhaps it had gone somewhere, to wherever Elise was.

She fell asleep that night, eventually, after fitfully checking the mirror every few minutes, before giving up in exhaustion.

In the morning when she awoke, the first thing she saw was a blood-red message on the mirror.

Athena felt the chill of dread in her gut. "Mum!" she called out. "Mum!"

Rosemary came running into the room. "What is it?" she asked.

Athena pointed to the glass. "Look. She did reply."

Rosemary looked from the mirror back to Athena. She gulped. "Are you sure it's Elise?"

Athena nodded. "I can just tell."

"What was the last thing you wrote yesterday?" Rosemary asked.

"We're coming to get you," said Athena with a shudder.

They both stared at two letters followed by an exclamation mark, written large and ominous:

NO!

Eleven

"Come on, love," said Rosemary, opening the curtains in Athena's bedroom. "You can't just stare at the mirror all day. It's not helping."

Athena groaned and threw herself back on her bed. "I've tried writing so many things that my finger is sore. I have no idea if Elise has seen them or if she's tried to respond. Maybe she won't know which to respond to. It's all such a mess. Hopeless."

"Let's go to Marjie's tea shop for some brunch," Rosemary coaxed, hoping her daughter would emerge from her overwhelmed state and not spiral further into despair.

"I'm not hungry."

"It doesn't matter if you're not hungry," said Rosemary gently. "You need your strength. How are we going to help Elise if you're not even looking after yourself?"

"Like I said. It's hopeless."

Rosemary gave her a sympathetic smile. "The Dreamweaver said she'd help us, remember. Besides, we can't just give up."

"I don't want to give up, but we don't know if that girl can even help and Ursula said she's away for the rest of the week. Elise needs us now."

"But our best hope to get to her isn't until the winter solstice anyway," Rosemary reminded her. "In the meantime we'll just have to do whatever we can to prepare."

Athena sighed. "You're right. Okay, fine. I'll come to Marjie's."

"Music to my ears," said Rosemary. "I'm craving a beef pasty and a scone."

Rosemary was just taking a second bite of her deliciously moreish beef pasty when she heard.

"Athena!"

Both she and Athena turned to see some familiar teenage faces. Sam, Deron, Ash, and Felix all stood outside the tea shop. They rushed inside, hugging Athena and scolding her for not returning their calls.

"We were so worried," said Sam. They had dyed their hair purple since the last time Rosemary had seen them, and they wore matching purple nose studs.

Athena looked at them guiltily. "I'm sorry. I just feel like I'm to blame."

"Don't be silly," said Felix.

"Felix's right," said Rosemary. "It's not your fault."

Athena looked down at her tea cup. "Well, actually..."

Sam looked at them quizzically.

"What on earth are you talking about?" Felix crossed his arms.

"Don't tell me that you intended for Elise to run away to the Underworld."

"Of course not," said Athena.

"It sounds like you're taking too much responsibility for this," said Ash.

"That's exactly what she's doing," Marjie said, bustling over to the table. "And I won't hear another word of it. Not unless you personally sent Elise to the Underworld to try to harm her."

"I would never do that," said Athena.

"Exactly," said Ash. "So stop being so hard on yourself."

The phone rang in the tea shop, and Marjie left them to answer it.

"So what's the plan?" asked Sam.

Athena and Rosemary looked at each other.

"What do you mean?" Athena asked.

"I know you. And I'm a hundred percent sure that you're not just going to leave Elise to rot down there."

"We're just talking about that," said Deron, putting a hand on Sam's shoulder. "We're sure you must be plotting some kind of rescue mission."

Athena studiously cut into her own pasty as if trying to avoid answering, but Rosemary decided it was unfair to keep Elise's other good friends completely in the dark, especially since a problem shared is a problem halved, or perhaps divided into many pieces in this case.

"We are trying to figure out how to get Elise back," she told them.

"Mum!" Athena said.

"You can't keep this from us, you know," said Felix. "Elise is our friend too."

"Sure, but we don't exactly have a plan yet."

"Aren't you going let us help?" Deron asked.

Athena shrugged. "Sure, if there's any way that you can, and it's not dangerous. We've already lost Elise. I'm not going to lose anyone else."

"We haven't lost Elise," said Sam. "Not really. I know she's alive."

Athena nodded resolutely. "I think she's sending me messages."

"Really!?" Felix exclaimed.

Athena explained to them about their words on the mirror. She was halfway through the rather frustrating story when Marjie came back towards the table, her eyes wet and rimmed in red as if she'd been crying.

Rosemary stood to hug her friend. "What is it?" she asked.

"Oh...terrible news," Marjie said. "I've just heard about a dear old friend, Ally McAlister, in the next town over. She was found dead this morning."

"How awful," said Athena.

"And that's not the worst of it," said Marjie, wiping more tears from her eyes.

A shiver of cold ran over Rosemary's skin. "Don't tell me she was frozen solid."

"I'm afraid so," said Marjie. "Neve just called to tell me. They found her in her shop, surrounded by her famous Yule cakes. There was no sign of a struggle. I had spoken to her last night. That's why Neve called, wanting to know if anything seemed amiss, but Ally seemed perfectly normal. I just called to put in an order of Yule cakes as I usually do. She makes the best in the county. I stock them here every year."

"You don't suppose..." said Athena.

Marjie looked at her curiously.

Athena continued. "Do you think she knew something important about Yule or the Winter Solstice?"

"Quite probably," said Marjie. "You aren't suggesting that's why she was killed?"

Athena and Rosemary both shrugged, but Rosemary silently agreed that Athena had a point. The other two mysterious deaths seemed to be winter-related, and the old historian had information about the key gods scattered all over his desk. If it was a secret they were killed over, perhaps Marjie's friend knew something about it too.

"How awful," said Rosemary. "Is there anything we can do?"

"You just keep being your wonderful selves," said Marjie.

"Come and stay with us again if you like," said Athena. "I don't want you to be all alone at this time of year."

"I'll consider it," said Marjie, patting Athena on the shoulder.

Marjie went back to the kitchen muttering that she wanted to distract herself by doing a few odd jobs.

Athena's friends were looking at them curiously, and it was only fair to share the story of the past few days. While Athena explained about the mysterious wintery deaths, Rosemary noticed that she stopped short of telling her friends about the Dream-realm and the possible lead.

Rosemary wasn't sure if Athena didn't want to give them false hope or lead them into potential danger if they insisted on coming with them. After all, the Dreamrealm was said to be a dangerous place.

Athena was almost finished with the story when Ferg came in to the tea shop wearing a blue paisley cloak and approached them.

"Rosemary Thorn," he said.

"Your Excellency," said Rosemary somewhat ironically.

"Majestic Excellency," Ferg corrected.

Athena and her friends stifled a giggle, but Ferg didn't appear to notice. In fact, he seemed rather pleased with himself. "I tried to deliver your tree," he said. "However you did not write the address as required."

Rosemary squinted at Ferg. "I wrote Thorn Manor on your little clipboard."

"My official clipboard," said Ferg. "Thorn Manor is not an address, however. So your tree has been delivered to my house."

"Oh dear," said Athena.

"Really, Ferg?" said Rosemary. "I mean, Your Excellency. Couldn't you have..."

"I'm afraid I'm far too busy to muck around," said Ferg.

"Oh, come on," Rosemary protested.

"Nope, you'll have to pick up the tree from my house yourselves."

He handed them a small card with his address.

Rosemary clenched her fists, vile anger rising of the kind that was usually reserved for couriers that failed to deliver packages. "Seriously, Ferg, you know exactly where we live. This is ridiculous. I expect more from you as mayor than just being a stickler for the rules and a pompous bureaucrat." She launched into a tirade before Athena kicked her under the table.

"Stop making a scene," Athena whispered. "It's not funny anymore."

Ferg paled, and then he turned on his heels and left the tea shop without another word.

"That man," said Rosemary. "I can't believe the hoops he insists people jump through for no good reason. And besides, I have no idea how we're going to get that giant tree home."

"We'll figure it out," said Athena. "I'm known to be quite a powerful fae-witch."

Rosemary raised an eyebrow, wondering if she should tell Athena about the prophecy relayed to her by Elspeth and Queen Áine. She hadn't wanted to burden Athena with speculation about some important chosen-one-type-role, but perhaps she should also refrain from telling her in case it went to her head.

It was a while before they finished the brunch, which was obviously followed by delicious slices of cake, another cup of tea, and plenty more conversations and reassurances with Athena's friends.

"I suppose we need to go get this tree then," said Rosemary as they got up from the table to leave. "Before Ferg fines me or something."

They drove a short distance to the address His Excellency had given them, which led to a street that they hardly knew existed, despite its proximity to town.

Ferg's house, it turned out, strangely resembled a series of shoe boxes painted slate grey. It was modern-looking compared to everything else on the street, except for the old-fashioned small square windows placed symmetrically along the structure, which were edged in a bright peach.

"Interesting choice," said Athena as they walked through the entrance way, guarded on either side by large, obnoxiously yellow painted lions.

The lawn was so tightly manicured and bright green that Rosemary wanted to check to see if it was plastic grass. But she refrained in case that also came with a fine.

They knocked on the front door, but there was no answer.

"I suppose he's being officious somewhere else," said Rosemary.

"Let's go home," said Athena, linking arms with her mother.

They arrived back at Thorn Manor only minutes later, to hear the sound of clinking coming from the lounge.

Rosemary's heart raced at the possibility of an intruder. They proceeded cautiously towards the lounge to see none other than His Excellency the mayor standing next to the enormous Christmas tree, hanging a bauble.

"What is going on?" said Rosemary.

"I took your complaint into consideration," said Ferg. "And I decided I would go above and beyond my duty and decorate the tree for you. These are my spares." He gestured to the decorations now adorning the tree.

"Are those tiny cardigans?" said Athena, sounding both amused and excited.

"You're welcome," said Ferg.

Rosemary admired the unusual decorations of not only tiny cardigans but also mandolins, pineapples, and typewriters. She wasn't sure whether she should be angry, frustrated, confused, or grateful. In the end, she just politely thanked Ferg and let him leave the house, and then of course, she put the kettle on for tea.

Twelve

Athena had been counting down the days until they could finally talk to the Dreamweaver. Due to time zones, and New Zealand being on the other side of the planet, the only time they could find that worked was seven in the morning in Cornwall.

Athena had slept fitfully with fragmented dreams. In one, Elise had transformed into a lion and chased her through Thorn Manor. In another, they'd been trying to call the Dreamweaver only to discover she'd vanished without a trace. Neither of these seemed to bode well for their path ahead.

Dreams had never made sense to Athena. Some nights, she'd wake suddenly after falling off an elephant or scaling a high-rise building. Some mornings she would lie awake trying to process the terror of swimming in the deepest ocean being pursued by an enormous squid. She could never make sense of any of it, and though she'd craved deep and meaningful dreams that hinted at a greater purpose for her life, she mostly just met confusion and bewilderment.

As such, Athena preferred to ignore her dreams. She liked consistency and order, not utter chaos, but this might be the only way to reach Elise, so she had to try.

That morning, she awoke far earlier than necessary. It was still dark outside and snow was falling again. Athena shivered as she looked out the window, hoping there hadn't been any more unexplained deaths in the night.

Athena paced back and forth in her room. It was too early to wake her mother and she was far too restless to read. She hadn't thought about the strange deadly winter magic much since Fleur had been so sure Elise wasn't responsible and Athena had to agree.

The deaths seemed too calculated and deliberate to be Elise accidentally trying to reach through, though perhaps there was some other missing link that she hadn't thought of yet. She glanced towards the mirror again, for what felt like the thousandth time, but there were no more messages.

She tried to reach out to Elise in her mind, but as usual, there was only static.

After what felt like an age, it was finally late enough to wake Rosemary, though it proved to be no easy feat.

Athena tried calling out first, then shaking her mother, and when that didn't work she resorted to magic. She reached out to touch Rosemary's hand and sent what she thought to be a tiny jolt through.

Rosemary sat up in bed, bolt upright, her hair sticking up in static. "What on earth!?"

"Sorry," said Athena. "But it's time to wake up or we'll miss our call."

"Did you just jump-start your mother!?" Rosemary screeched.

Athena couldn't help herself. She buckled over in laughter.

Rosemary was less impressed, and scowled from the bed, but she didn't fall back asleep so Athena considered her magic a success.

Rosemary and Athena had a quick breakfast of toast and a big pot of Earl Grey tea before settling down in front of Rosemary's laptop for the video call.

"Ursula said she's not sure how much Awa will know about the magical world," said Athena as they waited for the Dreamweaver to join the call.

"Isn't she magic?" Rosemary asked.

"I think her magic is a different kind from ours...so maybe don't say anything too weird in case we freak her out."

Rosemary feigned offence. "Would I do that?"

Athena nudged her mother playfully. "Remember the golden rule: if in doubt, keep your mouth shut."

Rosemary mock-glared at her daughter.

"Look, here she is," said Athena. The video screen popped up, revealing a young woman with shoulder length brown hair and tanned skin.

"Hi," said Athena, introducing herself and her mother.

"Nice to meet you," said Awa with a shy smile. Her accent was obvious with its clipped vowels, similar to the way Ursula, Rowan, and Hazel spoke.

Athena felt a stab of doubt. This girl was young. Too young. How could she possibly have the answers they sought? Then, she gave herself a reality check. Awa was only slightly younger than she was, and, according to Ursula's sister, she'd been on her fair share of epic adventures since taking her place as the Dreamweaver before she'd even turned thirteen. Athena cast her doubts aside and smiled at Awa. "Where do we begin?"

"What do you know about the Dreamrealm?" Awa asked.

"Not very much, to be honest," said Athena. "I've read a few bits and pieces over the last few days, but..."

Awa shrugged. "It's hard to tell what's true, isn't it?"

"Exactly. It's just like the Underworld," Athena said with a sigh.

"Well, that's just it. Both realms are mysterious. So much is unknown or unknowable. But I've got some friends who might be able to help," Awa continued. "I can introduce you to them..."

She frowned slightly.

"What is it?" Athena asked.

"Well, I was thinking if this is going to work, it might be easier if we could practice tonight, although it will be tricky for us to be asleep at the same time," Awa said.

"We could go to sleep anytime," said Athena enthusiastically. "We could even take a sleeping potion."

"As long as it's not too strong that you don't dream, give it a try," Awa said. "The only thing is..."

"What?" Rosemary asked. "Don't tell me you haven't done any of this before."

"No, not exactly," Awa said, looking a bit sheepish. "I've led a few people into the Dreamrealm, but they were all...what I've been told are called sensitives."

"Sensitives?" said Rosemary. "What does that mean?"

"I'm still not a hundred percent sure," said Awa. "I mean, they do tend to be people who are sensitive in one way or another, but I think it relates specifically to the Dreamrealm, like a sensitivity to dreaming. Some people can access it more easily than others who are much more stuck in the mundane world."

"Well, we're not exactly mundane," said Athena, looking at her mother.

"You're witches," said Awa. "I can tell."

Rosemary shot Athena a knowing glance, and Athena exhaled in relief. "So you know about that kind of thing?"

"Of course," Awa said. "I mean, I didn't know anything about it for a long time, but just recently I realised there's so much more than just the Dreamrealm. One of my best friends is...well, we won't go into that now. The thing is, I can't be sure if I can help you enter the Dreamrealm."

"We'll just have to find out, won't we?" said Rosemary.

They began to make a plan for a few hours' time. Rosemary and Athena would ensure they were asleep and Awa would be going to bed anyway as it would be the middle of the night in New Zealand.

A voice called through from the screen. "Coming, Mum!" said Awa. "Wait a minute."

She ducked away and returned moments later with a big plate of lasagne. "Dinner time," she said, and proceeded to douse her plate with an inordinate amount of chili sauce.

"Not very sensitive to spice, are you?" said Rosemary with a laugh.

"I've heard that before," said Awa.

"Is there anything that we should know about the Dream-realm before we proceed?" said Rosemary. "What can you tell us?"

"It's hard to explain," said Awa. "It took me quite a while to get used to it, and it's not going to be the same for everyone who goes there. But being a Dreamweaver gives me certain abilities. It creates a more stable plane when I'm there, and I can help navigate it to some extent."

"So you will help us?" said Athena.

"I'll do what I can to help you get to the gateway, wherever that is," said Awa. "But I'm not going to go further than that. I asked my guide. She said it's too dangerous."

Awa looked at them tensely.

"We know it's dangerous," said Athena. "But we have to try."

"Sorry about your friend," said Awa. "I really hope I can help."

"I hope so too," said Athena. She and Rosemary ended the call, not knowing very much at all about what they were getting themselves into, but at least they had something of a plan for their next steps.

Rosemary and Athena had taken a careful measure of Una's special sleeping tincture blend, and then, still dressed in their pyjamas, got into Rosemary's big bed. They figured it might be easier for Awa to find them if they were in the same place. They'd sent her a picture of the room and some other information about the location so that Awa could navigate there.

Athena lay in Rosemary's slightly too-soft bed, pulling the blankets over her, and closed her eyes. It wasn't long before she began to drift off under the power of the herbs and magic so skillfully brewed by Una.

Athena found herself in a house where she'd never been before. Only the floor was made of water, interrupted by protrusions of small icebergs. She had to navigate over them, jumping from piece to piece so as not to drown. She had to find Elise, but then someone was shaking her, waking her up. She opened her eyes. "No, I've got to sleep," she muttered.

"You are asleep," said Awa's voice.

Athena looked around. "But I'm in the bedroom...and you're here." It took a moment to dawn on Athena that she must indeed still be asleep. Rosemary was beside her, snoring softly, and the Dreamweaver girl was standing right in front of her, as if she wasn't really halfway around the world in New Zealand.

"So what now?" Athena asked.

"We wake your mother," said Awa.

"Good luck!" said Athena.

But it didn't take long before Rosemary was rubbing her eyes. "Did it work?" she asked.

"Yep," said Athena. "We're dreaming even though it seems like we just woke up."

"It's night time," said Rosemary.

"It's probably me," said Awa. "It's night time where I am, and like I said, my power influences dreams."

"What do we do now?" asked Rosemary.

"I have something for you." Awa produced a little golden pouch and reached inside it. She pulled out two pink berries. "One each," she said, holding them out towards Rosemary and Athena.

"What are they?" said Rosemary.

"Just eat them. They'll help you get to where we need to go."

Rosemary and Athena looked at each other, no doubt sharing questions about whether they should eat unusual pink berries from someone they hardly knew. But their doubts quickly evaporated. They'd come this far already and eating strange berries was probably the least of the dangers they faced. Athena popped a berry in her mouth and tasted the most exquisite flavour she'd ever experienced; it sent shivers down her spine, bringing dreamlike kaleidoscope visions and working its way through her very being.

"What is this?" Athena asked.

"It's a special berry from the Dreamrealm," said Awa. "It will help you to be able to get out of your regular dreaming states and deeper into the realm."

There was definitely no going back now.

"Do you think this is going to work?" Athena asked.

"Well, the fact that you woke up at all is a good sign," said Awa. "Come on, take my hand."

They all stood in front of the bed, holding hands. "I'm just going to focus on taking us through to the meadow. It might feel a little bit strange," said Awa.

There was a meow, and Serpentine Fuzzball walked into the room, followed closely by Nugget the squirrel.

"What is going on?" asked Awa.

"They're our familiars," said Athena. "But I don't understand. Do you think they're in the dream too?"

"They must be," said Awa. "But it's not safe for them to come with us."

Rosemary bent down. "Now, Fuzzball, I'm going to need you to stay here and protect us while we sleep. Do you understand?"

Athena gave Nugget a pat on the head. "You too. Be a good familiar."

"Right then," said Awa. "There's a special poem, a bit like a spell. Repeat after me..."

I am water, earth, sun, and sky.
I am dawn, noon, dusk, and midnight.
I am the whisper in the wind...
and I am here.

The earth beneath them began to shimmer like water. All of a sudden, they were in a wide open plain, with grass so vibrant it sparkled beneath a swirling purple sky. A flock of pink birds drifted overhead, wobbling in the breeze. It took Athena a moment to realise they weren't birds at all. They were airborne jellyfish. "Amazing!"

Awa smiled at her. "Welcome to the Dreamrealm."

"Is it...safe?" Rosemary asked tentatively.

"This place is fairly safe for now," said Awa. "At least, for the most part."

"You look really cool here!" said Athena. "Is that a superhero suit or something?"

Rosemary took a closer look at the dark purple outfit Awa was wearing, completed with an ornate belt containing multi-coloured stones that reminded Rosemary of something familiar that she couldn't recall.

"Come on," said Awa. "I want you to meet someone."

They wandered through the meadow towards a majestic tree that stood alone on a hill. As they drew nearer, Athena gasped as the gnarled roots of the tree resembled a woman with a beautiful, serene expression, like a goddess with her eyes closed. Athena's breath caught in her throat as those same eyes opened, deep with wisdom, and looked at them.

"Who is it you've brought me, Dreamweaver?"

"Priestess Tree," said Awa. "This is Rosemary and Athena. They're witches, and they're looking for their lost friend."

"Ah," said the tree. "You seek the Underworld."

"How did you know?" asked Rosemary.

"I am connected to all that is."

"Then tell us how to find Elise and bring her back," Athena said, somewhat desperately before adding, "Please."

The Priestess Tree looked at her through sad eyes. "I do not have all the answers, dear one, just whatever knowing flows through me."

"Is there a way we can get to the Underworld?" Athena asked.

"Yes," the Priestess Tree said. "There is a way, however you'd be wise to get familiar with the Dreamrealm first. As challenging as this realm may be to navigate, the Underworld may be even more so. It is a deeper and more mysterious place than most beings ever touch in their mortal lives."

"Do you have any advice for them?" Awa asked.

The tree looked at Rosemary and then at Athena. "The path is not meant to be easy. It is through the challenges that you will find *yourselves*. Do not waste energy wishing that it was something that it isn't."

Athena looked at the ground. She certainly had been doing that, so full of regret recently, wondering what she might have said or done differently so that Elise might not have left.

"Things are as they are," said the tree. "And you are exactly where you need to be."

"Thank you," said Athena. "I needed to hear that."

It was true. She felt some of the burden she'd been carrying easing at the words.

The tree looked at Rosemary. "I meant what I said about the journey being hard. If you can embrace it, it will work for you. The pressure and tension you feel will become powerful tools in your quest."

"Uhh...okay," said Rosemary, sounding somewhat baffled.

Athena took her mother's hand, knowing that she didn't really enjoy being out of the earthly plane and was putting on a brave face in not expressing total overwhelm.

"Thank you," said Athena to the tree. "How do we access the Underworld from here?"

"You'll find the gateway when the time is right. A way will be made," the tree said.

They looked at each other. "Doesn't sound very helpful,"

Rosemary mumbled under her breath and Athena elbowed her gently.

Awa giggled. "Things are often like that here. There's someone else I'd like you to meet. Come on. Take my hands."

"What are we doing?" Rosemary asked as they held hands.

"This will be easier if you lean on my power," said Awa.

Just then sparkles appeared in the air between them. A tiny creature popped into the air, almost like a fairy creature, but without wings. She hovered there emitting a glowing peachy light, frowning at them.

"What's going on?" said the creature.

"Veila, this is Rosemary and Athena Thorn," Awa said. "I'm helping them rescue their friend in the Underworld."

Veila spun around in the air, looking sceptical. "The Underworld? That's a dangerous place. You don't really want to go there, do you?"

"We have to," Athena said firmly.

"I'm taking them to Honu," said Awa.

"Alright then." Veila sighed. "I better come with you."

"If you concentrate on me, I can use my powers to fly us there."

"Fly?" Rosemary asked, looking sceptical. "Are you serious?"

"It'll be a lot quicker this way," Awa explained. "Just relax and don't worry about it. In fact, you might want to keep your eyes closed."

Athena shot her mother a worried glance. "Just keep your eyes closed and I'll tell you when it's safe to open them."

"I don't know about this," said Rosemary. "What if we fall?"

"You won't," said Awa. "Just trust me."

"This is like some kind of team-building exercise," Rosemary grumbled. "You know, there's a reason I don't work in a corporate job."

"Mum, just relax," said Athena.

Rosemary closed her eyes. Athena did the same. She felt a weightlessness and then the sensation of rising in the air that made her stomach flip. She couldn't help it. She opened her eyes to find that they were all floating higher and higher above the Dreamrealm, hands still clasped together.

"It's beautiful," said Athena, looking out at the majestic Dreamrealm spread out below them, with snowy mountains in the distance and a swirling purple sea to match the sky.

Rosemary kept her eyes firmly shut. "Just tell me when we get there."

"You're missing out," said Athena, whooping as they sped up.

Rosemary merely scrunched her face up more tightly as if to brace against the movement as Awa guided them over a dense forest towards a shimmering silver lake.

They touched down on the sandy shores of the lake and Rosemary opened her eyes and blinked with an astounded expression on her face. "We really flew, didn't we?" she said.

"Yes," said Awa. "Whatever you do, don't go over that way." She gestured to her left.

"Why not?" Athena asked.

"You'll want to avoid the sands of desire. People who go there get stuck there feeling incredibly happy for a very long time."

"That doesn't sound too bad, actually," said Rosemary.

Athena glared at her mother.

"What? I could do with some contentment, but obviously not until we rescue Elise," Rosemary reassured her.

"Why did you bring us here?" Athena asked as Veila somersaulted through the air around them.

"Like I said, there's someone I want you to meet," Awa said.

"And it's not that grumpy acrobat fairy?" Rosemary asked.

Awa laughed. "Veila's a dreamcharmer and I don't think she'd like to be called a fairy very much, unless she's in a particularly good mood. Then she might take it as a compliment. Dreamcharmers can be rather fickle, but she's a good friend."

"And this other friend of yours...?" Athena said.

"I think he's coming," said Awa, looking out over the lake to where a small island lay.

"Wait a minute," said Athena. "I swear that island is getting closer."

Rosemary laughed in surprise. "I think it is!"

It appeared to be moving towards them at an alarming pace.

"Don't worry," said Awa. "You'll see in a minute."

As the island drew nearer, an enormous head emerged that looked a lot like a turtle.

"You're kidding me?" Rosemary said, stunned.

"This is Honu." Awa introduced them.

"I thought you might be here soon," Honu said in a deep rumbling voice. "I've been expecting you."

"Really?" Athena asked in surprise. "But how did you know?"

"Here we are attuned to the collective unconscious and the realm of dreams that connects all beings. I sensed that you were navigating your way here, and here you are."

Athena stared at the ancient being, who was clearly incredibly wise, just as the Priestess Tree was. She wondered if he had any more useful and less cryptic messages for them.

"We need to get to the Underworld," Athena blurted out.

"Yes, you do," said Honu. "And you shall."

Athena breathed a sigh of relief. "Really? It's going to happen?"

"At the right time," said Honu.

"The winter solstice," said Rosemary.

"That indeed may be the right time," said Honu. "It is when time itself will stand still and you will have a window where you may traverse into the realm of the dead, though you are still living."

"It's really going to happen," said Athena, feeling a shiver run down her spine as the seriousness of the situation began to sink in.

"I believe so," said Honu. "Though your journey will not be easy. You risk losing everything you have."

Athena looked at her mother, who shivered.

"I can't lose you," said Rosemary.

"But I can't lose Elise," said Athena, and in that moment she woke up, back at Thorn Manor, just as Rosemary stirred beside her.

Athena lay there, overwhelmed by a sense of both hope and dread.

Thirteen

The next day, Rosemary was in the chocolate shop with Papa Jack. The Yule window display had brought in lots of customers. Even with the help from Papa Jack's family they were struggling to keep up with demand, leaving Rosemary wondering if she needed to hire more help. But that would have to be a question for another day.

She was busy filling orders for festive truffles; Papa Jack's special Yule-pudding-shaped bonbons with little tiny green and red chocolate holly sitting on top were a favourite among the customers.

"What do they do exactly?" said Rosemary, popping one of the tiny puddings into her mouth.

"Just a little seasonal cheer," said Papa Jack.

Rosemary tasted the brandy and spices and fruit. It reminded her of sitting in front of a fireplace, cosy and warm, with the anticipation of Christmas as a child. "Oh, these are great," she said. "I might need to take a box home myself. Goddess knows Athena and I need a little bit of cheer."

"Help yourself," said Papa Jack. "I made extra since they've been so popular this week. In fact, I had to come in early just to put on a new batch."

"I hope you're not overworking yourself," said Rosemary.

"I'm having a ball," Papa Jack assured her with his warm smile. "And I'm only happy to help. Just let me know if there's anything else you need."

Aside from the near constant stream of customers, Marjie popped in with a new scone she'd made flavoured with rosemary, feta, and olive, which Rosemary was only too happy to taste test and deemed them delicious.

Ferg stopped by to pick up an extra-large box of Papa Jack's Yule pudding truffles and handed Rosemary a box he'd carried in with him. "These are superfluous to my needs," Ferg said as Rosemary opened the pink velvet box to reveal several dozen decorations that appeared to be either tiny flamingos, poodles, or neck ties.

"Uh, that's great, thanks, Ferg," said Rosemary, trying to smile rather than grimace. No doubt he would be expecting her to hang every single one of them, and he would be by with his clipboard to check on the tree.

Aside from the regular cast, there seemed to be a lot of out-of-towners in Myrtlewood.

"Do you know if they're mundane people or...?" Rosemary asked Papa Jack.

"I think most of them are magical," he replied. "They've come back for the holidays, you know, or to have a change of scenery.

I've been chatting to them when they come in. Many are here for the big winter fair. It's a big magical event."

"Of course," said Rosemary. She'd been told that every year there was some kind of pantomime the week before winter solstice along with a special Yule market. She hadn't really been in the mood to be thinking about festivities, especially given that when she wasn't focused on helping Athena to reach the Underworld her thoughts kept drifting back to the mysterious deaths around Myrtlewood and the surrounding villages.

While Rosemary would love to be doing more to solve the crimes, especially with Neve hurtling towards being a new parent and Perkins being...well, Perkins. Despite all this, something told her that Agatha Twigg was right, there was a connection between the deaths and some greater mystery which somehow inexplicably involved their plight to rescue Elise.

It was about midday when a very strange sight distracted Rosemary from the peppermint truffles she'd been arranging in the cabinet.

A whole row of people dressed in bright sunshine yellow paraded down the street. They seemed to be stopping in at every shop. Rosemary took in their long hair and billowing yellow shawls. "Is it some kind of cult?" she whispered to Papa Jack.

"No idea," he replied.

It wasn't long before they came to call on the chocolate shop. A woman with long straight blonde hair entered the shop, holding her hands in a prayer position. She bowed.

"Greetings from the Fellowship of the Sun."

"Uhh, hi there," said Rosemary. "Can I help you?" She wasn't sure if she wanted to talk to these people or find out what they were peddling, but she didn't have grounds to kick them out, at least not yet.

"Of course you can help us," said the woman. "My name is Ariadne and I follow the great Oak King, Sage of the Summer."

Rosemary's ears perked up at that. The Oak King, from what she'd read, might be their natural ally if the Holly King, his nemesis, happened to be at fault for the winter deaths around Myrtlewood. Despite this possibility, Rosemary wasn't convinced these people knew what they were doing. "Oh yes, the Oak King...Do you have much to do with him?"

"The Great King works in mysterious ways," said Ariadne. "He tells us of the threat of eternal winter. Isn't it just freezing outside?" She looked Rosemary in the eyes as her companions rubbed their arms as if there was a frosty chill in the shop, which there most certainly was not.

"What threat?" Rosemary asked.

"But you must have heard of the perils of winter," said the bearded man standing next to her. "The deaths!"

"I'm pretty sure everyone's heard about those by now," said Papa Jack. "At least in the magical community in these parts."

"It's the Holly King, you see," said Ariadne. "He is our patron god's great foe and he's clearly fighting for an eternal winter."

Rosemary felt a shiver of fear. Her mind began darting about wildly, making all kinds of connections. Could the recent spate of mysterious deaths have been caused by a god? If so, fighting him could be a far more terrifying and dangerous challenge than they'd ever faced. She recalled how huge and formidable Belamus had been at Beltane, and even the Morrigan had possessed such power that no mere mortal would stand a chance against her. They'd been lucky in those former encounters, but this time fate might not be on their side.

"That doesn't sound good," said Rosemary, trying to keep the dread from her voice.

"We're simply here to raise awareness," said the man, holding out a pamphlet.

"Why do you think we can help?" Rosemary asked.

"Myrtlewood is an entirely magical town," said Ariadne. "You have such power here, and you are powerful, my dear." She nodded to Rosemary, who shrugged noncommittally. "If we all lend our magic to the Oak King he can defeat his brother and bring this evil to an end."

Rosemary frowned, still perplexed by these newcomers. "Is it really what you're here about?"

"Oh yes," said Ariadne. "Don't worry. The warm days are coming. The sun will return in all its glory and the Oak will triumph."

The fellowship bade them goodbye and left, leaving Rosemary puzzled.

"What do you suppose all that was really about?" asked Papa Jack.

"I don't know," said Rosemary. "It seemed pretty odd to me."

"But they were friendly at least," said Papa Jack. "Some people just need some kind of belief to keep them going."

"It's true," said Rosemary. "I feel like I've just been bowled over by a Californian yoga retreat, even though I'm sure that woman was Scottish."

"I can still smell the patchouli in the air," said Papa Jack, and they both laughed.

"I really hope they're totally bonkers and there aren't any gods committing homicides and trying to bring about eternal winter," said Rosemary. "But now that I think about it, all that talk of oak and holly...it reminds me of something. Those druids! Remember how I told you Athena and I met them at the Summer Ball? They were arguing about oak and holly. Maybe they know something about all this. They celebrate the solstices after all, but I don't know...Maybe I'm just grasping at straws."

"The thing about grasping at straws," said Papa Jack, "is you never know when you're going to draw the short one."

"I don't know if that's a warning or encouragement," said Rosemary. "But I suppose it's worth finding out, just in case they know something useful."

"Go on then," said Papa Jack. "And keep me updated. I need to know all the gossip."

Rosemary smiled at him. "Sometimes with the goings-on around here it's a lot better not knowing – if you want to sleep at night," she muttered.

Fourteen

Rosemary tried to contact the druids, though they were elusive beings. She left them a message as detailed as possible and hoped they'd get it. She also left messages for Burk, updating him on the situation. It was hard to keep track of where in the world he was when he was travelling for business.

Rosemary and Athena had both been glum and tense. Marjie tried to cheer them both up at every opportunity. She even brought by a new friend, Delia, a sassy woman around Marjie's age who was apparently new to magic. Delia had certainly brought a bit of excitement with her visit when she'd accidentally set the kitchen sink aflame. Fire seemed to be her speciality, not that she knew how to control it yet.

Marjie seemed more vibrant than ever, and Rosemary once or twice wondered whether new powers might be awakening in her dear friend in her crone years. She had become a bit secretive of late, and not only was she spending more time with Delia and Agatha Twigg, the three of them kept going off on little adventures that Marjie didn't care to explain. Rosemary and Athena merely shrugged, sure that they'd find out everything eventually, when Marjie was ready to tell them.

As the days wore on towards the winter solstice and Rosemary's approaching birthday, she began to feel a tightness in her chest and a sense of heaviness that she couldn't shrug off. Bearing in mind the words of the Priestess Tree in the Dreamrealm, as well as the wisdom shared by her ancestor Elzarie Thorn when they'd met at Samhain, Rosemary decided to work with these tensions.

"That's perfect for a Saturn transit," said Athena, taking a sip of tea over breakfast where Rosemary had filled her in on her latest thoughts. "That's exactly what you should be doing."

"I'm having a Saturn transit?" Rosemary asked. "I'm only forty. Surely I'm not supposed to have another one of those for quite a while yet?"

"Not a Saturn return," said Athena, pulling up an app on her phone. "But look here, Saturn is at a right angle to your Sun. That's called a square aspect and it's...challenging."

Rosemary shrugged. "I know better than to question you when it comes to the planets. What do you suggest I do about it?"

"Take a hike."

"Excuse me?"

"I'm serious. Go for a walk," Athena said, picking up another pancake and slathering it in butter and lemon sugar.

"How am I supposed to find the time to stroll around?" said Rosemary.

"Don't be silly, Mum," Athena said. "You've got lots of time. Burk's not even around to distract you."

"Don't remind me," said Rosemary glumly.

"I hope he's back in time for your birthday."

Rosemary groaned. "A walk, you say?"

"It doesn't have to be a very long walk. Either that or you could try taking up some other activity with a bit of structure and routine. How about journaling every morning?"

Rosemary shook her head. "Walking it is, and look at that, I've got twenty minutes before I have to leave for work."

"Off you go then," said Athena.

Rosemary began walking around the block. At first she'd just wanted to get away from the impending lecture she could sense Athena was embarking on. Her mind was scattered, just as it always was whenever she tried to meditate. But as she continued, one foot in front of the other along the side of the quiet country road edged in snow, careful to stick to the gravel so as not to trip, her head began to clear.

She went for another walk during her break at work, and then another that afternoon. Although her hip joints reacted to the new exercise, she decided it was a habit she needed to keep. She almost felt as if the planet Saturn and the other gods of difficult learning were walking with her. She could feel the energy and work with it, almost as if she was weaving it.

Rosemary explained her experience to her daughter over a cup of tea the next afternoon. Athena was immensely pleased that her mother was taking her advice for a change and smiled smugly.

"It's funny," said Athena. "This time of year used to be called Saturnalia by the ancient Romans."

"What did they do?"

"Lots of feasting," said Athena.

"That sounds about right for the Romans," said Rosemary. "That's what they're famous for, isn't it?"

"I suppose," said Athena. "Along with sculpture and literature and war...and their gods are pretty well known, including Saturn. In ancient times, people really believed the planets were the gods. And maybe there's some truth to that, not that I think there's really a god out there in the form of a planet. But there's some kind of correspondence between the energy maybe."

"Maybe," said Rosemary. "I kind of wish they'd leave us alone. I'd like to feel relaxed for a change, not so tense."

"It sounds like you're doing the right thing," said Athena. "One step at a time."

"What did they do during Saturnalia, besides feasting?" Rosemary asked, wondering if it held some kind of clue as to their current predicaments. "Come to think of it, if Saturn is all about structure and difficult learning, feasting sounds far too jovial just to be having a big party."

"That's the funny thing," said Athena. "In the ancient world Saturn was also associated with rulership and governance. Apparently, there was some kind of role reversal at Saturnalia. The masters and nobility would serve the slaves instead of the other way around. And that's a little bit like the planet Saturn, busting down the structures and flipping everything on its head."

"Is that what's going on with me lately?" Rosemary frowned. "Saturn's busting me down and making me re-build myself."

"Something like that," said Athena. "Making you stronger whether you like it or not."

Rosemary never expected that walking would become a preoccupation of hers. It didn't dissolve the tensions she felt, but it did somewhat ease them. She could only hope that it was strengthening her and making her magic more powerful and potent, though she wasn't in a hurry to test it anytime soon.

Fifteen

It was several days before Awa agreed to help them access the Dreamrealm again, insisting that they needed time to rest and process all they had experienced.

They went to sleep, just as they had last time, and Awa guided them back to the meadow.

However, instead of finding themselves in the same glowing and magical surroundings, they arrived to find a different terrain. The sky was stormy and the wind blew cold and icy, hitting them hard.

"I don't know what's going on," said Awa. "It's not normally like this. In fact, I don't remember it ever being quite so wintry."

Rosemary nodded. "Something tells me this is another one of those connections – the kind that Agatha Twigg told us about."

They began following Awa. There was a place she wanted to take them to – a sacred grove in the forest.

The wind buffeted them back, but they pressed on. The terrain began to shift and change around them.

"This is very strange," said Awa. And right before their eyes, she faded into thin air.

Athena gasped. "Awa!" she called out, but there was no answer.

They were left alone in the Dreamrealm with no guide amidst a raging storm.

"Do you think she woke up?" Rosemary asked.

"Maybe we should too!"

The ground became unstable beneath their feet. They reached out for each other's hands as a jagged and rocky hill emerged before them. Standing atop it were two ominous figures.

Lightning struck, illuminating an old woman in a ragged cloak adorned with bones. The man beside her looked a lot like an evil version of Father Christmas.

"This is not how I expected meeting Santa to go," said Rosemary.

"Now is not the time for jokes," said Athena. "I think I know how to get us out of here. Close your eyes and focus on being back at home in bed."

Rosemary nodded. "I don't know about you, but I don't want to face off against those two."

They both closed their eyes and Athena drew on her magic, willing it to zap through them both, just as she'd woken Rosemary up not so long ago.

With a jolt they both sat up in bed.

"That was not how I expected it to go," said Rosemary, trying to smooth down her hair, which was sticking up with static again. "Thank you for getting us out of there."

Athena shivered. "I'm sure that was the Cailleach and the Holly King. It's strange though, because from what I've read they usually work alone, not as a team. Do you think they were deliberately trying to stop us from reaching Elise? Are they even connected to the Underworld?"

"I don't know," said Rosemary. "But something tells me we were wise not to stick around and ask."

Sixteen

I t was the evening before Rosemary's birthday and she was
just about to settle in for a light supper in front of the fireplace with Athena when the doorbell rang.

Rosemary answered it to find two druids standing there. It
took a moment for her to recognise them as they weren't in their
robes, just regular clothes.

"Oh, hello," said Rosemary.

"We got your message," said Catriona, "and we thought it
would be wise to talk to you in person. Text communication can
lead to various misunderstandings, after all."

"Sure," said Rosemary. "But it's a lot quicker."

"Colla doesn't trust it," said Catriona, glancing at her friend
who was looking around as if somebody might be listening to
them.

"Can we come in?" Colla asked.

Rosemary gestured for them to enter the house and they

settled in in front of the fireplace, where fortunately there were plenty of fruit mince pies and tea to go around.

"So what is it you came all the way from Glastonbury to tell us?" Athena asked.

"The seasonal energy at the moment is uncommonly potent," said Colla. "We're worried some of the winter gods might be trying to reclaim the earth."

"Err, yes..." said Rosemary. "We've had similar suspicions."

Athena frowned. "Unfortunately we have other things to focus on."

"Rosemary told us about your friend," said Catriona. "We understand. Only the winter solstice might be the key."

"So we've been told," said Rosemary. "Time will stand still for five days and it'll be safe to enter the Underworld, or safer at least. We can hopefully get out without being crushed by the forces of time."

"Not only that," said Colla. "The solstice is a powerful time. That's what we came here to tell you. Are you planning on attending the winter solstice festivities in Myrtlewood?"

"We can't," said Athena. "That's our opportunity to rescue Elise."

"You can't afford not to," said Colla gruffly.

Catriona cleared her throat. "What he means is, if you go to the solstice ritual, which the druids will be in attendance at, we can lend you our power. The energy of the ritual itself will help you."

"Unfortunately we need to be sleeping," said Rosemary.

"This causes some complications," said Colla, crossing his arms.

"We need to sleep to enter the Dreamrealm," Rosemary continued. "And it'll be difficult enough as it is, when our guide is on the other side of the world. It'll need to be early enough that she can still reasonably be asleep."

"Sunset is early on the solstice," said Catriona. "Perhaps we can create you some kind of magical dome inside the ritual itself, where you can sleep in your physical form and enter the Dreamrealm."

"It doesn't sound the most comfortable," said Rosemary slowly.

"Or someone else can transport you back in with magical flight," Catriona suggested.

"You mean teleport us?" asked Athena.

The druids nodded.

"I wonder if Juniper will be around," said Rosemary. "She might lend a hand."

"It's worth investigating," said Colla. "Go straight from the ritual to your house, carrying the energy with you, and then fall into a slumber where you can reach the Underworld."

"It sounds so poetic when you put it like that," said Athena.

"It's the best advice we can give you," said Catriona. "The Oak and Holly kings have been at war for centuries. And it seems with the deaths reported recently, the Holly King himself may be trying to take over, using this time of year, his time of greatest strength, to gain a foothold in the world of the living."

"Do you think that could have anything to do with the Underworld?" Athena asked. "Our local historian seems to think there's a connection somehow between our quest to find Elise and all this winter stuff."

"It's possible," said Catriona. "After all, the Underworld and the divine realm of gods are connected, with no easy passage for mortals into either, beyond death itself."

"I didn't know that," said Rosemary. "But I suppose it makes sense."

"There are far too many realms to get your head around, I'm afraid," said Colla.

Rosemary smiled and then her expression turned into one of concentration. "If the Holly King is involved and we face him, whether in the Underworld or Myrtlewood itself, how do we fight him?"

Catriona and Colla looked at each other and shrugged. "You don't," they both said.

"He's a god. How do you fight a god?" Catriona added.

"That's true," said Athena. "The only time we've been able to best a god is with another god."

"Well, there's a thought," said Catriona. "Maybe the Holly King could be bested by the Oak King, or some of the other gods associated with light and the sun and summer. And you could pool the magic together to bind him. It won't last, but temporarily it might help you. Although, I wouldn't risk it if you didn't have a bigger plan. Gods don't tend to like being bound, especially not by mere mortals."

"Thank you for your help," said Rosemary. "I suppose we'll see you at the solstice."

"May the power of the Four Winds be with you," said Catriona, and the druids bade them farewell.

Seventeen

Though the days had passed in an agonisingly slow fashion, the morning of Rosemary's fortieth birthday still dawned far too soon. She woke up feeling groggy, not ready to face the music, but there was music playing...She got out of bed and drifted downstairs. The sound reminded her of an old gramophone.

As she entered the kitchen, she saw Athena, who smiled and held up a plate.

"Waffles?" said Rosemary.

"I was about to bring them up to you, sleepyhead," said Athena, giving her a big hug and a kiss on the cheek. "But you beat me to it." She gestured to the tray that she'd just placed the waffles onto. They looked perfectly crisp, with sides of fruit and cream and syrup.

"But we don't have a waffle maker," said Rosemary.

"You don't need one when you have magic," said Athena with a wink. "Where do you want to eat?"

"Here is fine," said Rosemary. "I'd rather not risk crumbs in bed. This is perfect. Thank you."

They sat down at the kitchen table and Rosemary smiled across at her daughter. "I'm very proud of you. You know?"

"If I knew all it took for you to be proud of me was to make waffles..."

"It's not just the waffles," said Rosemary. "It's everything. Look at you, look how competent and strong you are. The waffles are just a bonus."

She bit into a delicious mouthful. "Mmm, especially when they taste like this. Thank you."

"Do you have any plans for the day?"

Rosemary eyed her suspiciously. "I know you're planning something for tonight, but I was hoping just to lie around and read today."

"That sounds wonderful," said Athena. "And look, you can open your present." She handed Rosemary a parcel.

Tearing back the tissue paper wrapping, Rosemary discovered the most exquisite silk dressing gown she'd ever seen. It felt amazing against her skin and was a peach colour with green and lavender roses and a subtle tassel trim – just enough to be elegant but not long enough to be annoying.

"It's perfect. I love it," said Rosemary. "If only it was warm enough outside for the hammock."

"Aha!" said Athena, clapping her hands. She gestured over to the window seats where Rosemary's hammock had suddenly appeared, hanging by the bay windows.

"I never thought of that," said Rosemary. "You're brilliant! And you know me so well."

"And don't you forget it," said Athena.

They smiled at each other.

It was a wonderful peaceful day, exactly what Rosemary needed. And Athena seemed to be in good spirits despite everything. They lounged around, drank plenty of tea, ate delicious snacks, and read books together in companionable silence.

"This is one of the best days ever," said Rosemary.

"And it hasn't even finished yet," said Athena. "You might want to have a nice bath. In fact, I'm just going to pop upstairs and draw you one."

She returned moments later with the smell of roses wafting with her down the stairs. "Bath's ready," said Athena with a sly smile.

"What's going on with my bath, exactly?" Rosemary asked.

"Nothing," said Athena innocently. "Just go and enjoy it."

Rosemary did have a lovely luxurious bath and washed her hair. When she got out, she found a large cornflower blue package sitting in the middle of her bed. She opened it to find an exquisite evening gown made of luscious silky fabric and lace that looked as if it had been hand-stitched by pixies, and perhaps it was, knowing Athena's family connections.

Rosemary decided not to look a gift horse in the mouth since she wasn't in a war – with Trojans or with her daughter.

She put on the dress, which slipped over her body effortlessly and made her feel gorgeous. She looked in the mirror, admiring it.

"Not bad," she muttered to herself. "Might be forty, but I'm glorious."

"That's exactly right," said Athena from the doorway.

"I didn't know you were there," said Rosemary, shocked.

"I didn't want to miss you finding the dress. But don't worry, I turned away when you were actually getting changed. I don't want to see that!" said Athena.

"Of course not," said Rosemary, rolling her eyes. "It's perfect. I love it."

She gave her daughter another hug.

"Now," said Athena, "I'm going to give you a warning that you're about to be picked up by a handsome gentleman. And then I'll see you a little bit later on."

"A handsome gentleman," said Rosemary. "Well, as long as you're not trying to set me up on a date with your father, I think we'll be okay."

"Don't worry. Not in a million years would I do that. You know what he's like."

There was a knock at the door and Rosemary smiled. Athena nodded to her and said, "Go on."

Rosemary walked down the stairs feeling like a debutante despite her years. She opened the front door to find none other than Perseus Burk standing there, wearing a debonair suit with a cornflower blue cravat to match her dress.

"Why, Rosemary," said Burk, "I do believe it's your birthday, and I hope it's been a happy one."

Rosemary smiled. "It's been a pretty good day so far," she said.

"Will you do the honour of accompanying me?" Burk offered her his arm. She took it, and he guided her down the stairs to an old fashioned limousine.

"This is not your usual ride," said Rosemary.

"No," said Burk, "I borrowed this one especially for the occasion." He opened the backdoor and held it for Rosemary to enter, then got in beside her. Rosemary couldn't see the driver, but the vehicle started up and began moving.

"Where will we be going this evening?" said Rosemary.

"It's a surprise," said Burk with a twinkle in his eye. "Champagne?"

He popped an incredibly expensive looking bottle and poured it carefully into a crystal flute. Rosemary took a sip and it was divine, buttery and mellow, exactly what good bottles should be.

It was early evening and the sun was already setting, though apparently in mid-winter it bothered vampires a lot less.

"Do you remember our sunset date?" asked Burk.

"How could I forget?" said Rosemary. "You mean the one where we found the dead vampire in the field?"

"I was hoping that wouldn't be the first thing that came to mind," Burk admitted.

"But before that it was a lovely date."

"Well, I thought we might watch the sunset together again."

The limousine drove up a steep hill, parked, and Burk led Rosemary out towards what looked like an old castle or battlement, with a stunning view of the sea.

"It's gorgeous," said Rosemary, watching the sun dipping close to the horizon.

"I have a gift for you." Burk handed her a medium-sized box, which she opened to reveal a stunning set of pale blue sapphire earrings and a matching pendant.

"Oh no," said Rosemary, "they're so expensive. You can't be giving them to me."

"They're family heirlooms," said Burk. "Please do me the honour of accepting them. I chose them especially for you."

"From the vault?"

"How did you know there was a vault?" said Burk with a wry smile.

"Woman's intuition," said Rosemary.

"They go perfectly with your dress. Will you at least wear them for tonight?"

"As long as you promise they're not cursed, I'll give them a whirl."

Rosemary felt a flutter of happiness. She put the necklace and earrings on. "Tell me. You've brought another picnic dinner," she said, looking around.

"I'm afraid not," said Burk. "Dinner is a bit later, but I do have some hors d'oeuvres."

He produced a small basket that Rosemary didn't realise he'd been hiding. Out of it, he drew out some fancy canapes that all tasted divine.

Rosemary sipped more champagne and nibbled.

Burk stood behind her, holding her as they watched the sunset over the ocean.

"It's not a bad place," said Rosemary.

"Not a bad life, either," said Burk.

"You don't think I'm getting all old and decrepit, like my insecurities never fail to tell me?"

"Your age is a blessing," said Burk. "Many people never live as long. And with age comes wisdom."

"I love it when you call me wise," said Rosemary, grinning at him.

As soon as the sun had set, Burk looked at his watch. "Time to go, I'm afraid," he said.

"I could stay here all night," Rosemary said. "Have you got any more of those delicious treats?"

"Unfortunately, the universe has other plans for us."

"The universe, or my daughter?"

Burk shrugged. "Both, it would seem." With that, he led her back to the limousine and they set off in the direction of Myrtlewood.

As they drew closer, Rosemary caught a glimpse of the town. It looked different. As they drove towards the centre of the village, she saw an enormous dome had formed right over the whole town circle.

"What is this magic?" Rosemary asked. "Please tell me it's supposed to be like this."

Burk pulled her close and kissed her, before explaining. "It happens every year. The dome is put up for the duration of the winter festival."

"But that starts tomorrow night."

"Exactly," Burk said. "It turns out your daughter is in cahoots with Marjie, who convinced the mayor to put it up a day early so we could have a special dinner inside."

"No way!" said Rosemary with a giggle. "That's outrageous! I'll have to take back every bitter thing I've ever said about Ferg."

"Well, it takes a lot of bravery to stand up to Marjie."

"That's for sure," said Rosemary. "How perfectly sweet of them to go to all that trouble for me."

"You mean the world to them," said Burk, his eyes glinting. "And to me."

Rosemary felt a blush creep across her cheeks. She gave him one last kiss, and then exited the limousine to the sound of cheering.

Athena, Marjie, and all of their closest friends stood in front of the dome's entrance, all dressed up in their glad rags. Ursula and Ashwyn were there with Harry and the twins, Clio and Thea. Neve and the heavily pregnant Nesta were there, of course, with little Mei, along with Liam, Dain, Tamsyn, Elowen, and Sherry. Rosemary smiled and greeted all the people that she and Athena had come to think of as family over the past year. They'd all gathered there for a special birthday dinner for her. It made tears spring from her eyes, which she wiped away quickly before hugging everyone.

"Thank you both so much," she said to Marjie and Athena. "This is really special. I know I said I didn't want a surprise party, but..."

"Perhaps you just didn't realise you wanted one like this," Athena offered.

"Exactly!"

"Wait until you see what it's like inside!" said Marjie.

As they walked inside, Rosemary gasped at the sight of thousands of luminous ice crystals hanging from the ceiling. There were also streamers and balloons everywhere in typical Marjie style.

"Spectacular!" said Rosemary.

Marjie flushed with pride. "Oh, it's nothing really."

In the middle of the dome sat a long table set with an elaborate feast, the food kept piping hot by Marjie's spells.

It was a wonderful evening, and Rosemary enjoyed herself immensely with her friends and family. The food was divine and the atmosphere enchanting. However, she couldn't shake the feeling that something strange was about to happen.

"That's odd," said Neve. "My feet are getting wet." She turned to Nesta. "Your waters haven't broken, have they?"

Nesta looked mortified. "I think I might have noticed if that was the case!"

"But..."

"Look!" said Athena, pointing towards the back of the dome. "It's melting!"

Water was dripping from the ice and a hole had appeared which was quickly growing. There was a cracking sound and Rosemary braced herself in fear that the structure would collapse on them. She only hoped her magic could hold it up.

"Ho, ho, ho!" said a jolly voice.

"Don't tell me it's Santa Claus," said Rosemary.

Marjie frowned. "He's not real."

"No, but I am!" The ice melted away to reveal a tree, or at least, that's what Rosemary took it to be at first, except that it was moving rather like a person.

"The Oak King!" cried Ashwyn, and bowed as he entered.

"Indeed, it is I," he replied, and Rosemary noticed that he did, indeed, seem to be a walking, talking oak tree, with a face a lot like depictions she'd seen of the Green Man.

Rosemary's mind raced with questions, but she didn't know if it was rude or wise to ask them of a god. She and Athena looked at each other in confusion.

"To what do we owe this visit?" said Marjie, after standing and bowing.

The Oak King moved further into the dome and Rosemary noticed an array of flowers followed in his wake, both on the ground and floating in the air, drifting in alongside a summery breeze that brought with it a happy and relaxed feeling.

She stood and bowed, following the lead of the other guests. After all, this was the god of the summer months and she wanted to be on his good side.

"I'm afraid it is not good news that brings me to your fair town, my dear lady," said the Oak King sadly. "I fear my brother, the Holly King, is up to no good."

"That's what we fear as well," said Athena.

"You have heard about the deaths, then," he said gravely. "I normally would slumber at this time of year, and yet my followers, the Children of the Sun, have awoken me with news of his malicious undertakings. I fear he has joined forces with the Cailleach, that cruel old crone goddess. They're trying to bring about eternal winter!"

Marjie frowned at that.

The Oak King raised his hands. "I mean her no disrespect. It is simply that we are always at odds, you see. And now the two of them threaten to steal the summer itself from this world, creating an eternal winter!" He raised his arms dramatically.

"That's what we thought, more or less," said Rosemary. "But why are you here?"

"Ah, I believe you hold the key to that."

Rosemary's jaw dropped. "Me?"

"You are the powerful witch, Rosemary Thorn, are you not?"

"I am, but..."

"And your magic is strong, and connected to this town, which in turn is connected with the seasons themselves."

"Okay...but I'm just a person, not like a god or anything."

"I fear the Holly King has gone well beyond the bounds of the gods," he said, bowing his head in sadness. "What we need, in order to stop him, is a catalyst."

"What do you mean?" Athena asked.

"Someone from this realm with the power to draw the magics together and...stop him."

"That doesn't sound like a catalyst to me," Rosemary mumbled.

"Call it whatever you like," the Oak King said flamboyantly. "I am merely here to offer you my help."

Rosemary nodded. "That could come in handy."

"We're trying to get our friend back from the Underworld," said Athena. "Do you think you could help us with that?"

The Oak King raised a twiggy finger to his chin in contemplation. "Perhaps we can help each other," he said. "I cannot transport you safely to the Underworld, but I do believe that is where my brother is hiding out with the Cailleach – it's her preferred home, you see. She likes the dark."

"Are you sure you can't try?" Rosemary asked. After all, their Dreamrealm adventures hadn't yielded a doorway or even a window yet.

He raised his arms again, releasing a cloud of butterflies that fluttered wondrously around the room.

"One cannot simply take a little mortal to the Underworld," he explained with a chuckle. "The divine realm, perhaps. I've heard of gods taking mortals there to keep as pets. But even that is dangerous. My powers are too immense. I could not protect you from them. However, if you are able to find a way in yourselves, I could meet you there, and together we could stand a chance of defeating my brother and bringing balance to the world."

Athena's eyes lit up with hope. "That's exactly what we need," she said. "Isn't it, Mum?"

Rosemary felt a surge of optimism. After all, as the druids had said – the only way to fight a god was with another god. They didn't know why, but the Holly King and the Cailleach seemed to be standing in their way, given their appearance in the Dream-realm. If the Oak King was on their side it could be a secret weapon in an otherwise insurmountable challenge.

"It seems we're natural allies," Rosemary said.

"It's settled then," the Oak King announced, and disappeared into thin air, leaving nothing but a pile of flowers in his wake.

"Oh, wow!" said Nesta.

"That was quite something." Neve smiled at her.

"No – I think it's a contraction. I'm having the baby!"

A flurry of activity followed in which the two of them were escorted away by Ursula and Ashwyn, who both performed magical midwifery roles from time to time. Tamsyn agreed to look after Mei and the other foundling children.

Sherry and Liam insisted that they'd clean up and sent Rosemary home. Eventually, she, Athena, and Burk climbed back into the limousine and drove back to Thorn Manor feeling rather tired but pleasantly satisfied.

"You know," said Rosemary, "I'm starting to think forty isn't that bad, after all."

Burk smiled at her and Athena looked particularly happy with herself.

Eighteen

It was the middle of the night, and Athena couldn't sleep. She'd been tossing and turning for hours, in dread, her mind circling over and over again about Elise.

Fleur had come to visit them again that afternoon with desperation in her eyes.

Athena offered her tea and comforting words, but Fleur, whose hair had turned jet black again, had not responded well.

In the end, Athena sent her away with one of Una's tonics to calm down. She wouldn't be much help in a panicked state. Athena also gave Fleur some tasks to keep her occupied, such as trawling through any books in Liam's shop for information on the Underworld and going back to visit Agatha Twigg in case the old historian had any further wisdom for them.

Fleur had slunk away with a dead look in her eyes, as if she was beginning to give up hope. Athena tried to assure her they were still doing everything they could and that the winter solstice was their best bet, but Fleur merely nodded and left. Her dread had stirred Athena's dread. She heard nothing from Elise and wondered if she would ever again. Still, she couldn't give up.

A thought occurred to Athena as she lay in bed staring at the ceiling. She slipped out of bed, tied her dressing gown on, and wandered out to the back garden.

Near the forest, she held out her hand and, drawing her magic near, cut a doorway to the fae realm.

She allowed herself to enjoy the familiar rush of soothing energy, that floaty feeling, the satisfaction of homecoming. It seemed wrong to enjoy it too much with Elise gone, but Athena could spare herself this small indulgence.

With the door open, but her feet firmly in the Earth realm, Athena reached out with her magic.

Grandmother, she called, sending a message as far as she could across the realm.

Queen Áine was powerful and could come at short notice if she wanted to.

Athena knew that, but would she? A silence followed and she wondered if she was merely bothering an ancient and powerful queen who had more important things on her mind.

Athena had to try. The queen of the fae had been around for a long time and while she might not have all the answers, there could be something of use that she could tell Athena, something that would help in their quest.

The silence continued, and Athena looked into the purple light of the fae realm. Disappointment bloomed in her chest, heavy and bitter.

Just as she resolved to return to her bedroom, a golden light shone through, and Athena smiled as her grandmother appeared before her.

"My dearest," said Queen Áine, "I sense you summoned me for a crisis or emergency. Are you under threat? Do you need my help?"

"It's not exactly that," said Athena, "but sort of."

"It's your friend, isn't it? The one you call beloved?"

Athena nodded. "It's Elise. We're going to the Underworld to rescue her."

"Dain told me of your plans," said Queen Áine. "But it is treacherous. You will be risking everything."

"I know," said Athena. "I was wondering if there's anything you could tell me that might help," Athena said. "We have so little information."

Queen Áine was silent for a moment as if pondering the question. "It is indeed a shadowy and mysterious place. I myself have been to the divine realm once or twice, but not to the Underworld. Though, they are joined."

"I've heard that," said Athena. "How did you get to the divine realm?"

Queen Áine's mouth twitched. "I may have had a fling with a god or two in my time," she said with a hint of amusement.

Athena blushed, not wanting to know the details.

"The darkness of the Underworld is said to be impenetrable," said Queen Áine. "I do have something for you." She reached to her chest and plucked a gem from her gown. It glowed like yellow sunshine. "This is a sacred stone of the fae, holding the luminescence of the sun from this realm. My intuition tells me that it will help you. Perhaps it will guide you or light your way in the dark." She dropped it into Athena's waiting hands.

"Thank you," said Athena. "Thank you so much."

"I fear this is the prophecy coming to pass," said Queen Áine.

"What prophecy? What are you talking about?"

"Why, child, did your mother not tell you?"

"Tell me what?" Athena asked.

"There is an ancient prophecy about a powerful being, both fae and witch, who will right the balance of the world, weaving together the fabric of time itself."

"Oh," said Athena. "That sounds a bit like..."

"Oh yes," said Queen Áine. "That's right, you read the diary of my sister, before she became the Morrigan. She was obsessed with that prophecy."

"That's right," said Athena. "The Morrigan's diary went on and on about a prophecy. I can't remember the details, but that was such a long time ago, and wasn't that prophecy about her?"

"She certainly thought so," said the Queen. "But my sister has always favoured the dark. She relishes it and revels in it. However, you have the ability to weave both together, which is a great power indeed."

"I don't understand," said Athena. "Are you saying that the dark isn't evil?"

The Queen laughed. "Evil is a funny concept, don't you think? The dark is the unknown. The dark is what we suppress, our shadow, the things we hide from, the things we are frightened of in our lives. The dark is the absence of light, but it is not evil. It is necessary, it is powerful. My sister and I were born different,"

122

said the Queen. "I am naturally drawn towards the light and she towards the darkness. However, both are necessary for life."

Athena nodded. "I think I understand. And my mother knew about this?"

"I told her at the wedding," said the Queen.

"Why didn't she tell me?" Athena felt a surge of anger. She didn't like being kept in the dark about something as important as this.

The queen smiled sympathetically. "Perhaps she felt you had enough to deal with without the burden of ancient prophecy."

Athena took a deep breath and tried to calm herself, not wanting to lose her composure in front of the queen. She would save that for the next conversation with her mother.

Nineteen

Athena stormed into the kitchen the next morning, her anger palpable.

Rosemary stared at her, perturbed. "You've got a bee in your bonnet."

"I can't believe you're keeping secrets from me," Athena exclaimed.

"What are you talking about?" Rosemary asked, confused.

"Last night I talked to my grandmother."

"You went to the fae realm without me? That's incredibly dangerous and irresponsible!"

"Don't be silly, Mum. It's hardly dangerous now, and besides, I did not leave this realm without telling you. I simply cut a door and called to her and she came."

"Oh," said Rosemary, her own anger dissipating somewhat.

"You knew about the prophecy. She told you. And you didn't say anything to me," Athena accused.

Rosemary sighed. "Oh, that."

"Don't 'oh that'! Don't dismiss me."

"No, it's just I really can't abide that ancient gossip. I mean, seriously, whoever made predictions like that – did they actually know what they were talking about? Besides, it's probably been changed over time to be unrecognisable. And on top of all that, don't you have enough to worry about with Elise without having to be the chosen one?"

Athena crossed her arms and pouted. "That's what my grandmother said too," she grumbled. "And I'm *not* the chosen one. It might not be about me at all. I just want to know these things."

"Fine," said Rosemary. "Now you know. What's the big deal?"

She poured their tea from the teapot but Athena refused hers, still clearly too furious.

"The big deal is that you're keeping things from me. You don't want me to go to the Underworld, do you?"

"In an ideal world, no," Rosemary said. "Of course, nobody wants to send their child to the realm of the dead."

"That's why you didn't tell me. You didn't want to encourage me."

"It's not really that," Rosemary argued.

"Stop trying to protect me!"

"Look," said Rosemary, putting her hands on her hips. "It's my job to protect you so long as I live and I'm really doing my best here. I've bent over backwards to try and find out everything we can about Elise, and I'm determined to go with you into the Underworld. I promise, I'm not trying to stop you – as tempting as that is. I promise."

Athena let out a long, slow breath, her anger dissipating. "Okay, fine," she said. "As long as you promise."

"I promise," said Rosemary, holding up her pinkie finger.

Athena smirked and hooked her little finger around her mother's.

"I know you're growing up," Rosemary said with a smile. "And I do want you to. I want you to make your own decisions, even if it means getting into danger. And I'll help you every step of the way when I can. I'm sorry I didn't tell you about the prophecy. It slipped my mind, and even when I remembered, I wasn't sure if it would help or just burden you."

Athena shrugged. "I don't really know what it means anyway. It's not like it's a particularly specific prophecy, is it? It's not like 'you'll go to this street and find a treasure on a map and unlock the key to the universe'."

"Although that would be quite handy," said Rosemary. "It might solve our other problems too. Perhaps we could petition for more specific prophecies in future."

Athena laughed. "Alright. I'm ready for that tea now."

Twenty

Athena felt her bones growing wearier with every passing day. It was the evening before winter solstice while they were sitting at the kitchen table over a humble dinner of roast vegetable soup, when Rosemary's phone rang, sending a strange ringing sensation through Athena's torso.

"Aren't you going to get that?" Athena asked.

"I'll check it later," said Rosemary. "It can wait."

"It might be important. I have a feeling it is."

"Oh, alright then." Rosemary got up from the table and picked her phone up from the kitchen bench. "Hello."

Athena waited in anticipation. She wasn't sure what was going on, but her intuition told her it was exciting news.

"Wow!" Rosemary exclaimed. "Congratulations." She turned to Athena. "It's Neve calling. The baby was born just a little earlier this evening."

Athena beamed at her mother. "I knew it was important. I take it everything went okay."

Rosemary nodded and continued the conversation before pausing and pressing the phone to her shoulder, turning back to Athena. "I've never heard Neve sound so excited. They want us to visit. Are you keen?"

For a moment, all the heavy worries of the past few weeks rushed back and Athena felt she couldn't possibly spare a moment to do something nice like visit a new born baby, but she let the feeling subside and she half-smiled at her mother. "We can't possibly get any more prepared for the winter solstice than we already are, can we?"

Rosemary shook her head. "Besides, worrying and fretting will just drain us and do us no good."

"Okay, then."

Rosemary held the phone back up to her ear to confirm with Neve. "We'll be over after dinner. Is there anything special you're craving?"

They quickly gulped down the last of their soup and put warm coats on before leaving Thorn Manor.

There was a thrill in the air and Athena couldn't tell if it was just her emotional state lifting or whether it was general festive cheer. It was nice to focus on something exciting for a change, not just the hopelessness of the situation with Elise.

Rosemary even let Athena drive the Rolls Royce, which she did with careful attention. They stopped in at Myrtlewood Chocolates to pick up all of Neve and Nesta's favourite treats before arriving at the cute cottage with the wild garden.

Athena couldn't help but think back to the wedding, which had been a wonderful occasion, aside from the tensions with Elise. It was like she was doomed – no matter what she did, she always messed things up with relationships. She still did not want to admit to herself that Elise might really have chosen to go, but in her darker moments, Athena feared that Elise had indeed run away and that she was the reason for it. She shook herself.

Now isn't the time for self-pity or melodramatic agonising over my girlfriend going to the Underworld just to get away from me. Besides, I didn't do anything that bad, did I?

There was a knock at the window "Are you alright, love?" Rosemary asked.

Athena realised she was still sitting in the car, lost in thought. "I'm fine," she replied, plastering on a smile before scrambling out of the car.

The whole house looked as if it was lit up by candlelight.

Rosemary knocked on the door and Neve answered quickly. "Come in!" she called out, hugging them both warmly as they entered.

"I've never seen you so happy," said Athena. "And you're wearing a dress."

Neve looked down at the red velvet slouch dress as if seeing it for the first time. "Oh yes. This is Nesta's. I was in the shower when she went into labour and it all just happened so fast. I had to throw something on and this was the first thing I found." She beamed at them.

"It suits you," said Athena.

"The dress?"

"Yes, and all the smiling," Rosemary added.

They followed Neve down the hallway. There were no candles in sight, and no lights seemed to be turned on either. "Are you doing some kind of magic lighting thing?" Athena asked.

"You'll see," said Neve.

She opened a door and bright golden light streamed out into the hallway, bringing with it a warm happy sensation.

"It's like sunlight," said Rosemary. "Lovely..."

As her eyes adjusted to the brightness, Athena recognised Nesta. She was serene, sitting up in bed, with light shining out around her like a halo from a Renaissance painting.

In her arms was the most exquisite cherubic baby Athena could ever imagine, glowing with bright light.

It would have been alarming, if it didn't feel so special and wonderful.

Athena took a step forward. "Your baby is glowing..."

Those weren't the right words, but she wasn't sure what else to say.

"Yes," said Neve. "Isn't it amazing?"

"The doctor visited earlier," said Nesta. "And so did Ashwyn from the Apothecary. They don't know exactly what's happening, but she's healthy."

"That's what's important," said Neve. "The theory is that because she was a Beltane baby, she's absorbed some of that powerful magic of the summer."

"She's our miracle," said Nesta. "So we're naming her Gwyn. It means miracle in Welsh, which is my ancestry, of course."

Rosemary nodded. "I always thought you had traces of a Welsh accent."

"That's beautiful," said Athena. "She's beautiful."

And in that moment, despite all the challenges they faced, Athena couldn't help but feel hopeful.

Twenty-One

Though the recent days had passed agonisingly slowly, Athena couldn't help but feel a flutter of excitement on the morning of the winter solstice, especially when she got out of bed to find a heart on her mirror, drawn in the steam.

"Don't worry, Elise, we're coming," she wrote back, not waiting around for an answer.

She and Rosemary had spent a lot of time preparing for this day. As they were travelling via dreams, they didn't know how to bring anything with them. Over the past few days, they'd had a few conversations with Awa, who had explained that sometimes things could be transported through the realms, but it wasn't always consistent.

Athena decided to pack a bag just in case it somehow managed to make it not only through her dreams but also into the Underworld with them. She also packed one for her mother because Rosemary had been reluctant.

They'd scoured through dozens of Granny Thorn's books, as well as Athena's personal collection, trying to find out any more information that might help them. And though they'd read a lot of mythology relating to the Underworld and the winter solstice, they were none the wiser on what awaited them this fateful night.

Fleur had been around to the house every day. She wanted to come with them, but Athena and Rosemary had discouraged her. Both Agatha and Marjie had suggested that only very powerful witches or Underworld creatures themselves stood a chance in that dangerous plane.

Awa had guided them back to the Dreamrealm again, twice, and though they hadn't been accosted by any wintery guards, they also hadn't discovered any new information or any paths forward. It was discouraging, and Athena was worried her mother would withdraw support for the entire campaign. But just that morning, Awa had sent them a message. She had a lead on where they needed to go to reach the Underworld itself. Her wise Dreamrealm friends had told her where the gate might be. It was still all hypothetical, and there were no guarantees that any of their work would pay off, but Athena was determined to try.

Her heart ached every time she thought of Elise. She couldn't help but wonder what kind of horrors she faced in that desolate world of the dead.

As Athena came downstairs for breakfast, she found Rosemary had already made toast. She was sitting at the kitchen table, sipping her tea pensively.

"Don't ask me whether I've changed my mind," Athena said with a warning in her voice.

Rosemary shook her head. "I wouldn't dream of it, at least not until things get hairy."

"Good," Athena said. Satisfied, she sat down and began to butter toast for breakfast.

"Do you want to go to the Winter Fair later?" Athena asked. "It goes all afternoon. We might be able to see the pantomime."

Rosemary frowned. "We should save our energy," she said.

"But the winter fair is part of the solstice in a way. If we don't go and experience it, maybe we won't make the most of all of the solstice energy floating around."

Rosemary sighed. "Oh fine. I suppose it will at least distract me from my growing sense of doom."

"Exactly," Athena agreed, pouring her mother more tea. "The less doom we have, the better."

They dressed in their warm coats and made their way into the centre of Myrtlewood.

The icy dome covering the middle of town was even more elaborate looking than it had been on the night of Rosemary's birthday, covered in patterns made by many thousands of snowflakes in varying sizes.

Hundreds of people milled about town, dressed up in warm clothing and scarves.

"It would all be quite nice if it wasn't for the circumstances," said Rosemary. "Festive."

"You should be doing something with your shop – like a hot chocolate stall," said Athena.

Rosemary laughed. "Don't worry, Papa Jack has already taken care of it."

Indeed, Athena noticed that outside the chocolate shop there was an extra little awning with a stand serving hot chocolate and a long line of customers waiting to be served.

"Don't think we'll be able to get one ourselves with that queue," said Rosemary.

"I'm sure he'd let you cut the line," Athena said.

"Never mind, let's go into the dome," said Rosemary excitedly, pulling her daughter towards the enormous ice structure.

The dome was far bigger on the inside than it had been on the night of Rosemary's birthday, like a large cricket field in diameter, but a lot more glimmery.

They walked around, through the excited crowd, taking in the sights and sounds. One side had rows and rows of market stalls filled with magical winter treats, huge stacks of Yule crackers that were supposed to turn into tiny objects of the winner's choosing, elaborate festive desserts, bottles of fae wine promising to bring about different flavours of bliss, and a stunning array of gifts.

As Rosemary and Athena meandered through the bustling market, the scent of Yule spices mixed with the crisp, pine-tinged air filled their senses. The glow from the icy decorations cast a magical light that danced across the crowd.

A cluster of Spellweaver scarves in hues of twilight purples and midnight blue immediately caught Athena's attention. Each thread seemed to hum with an enchantment, while apparently emanating a gentle warmth that could shield the wearer from the coldest winter chill. She bought two, just in case they were needed, though like everything else she planned to bring with her, she doubted whether they'd make it through to the Underworld.

They paused briefly to chat to Marjie, who had arrived late, looking a little dishevelled with her new friend Delia, Agatha

Twigg, and a couple of other women of a similar age who Athena didn't recognise. Marjie chatted somewhat frantically to Rosemary with a gleam in her eye while Athena surveyed the stalls nearby.

Just around the corner, a collection of glistening ice-flower earrings twinkled with crystalline petals. Each pair, when worn, whispered a soothing melody that only the wearer could hear, like the soft lullaby of a gentle snowfall.

Nestled between a bookbinder and a silversmith, Rosemary spotted a vendor selling the most extraordinary Yule phoenix candles with the fragrant scent of sacred resins. A sign explained that they held a flame which danced but never burned out.

Athena couldn't help but long to experience all of this with Elise. She imagined a year in which they could buy each other presents and spend a lovely time together, but she knew it wasn't going to happen anytime soon.

She felt a momentary surge of anger.

How dare she leave us? Leave me?

Though Athena mostly felt bad for Elise, having made an unfortunate decision to go to the Underworld, Athena couldn't help but have moments of rage. Elise chose to leave, after all. She chose to leave their entire world behind, even if she had been affected by a curse and must not have been in her right mind.

It all just seemed so unfair. And it wasn't just Elise she was mad at, perhaps it was the gods and the whole world which seemed to be plotting against her.

Athena quickly shook herself, pulling herself out of her resentments, for she knew they would do her no good.

She and Rosemary found seats on the other side of the dome,

where the pantomime was about to start. The pantomime told the story of Taliesin the hero, played by a rather overly enthusiastic Ferg, who started off a mortal boy, becoming servant of the great mother-crone goddess, Cerridwen, played by the tiny and terrifying Marla Twigg. Athena knew the story, or some of the versions of it. While tending Cerridwen's cauldron, Taliesin mistakenly drinks three drops of a special potion intended for the goddess's son, bringing with it the gifts of awen: inspiration and wisdom. He runs away, shapeshifting with magic from the potion and pursued by Cerridwen who also shapeshifts to catch him.

Athena was more impressed by Ferg's magical costume changes than she was by the over-done acting, but something in the story seemed strangely relevant in a way that Athena couldn't quite rationalise. When Taliesin-Ferg turned into grain and was finally caught by the goddess who gobbled him up in her hen form, only for him to be reborn as her own child, Athena wondered whether the story itself was a metaphor for the rebirth of the seasons after winter. She couldn't help but feel there was something else hidden in the story, something important she was missing.

Twenty-Two

T he pantomime came to an end and Ferg took to the stage, now dressed in a bright purple velvet cloak with embroidered gold panels and a matching hat that reminded Rosemary of the Pope.

Standing next to Ferg was a druid woman he introduced as Clodagh, who had wavy sandy-coloured hair. She wore robes embroidered with golden symbols. Rosemary thought she recognised her from the summer solstice rituals.

"Fine people of Myrtlewood and our treasured guests," said Ferg, waving his arm elaborately. A golden staff that matched his outfit appeared in his hand, and he thumped it down onto the stage. "Thank you all for coming to our winter solstice celebration. The grand event – the ritual itself – is about to commence. We welcome the druids, including lady Clodagh here, who have come to support Myrtlewood at this time, as it has been throughout our long history of alliance."

Ferg paused, looking sombre. "Some of you know there have been unfortunate occurrences in town recently." The audience hushed. "It is our hope that this rite of winter solstice will appease our kind and gracious gods."

Athena and Rosemary looked at each other, unconvinced.

"Let us begin," said Ferg, tapping his staff. "Please stand!"

The audience did so. Ferg thumped this staff down again and the seating disappeared. The market stalls must have been hidden somehow.

They were all left standing in the vast icy dome. It was a spectacular sight with the light dancing through the ice crystals.

"If you all will, please make a circle," said Ferg.

Ashwyn cast the circle and the druids chanted their awens. Pronounced ah-oo-wen, the sound reminded Rosemary of a resonant gong or singing bowl. Clodagh had explained to everyone that the word meant inspiration and sacred wisdom.

"We're certainly going to need some of that," said Rosemary, before Athena hushed her.

The druid priestess Clodagh stepped into the centre of the circle and began to greet the powers of winter and thank them.

Ferg began to speak again in what Rosemary had come to think of as his ceremonial voice:

In the grip of winter's sombre reign,
We converge 'neath Yule's ember flame.
Longest shadows of the solstice night,
Bear witness to Cailleach's sacred rite.

. . .

In the glow of candles' hopeful sheen,
   We honour thus, the Winter Queen.
   Her frost-kissed touch, a boon we crave,
   To guide us through the sunless days.

Gifts we offer, blessings true,
   Echoes of our reverence and gratitude.
   To bide winter's frost-etched tableau,
   And the spellbound magic in its snow.

We whirl, we chant, we weave our spells,
   Under the star-kissed canopy that dwells,
   In the Winter Queen's icy might,
   We find joy in Yule's deepest night.

So, raise a toast, let voices rise,
   In the darkest winter skies.
   We praise the Cailleach as she draws near
   And the mystical secrets she holds dear.

As the longest night surrenders to dawn's soft glow,
   And the promise of lengthening days doth show,
   We call forth blessings, a triad divine,
   For health, harmony, happiness, in time's design.

. . .

And so, by powers of land, sky, and sea,
  As we do will it, so mote it be.

Rosemary could feel the stillness of the Earth as it rested at this time of year. Though she didn't personally enjoy the bitter cold, she could understand the value of the season itself; the earth needed to rest.

There was something beautiful about the peacefulness and stillness of the ritual. It was different from the other seasonal festivals she'd been to – such silent reverence here, despite the large crowd.

Rosemary took Athena's hand, just as they'd planned, connecting with the magic of the ritual, allowing it to bind with their magic in the hopes that they could capture some of its power and essence for whatever lay ahead.

"From our darkest night, a new day will dawn and a new spring will come," said Clodagh, raising up her hands. "We thank the gods and goddesses and we ask that they lend us their power, so that we may face our own challenges with strength and wisdom." She shot Rosemary and Athena a meaningful look.

Rosemary nodded subtly in acknowledgment. The druids would help. Rosemary didn't know what that meant. She just hoped that whatever assistance they offered would be useful. Something told her they were going to need it.

Twenty-Three

They left the solstice festivities as soon as the ritual finished and hurried home to Thorn Manor to find that the house had set up cosy looking beds for them in the living room and the fire was burning bright and warm in the hearth.

Rosemary smiled. "Darling house. What would we do without you?" She gave the mantlepiece a little pat.

"I suppose this is where we're setting up then?" said Athena, gesturing to the beds that sat in the middle of the room, complete with purple feather-stuffed eiderdowns and fluffy pillows.

Rosemary nodded. "It would be rude not to, after Thorn Manor has put in so much effort to accommodate us." She wondered whether the house could think and feel, or whether it merely responded to their own conscious or subconscious needs. Either way, it was brilliant.

Both Serpentine and Nugget hung around, begging for pats

and cuddles, as Rosemary and Athena prepared for a long and busy sleep.

"You stay here and protect us," Athena said, scratching both familiars lovingly behind the ears.

Rosemary smiled and gave them pats too, before turning back to the preparations.

They both took two teaspoons of Una's special sleeping draught that she'd prepared with extra *Artemisia Vulgaris* for vivid dreaming, then they got into the beds and relaxed.

Rosemary felt herself quickly drifting off to sleep while she repeated the Dreamweaver's chant in her head, just as they'd practiced.

I am water, earth, sun, and sky.

I am dawn, noon, dusk, and midnight...

Athena's telepathic voice mingled with her own as she found herself floating through the sky, gently alighting on the ground. The green grass of the meadow was vibrant against her feet, the sky a brilliant swirling purple above. As surreal as it was, this was exactly where they needed to be, even if the thought of the journey ahead brought no small amount of trepidation.

"Here we are," said Athena's voice.

Rosemary turned and smiled at her daughter's slightly transparent dream form as it solidified next to her. "What now?"

"Awa?" Athena asked.

Her voice echoed around the meadow.

"Maybe we can go to the tree?" Rosemary suggested. "I quite liked her. She might know something."

Just then, sparkles appeared in front of them and Veila burst into the air with a tinkle of bells. "Oh, there you are!"

Rosemary smiled at the strangely enthusiastic fairy-like creature. "Uhh, yes. And where is our guide?"

"Awa is coming. She was here before but got woken up. It's Saturday morning where she is and she's trying to sleep-in now, as far as I can tell. She can be a bit unpredictable sometimes!" Veila giggled and flipped around in the air.

"Who are you calling unpredictable?" said a familiar voice.

"You made it!" Athena grinned as they greeted the Dreamweaver.

"I said I'd do my best, but we don't have much time. Mum's making pancakes and says I'll probably have an hour. She usually burns the first batch." Awa laughed and then her expression became more serious. "This first part, through the Dreamrealm, will be easy, but I can't help you with what comes next. Are you completely sure you want to do this?"

"Yes," said Athena.

"And I'm not letting you go alone," Rosemary added, resting her hand on her daughter's shoulder. She'd learnt that lesson the hard way. Athena had a will of steel. Opposing her would only fuel her determination, but at least going with her meant her heartstrings would stay intact. She needed to know Athena was okay, no matter what.

Awa led the way, guiding them through the meadow. There was no flying this time – it seemed their intended destination was closer than anticipated.

"I didn't realise it," said Awa, as they moved towards what looked to be a giant crater in the ground, "but I know this place... this gate. I've never been through it, of course, but it seems I helped to unearth it when I was mastering my powers."

144

"And you're sure this is the right place?" Rosemary asked.

"Honu told me it is," said Awa. "And I trust him with my life."

Rosemary's feeling of unease intensified as they drew closer. The crater looked deep and ominous, but perhaps that was to be expected where the Underworld was concerned. They reached the edge of the crater and began to clamber down, following Awa who was much quicker, and Veila who preferred to dart around in the air and occasionally call out encouragement or giggle at them.

Awa turned and waited for them to catch up. "If you need to get back through here, try to make your way back to the gate and call out to me. I can't guarantee I'll be nearby, and I might not be asleep, but I'll help if I can."

"Thank you," said Rosemary. It was only slightly reassuring, but it was good to have some kind of escape plan, however tenuous it seemed.

"This is where I leave you," Awa said.

They stood amid the ruins of an ancient labyrinth.

"But what if it doesn't work?" Rosemary asked.

Awa shrugged. "This is where Honu told me to take you. The Priestess Tree agreed. I can't go any further. Down there is no longer my realm. Head to the centre of what used to be the Labyrinth, that's my guess."

They thanked the Dreamweaver and continued on, clambering over the rocks, deeper into the chasm.

The purple sky swirled above them, deceptively peaceful compared to the turmoil Rosemary felt.

It had all been fine when it was hypothetical, when they were doing what they could to help rescue Elise, but now she was afraid that it wouldn't work and even more afraid that it would – and that they'd find themselves in the Underworld, awaiting some dark fate with no friends to help them.

"Over here," Athena said as she climbed over a large rock and held out her hand for Rosemary, to help her over.

They stood on what looked like an old mosaic floor with a Celtic pattern weaving in and out of a circle.

"There's nothing here," said Rosemary.

Athena sighed. "Maybe Honu was wrong." She stood in the centre of the circle of tiles, closed her eyes, and added, "But he can't be wrong. We've just got to figure out how...."

Athena took a deep breath and Rosemary could see she was connecting her own magic with the magic of the place, willing it to reveal a way forward.

With trepidation, Rosemary lent her own magic to help her daughter, as much as she wanted to run back to the waking world and forget all about this place.

The earth began to tremble. Rosemary reached for Athena and they both ducked down and scrambled back as the rocks rose to reveal a dark opening of a cave.

"This is it then," Athena said in a high tone of voice. "It's just like Honu said. We've done it."

They looked at each other and Athena's expression of triumph turned into one of fear.

"It's okay if you don't want to come, Mum. I understand."

Rosemary shook her head. "There is no way I'm letting you go in there alone. And as much as I want us both to turn back, I know you can't. We've got to do this."

Athena shot Rosemary a grateful smile. "Thank you. I can't say I want to go in there alone."

They couldn't see anything in the darkness as they peered into the cave.

They continued holding hands as they stepped forward into the shadows. They were enveloped by the darkness almost as if it was a kind of liquid, icy cold and terrifying.

They continued on walking slowly, deeper and deeper into the cave.

Icy wind whipped past them, chilling Rosemary to the bone.

Athena shivered next to her. "I can't see anything." She held out her hands as if to summon magic, but nothing came. "Can I not use my magic in here?" Athena asked. "We're going to be completely helpless..."

Rosemary shook her head. "I don't know...It might not be too late if you want to turn back."

"Don't be silly," Athena replied. "We have to try."

They pressed on through the darkness feeling out each tentative step in front of them in case the ground gave way.

They could see nothing of the terrain through which they walked. Every step was a risk that could prove fatal.

However, as they continued on, Rosemary breathed a silent prayer to their guardian gods and goddesses, as whatever path they were on seemed to remain stable.

They continued walking through the darkness and the bitter freezing cold.

Rosemary grew weary; though she knew technically she was asleep back in the earth realm, this was not the restful slumber that she craved at all.

Her entire being was heavy with exhaustion. The thought of crumpling to the floor in that darkness and just giving up was tempting, though it would do no good. Nor would it help to complain to Athena, who was no doubt experiencing the same turmoil.

"No wonder people don't come here on holiday," Rosemary joked, trying to lighten the mood.

Athena laughed, her teeth chattering. "I don't know if I can go on," she said in a tiny voice. "But if we turn back now, who knows if we'll ever make it back to the entrance. I can't see anything back there."

Rosemary nodded. "I think we're past the point of no return now. We'll have to keep going into the darkness, but I do believe that we will find a way out eventually."

They held each other closer as they continued on into the unknown.

Twenty-Four

In the cold, devastating icy darkness, Athena longed for comfort. She wished that her backpack of supplies had made it through the realms, but nothing had.

She didn't even know what she was wearing anymore. In fact, the whole universe seemed to be nothing but inky black night, so desolate it was almost as if daylight had been just a dream, and darkness was all that ever was.

She held tight to Rosemary's hand. Her mother gave her palm a squeeze, and in that moment, the small comfort it gave her reminded her of the gift that Queen Áine had bestowed upon her: the glowing faerie crystal.

Surely, that could light the way in the darkness, and maybe there was even a way it could make it through.

There was nothing for it. Athena raised her free hand to her solar plexus, where Queen Áine had plucked the crystal from her gown, imagining its glowing radiance.

149

"What are you doing?" Rosemary asked as Athena paused. "Wait, what's that?"

Athena opened her eyes to see a subtle glow. The small golden stone slipped into her hand.

"How did you do...?" Rosemary asked.

"This is what my grandmother gave me," said Athena. "I didn't think it was going to work, but I've somehow managed to summon it. Maybe it's connected to my fae energy, my power."

"Well, whatever it is, I'm glad for it."

Athena held up the stone carefully. It illuminated only a tiny circle of the ground in front of them, but still, it was better than walking into complete uncertainty.

They walked much more confidently, grateful for every shred of light emanating from the crystal.

"How long do you think we've been walking?" Rosemary asked.

"An age," said Athena, "or an eon. However long that lasts. Seriously though, I have no idea."

"It can't possibly have been days. Could it?" Rosemary said. "I mean, surely we would have collapsed by now. Or somebody would have tried to wake us....if it gets too far past the solstice."

"Can they, though?" Athena asked, trying to suppress the chill that rose up when she thought of the consequences. "We might well have been walking in this darkness for years, never to return."

"Don't say that," said Rosemary. "We're going to find Elise, and then we're going to get back to our own realm. Everything is going to be just chipper."

"I don't think that's how that word works," said Athena. "But I appreciate your enthusiasm."

They continued on for what seemed like miles. Eventually, the darkness all around them began to subtly give way to a faint light, grey on the horizon, that revealed they were walking across a wide flat plane. Athena was grateful for it. They hadn't had to stumble over any rocks or risk falling.

Still, it was eerie. A biting wind continued to whip past them as they walked.

"What's that?" Rosemary pointed out to the right.

A cluster of lights floated through the air, emitting a sound a little bit like humming in harmony.

Athena gasped. "I think it might be souls."

"Souls of the departed?" Rosemary asked. "Aren't they supposed to be drifting towards the white light?"

Athena shrugged. "Perhaps they're just going for the soul equivalent of a walk."

"I'm still feeling ripped off about the white light thing," Rosemary muttered. "Isn't that what everyone always says about death?"

"Oh, Mum, I don't think this is the normal path to the Underworld. We've entered through the back door. They must reserve the light show for the official entrance."

Rosemary gazed up at the twinkling lights. "It looks kind of nice though. They do seem to be having a good time."

Athena smiled for the first time in what felt like an age. "Come on. Let's keep going."

She felt increasingly exhausted as they continued on. Rosemary, too, appeared weary, but she wasn't complaining, for a change.

"What's that up ahead?" Athena asked as a shimmer on the ground caught her eye.

In the low light, it took a few moments to realise that they'd reached an enormous ocean of water that went as far as the eye could see in both directions.

They neared the shore. "What now?" Athena asked.

"I don't fancy swimming in that, whatever it is," said Rosemary. "I don't even want to dip my toe in. What if it's poisonous? Are we even technically dead...I mean, temporarily?"

"I have no idea," Athena replied. "Maybe we're not technically anything. This is all highly unconventional, after all."

"How do we cross? Do we pay the ferryman with coins on our eyes?"

"I think that only works for the dead," said Athena. "And besides, we're not Greek."

Rosemary shrugged. "I assume Greek mythology is somewhere around here. I mean, it would be expensive to have multiple Underworlds, wouldn't it?"

"You're probably right," Athena agreed. "Aside from the expense thing, I mean. I get the feeling there's no one right way of seeing things. No one true pantheon. They're all just kind of out there somewhere, these incredibly powerful sentient beings, doing their godly things."

"What if we send out some kind of pulse into the water and see what happens?" Rosemary suggested.

Athena hesitated. "That sounds dangerous. What have you done with my mother?" she joked, trying to lighten the mood.

"All of this is dangerous," Rosemary said, her voice firm. "Come on, let's give it a try." She made a fist with her hand and they both concentrated on the water, sending out their intention over the surface in hopes of finding a way to cross.

Twenty-Five

As they stood before the vast ocean in the Underworld, a low resonant sound echoed around them, rippling across the water.

"What was that?" Rosemary asked.

Athena shrugged. Suddenly, the scent of salt and mint rose up through the air, and the water in front of them began to gurgle and spout like a fountain.

From the depths, a figure emerged, scaly green and blue and gold and silver – the colours of the sea, rippling across like paint. A great, long-bearded man of the sea stood before them.

At first, Rosemary thought it was a statue, but then he spoke.

"Who summons me, Manannán of the sea?"

Athena and Rosemary exchanged a quick glance, unsure of how to respond. Before Rosemary could say anything, Athena answered, "My name is Athena Thorn, and this is my mother, Rosemary. We seek passage to the other side."

"You choose to go willingly into the realm of the dead, witches?"

"We do," said Athena. "We must."

"And what would you give me in return?" he asked.

Athena looked down at the stone in her hand, wondering if that was the price she needed to pay. But Manannán shook his head. "Not an object. I have no need for baubles."

"What about a story?" Rosemary suggested.

"Ahh...That would be marvellous!" Manannán grinned. "You must tell me a story as we go across."

"But how?" Rosemary began to ask.

Manannán snapped his fingers.

More gurgling erupted from the sea and a boat began to emerge next to him, big enough to seat the two of them.

It was oddly dry inside, as they clambered in.

"Now," said Manannán. "You must tell me a story that is interesting or we might not make it to the other side."

Rosemary gulped.

"What makes a story interesting to you?" Athena asked.

"Ahh, that is a good question. I will answer it with ancient wisdom: the ring of truth, the soulfulness of heart, and the grace of God," Manannán explained. "These three things make a great story."

"It's a triad," said Athena.

Rosemary looked at her, questioningly.

"It's something the druids like," Athena explained. "It's like a poem, a way of imparting wisdom concisely."

"I like little bite-sized chunks of wisdom," said Rosemary. "I approve."

"Well, in that case," Athena said, turning her attention back to Manannán, "I will tell you a story that is very personal to me."

"Then it is already soulful indeed!" he announced. Raising his arms, the boat began to glide seamlessly across the water as Athena began to tell her story.

Rosemary smiled at her daughter as she articulately recounted their journey of moving to Myrtlewood, her first taste of magical power, her meeting with Finnigan and Elise, her forays into the fae realm, her great heartaches.

The boat moved so swiftly across the water that Athena had only reached the point in the story where Elise had vanished to the Underworld by the time they reached the other side of the shore.

"Oh, how I wish this story would go on," said Manannán. "You have done what you promised, and entertained me across the sea."

"Perhaps you'll meet me here for your return journey then," said Athena.

"I would be delighted," he replied.

They disembarked onto a rocky shore and Manannán disappeared back into the water. Rosemary and Athena were left staring at the bright, new world that they encountered around them – white, sparkling sands beneath their feet and wispy colours drifting through the air like clouds of silky mist.

"It's beautiful," Athena said.

"It is," Rosemary agreed. "But that doesn't mean it's not dangerous."

Twenty-Six

As her eyes adjusted to the brightness of the light, Athena noticed that it was all shining from one side, to the left of the sea, whereas there was darkness on the right.

Through the wispy colours, a path emerged before them.

Not knowing what else to do, they began to walk it tentatively, at first looking around for any potential dangers.

"I can make out rolling hills in the light to the left," Athena said, "whereas, to the right is only darkness and rugged terrain."

"What do you think is going on?" Rosemary asked. "Where are we?"

"My guess is that over that way towards the light is how you get to the divine realm of gods," Athena said, pointing in the direction of the light.

"Does that mean we head that way?" Rosemary asked darkly, pointing in the direction of the dark, rugged landscape.

"I think so," Athena said.

As they continued, the path began to wind more narrowly and split into three. One way looked glorious and meandered into the light through the charming hills. On the other side, there was barely a path at all and it descended down into the darkness.

In the middle the path became increasingly narrow as it wound along the steep ridge towards a mountain.

"I can just make out some sort of structure," said Rosemary.

Something in Athena's gut told her she knew to whom it belonged. "I have a feeling that's where Cerridwen, the old crone goddess, lives."

"Like in that Yule play?"

"Yes, but I can't believe that's all you recognise her from, Mum. Cerridwen is a very important goddess. Keeper of the cauldron of knowledge...her magic is important for transformation and rebirth."

"What makes you think that's her house?" Rosemary asked.

"Good intuition?" Athena suggested. "I don't know. The thought just occurred to me and I'm sure it's true. And besides, I've read that she lives in a house like that. An old cottage between the worlds, though I think there's also supposed to be a cave or something."

"I'd rather go to a cottage than into the darkness," Rosemary said.

"I don't think we have much of a choice," Athena said. "I'm sorry, Mum. I know it's scary. I can go on alone..."

"Not in a million years, kid," Rosemary said. "Let's do this."

They held hands again, unsure of what was coming and afraid they might be separated.

As they descended the path into the inky blackness, they

entered a cavern of rock. It wasn't quite as pitch black as when they'd first entered through the Dreamrealm, but it wasn't far off.

As their sight adjusted to the lack of light, Athena noticed that the cavern gave way to what appeared at first to be glow worms, but they soon realised it was in fact a vast skyscape, lit not by stars but what appeared to be souls drifting around, some in groups, some individually. Their singing was quite beautiful, like a heavenly celestial choir, creating harmonies that filled Athena's tired heart with wonder.

"I don't feel like it's dangerous," Athena said. "I feel safe."

"I know what you mean," Rosemary said. "But, remember, this realm is not for the living."

As they continued to walk into the darkness, a chill returned to the air around them.

"Look!" said Athena, pointing up. A snowflake drifted through the air.

"Watch your step," said Rosemary. "The ground looks icy down there."

The earth beneath them, or whatever it was that they walked across, was frosted with ice.

"Do you think they might be near?" Athena asked. "The Holly King and the Cailleach?"

"Possibly," said Rosemary. "But I hope not. I don't like our chances against them."

"We could summon him, the Oak King," said Athena.

No sooner had she spoken the summery god's name, than the snowflakes above them were replaced with flowers and butterflies.

"You called," said the Oak King, bursting into the air in front of them, five times larger than he'd appeared on earth, in all his green, glowing glory. "Ahh, witches, you made it! How marvellous! And, by the looks of the ice here, you have led me right to them as I intended. Well, come. We must stop the winter treachery before it's too late."

It felt as if they were being diverted from their most important mission; perhaps that explained the creeping dread in Athena's gut. She felt as if she were being pulled, gliding through the air with Rosemary next to her.

In front of them a structure emerged – a vast and impressive castle of ice to rival anything she'd seen in fairy tale books.

"Ahhh, here it is," the Oak King said. "But what is this? The energy around you." He shivered. "Why is it that you bring the energy of winter when what we need is the opposite?"

Athena felt a chill of suspicion that had nothing to do with the temperature.

"The druids told us that we needed to connect with the winter solstice in order to rescue our friend," Rosemary said.

"That is not the answer," the Oak King said sadly. "Look around you! This bleak wintery landscape is lifeless and barren. This is the world my brother the Holly King seeks to create on Earth. Quickly, lend me your powers. Let us destroy their mansion and dilute their power before they realise we are here."

"Wait," Athena said, but before she had a chance to voice her doubts, the Oak King raised his arms, and the Thorn witches fell to their knees. Athena groaned and Rosemary whimpered as he drew upon their innate ancestral magic, draining them of the powers they could not even properly use themselves, in this realm.

Something about this was dreadfully wrong, but they were powerless to stop it. Even in the earth realm, gods were too powerful. Here they were even stronger. Athena wracked her brain, but the only thing she could think that could help them now was another god.

She reached for that wintery energy, hoping that it could act as a beacon for the gods nearby. Eternal winter or not, she couldn't risk this arrogant summer god draining and destroying them – at least the Oak King's nemesis would be a strong distraction.

Just then, a blustering gust of snowy wind hit them, knocking Athena and Rosemary to the ground.

She scrambled upward, helping her mother to her feet as the Holly King emerged, floating above the castle, again giving the impression of a horror-story version of Santa Claus with a big white beard, clad in animal furs. His muscular form was enormous and surrounded in an orb of fluttering snow. It would have been a beautiful sight if it wasn't for the terror it elicited.

Athena and Rosemary looked around, but the Oak King had vanished.

"Who dares approach?" the Holly King bellowed from the sky. "Witches!" he cried, swooping closer.

"He's been here," said another voice, cold and brittle and old. The Cailleach emerged from the front of the ice castle, almost as tall as the Holly King, but stooped over a long white gnarled walking cane. Her long grey-and-white hair was matted and twisted with bones, and her clothing appeared to be made of rags. She moved swiftly towards them in an unnatural way that reminded Athena of an insect.

"Why are you here?" the Holly King growled from the sky.

Athena took a sharp inhale. "We came to the Underworld to rescue my friend."

"Lies!" cried the Cailleach. "*He's* been here! Your brother...and they are in league with him!"

"Err, actually..." said Rosemary, before Athena could stop her, "he was here, but he was kind of awful and we only said we'd help him because there've been a number of deaths in Myrtlewood attributed to winter magic. You wouldn't happen to know anything about that?"

"Shh!" said Athena. The last thing they needed now was to rile up angry and potentially murderous gods.

The Cailleach pierced Rosemary with cold wintery eyes. "What nonsense you speak, child."

Rosemary blanched, clearly not used to being called a child, but then again the goddess before them must be ancient.

The goddess thumped her bony cane on the ground, sending forth a blast of ice that rattled right through to Athena's bones. She gasped, drawing on her own energy to buffer her mother against the chill. She felt Rosemary do the same. Their magic was still there in this world – it was just different, muted.

"Please, if you just stop killing people, we have nothing against you," said Athena.

"Enough!" another voice broke through amid glowing sunshine. The Oak King, opposite his brother. "It is time, brother! We must fight to the death!"

The Cailleach shook her head. "Not this again," she muttered and stalked off into the darkness.

The Oak King raised his arms and the bright light of summer beamed forth, bringing with it a chorus of birdsong and waves of budding flowers, blooming through the air as his magic burst out towards his brother.

The Holly King moved away from the ball of wintry energy he was hovering in and sent it crashing towards the Oak King.

As the two opposite forces met, a thunderous blast of energy shot out all around sending waves of force through the air.

Athena felt herself sailing back in the darkness, losing her grip on her mother's hand with nothing else in sight but the terrible endless night.

Twenty–Seven

The blast blew Rosemary deep into the darkness. She looked around for Athena, but there was no one in sight. She was cold and alone, and while she heard the thunder of what was probably the continued battle between the gods, she had no idea which direction it was coming from or where Athena was, or whether she was even safe.

Rosemary struggled through the darkness, calling out Athena's name. She must have been blown back some distance from the scene of the icy battle, as she could see nothing.

With no light to guide her and her desperation increasing, she almost called out to the Morrigan but held back for fear of the consequences.

Athena was out there somewhere and hopefully safe. Rosemary prayed to all the divine powers that existed.

"Please, whoever's listening," she said. "I don't want to cause any more trouble. I just want to know she's okay. I *need* her to be okay."

She tried to call on her own magic to light the way, but it didn't work. Not even a subtle glow emerged through her hands in the inky night.

"Somebody help me…" she whispered into the darkness.

"You could have just said something earlier," a familiar slightly croaky voice replied from right beside her.

Rosemary jumped as Granny's form, ghostly and opaque, emerged.

"Granny! I've never been so happy to see you in my life!"

Granny raised an eyebrow.

"Trust me," said Rosemary. "It's been a hard day."

Granny began to become more corporeal, right in front of Rosemary's eyes.

"You can be a physical being here?" Rosemary asked.

"It takes a bit of effort," Granny said. "But I thought we could both do with a hug."

Rosemary smiled weakly and gratefully. She felt a subtle warmth fill her at the thought of embracing her grandmother. She leaned in and inhaled the herby mysterious scent of Galderall Thorn.

Rosemary tried to pull back, but Granny held her there a moment longer.

"I think you need this for strength," Granny said, patting Rosemary on the back.

Rosemary felt a single tear roll down her cheek as she leaned into her grandmother's shoulder.

After a moment, Granny let her go, and Rosemary felt much calmer and more stable.

"Thank you," Rosemary said. "But what on earth am I going to do now? Can you find Athena?"

"*You* will find her," said Granny. "I know it to be true. But you do need to trust your intuition."

"Of course I do," said Rosemary, rolling her eyes.

"Alright, then. Where does your intuition tell you to go?"

Thoughts swam through Rosemary's mind, the image of a winding path leading up to a dark, eerie cottage. "Cerridwen's house?" Rosemary was puzzled.

Granny nodded. "That's where you should go," she said. "I cannot stay in this form much longer. But I'll be with you in spirit one way or another."

"Thank you."

As Granny disappeared, Rosemary noticed a tiny trail of light illuminating the path in front of her.

When you're ready, a way will be made. Granny's voice drifted through Rosemary's mind, telling her she had to follow the path.

Rosemary didn't understand this place. Why could the gods appear as solid forms whereas Granny could only maintain it for a minute? She had so many questions, but the old woman had disappeared before she could ask them.

Oh stop your complaining, said Granny's voice in Rosemary's head. *This part of the Underworld is a liminal place. I can only stay here briefly in any kind of obvious form before I have to go back to the land of spirits, or the spirit realm, as it's sometimes called. I can do whatever I like there. It's marvellous! You'd love it. Though don't go there in too much of a hurry.*

166

"I'm not trying to," said Rosemary as Granny's voice faded away again.

After some time, Rosemary found herself in front of the winding path again.

A cold wind rushed past her, bringing with it a shiver, a feeling of unease, suggesting she should turn back. But she couldn't. If Granny couldn't help her find Athena, maybe Cerridwen could.

Rosemary knew very little about the ancient crone goddess, except that she was highly revered, connected to inspiration, and had a big cauldron. It wasn't very much to go on.

As she embarked over the windy ridge, Rosemary braced herself, apprehensive, not knowing what would befall her if she stumbled and fell off into the cavernous darkness below.

A murder of crows, or perhaps bats, fluttered about, but it was too far away for Rosemary to tell if it was a bad omen.

As she progressed, the sky was lighter but still dark and grey; visibility was poor against the dull landscape.

Rosemary's foot slipped, knocking some loose stones from the edge of the path. They fell but made no sound, suggesting it would be a long tumble down to wherever the fall would lead her.

I've just got to keep going. She reminded herself to trust her intuition. *One step at a time.*

The cottage had seemed rather small from a distance, but as Rosemary drew near, it grew bigger and bigger.

The steps loomed large and Rosemary had to hoist herself up to climb them. It helped that she didn't have her physical body with her – the spectral dream-like form she currently occupied was far easier when it came to climbing.

Finally, she reached the cottage door, towering above her. She reached up and jumped towards the blackened brass knocker. Fortunately it slid down the door towards her. Rosemary grasped it and rapped on the door three times.

All was silent and she wondered if anyone was home.

A banging sound jolted Rosemary backwards and the enormous door began to slowly creak open toward her.

At times like this, Rosemary wanted to look to Athena and share a reassuring glance, but there was nobody else. She was alone in whatever danger she was walking into. She only hoped that Athena was safer.

"Hello!" Rosemary called out, introducing herself to the house and whoever was inside.

"Who dares approach my cottage?" a loud, reedy voice rang out.

Rosemary's eyes widened, but she couldn't see anything inside. "Uhh...My name is Rosemary Thorn, and I'm a witch from the earth realm. I need your help." Her voice echoed in the silence.

A deep resonant cackle rang out. "In you come," said the voice. "Let me take a look at you."

Rosemary stepped tentatively through, and then quickly scrambled to get out of the way as the huge door closed behind her.

Inside the cottage, everything appeared to be grey and sterile. It wasn't what she expected.

A small, hunched figure approached her with wild grey hair, frizzing all over the place. She was dressed in black baggy clothes.

Rosemary bowed her head in respect. She did it automatically, without thinking or knowing what the appropriate thing to do might be upon meeting an ancient crone goddess such as this.

"Let me look at you," the voice spoke again. "Ahh, you are a witch. Though, you're a late bloomer, I see."

Rosemary pursed her lips, biting back a retort. She didn't know how to respond.

Her nerves trembled in the presence of Cerridwen. The goddess appeared tiny and demure, but had a powerful presence that almost made Rosemary want to bow again, right to the floor on both knees, in respect. Something told her that would be excessive, so she remained standing, centring herself and her energy as her intuition advised was the wisest thing to do.

The crone goddess would not take any nonsense. Cerridwen could be dangerous and was certainly powerful. Rosemary needed her power now to find her daughter.

"What is it you seek my help for?" Cerridwen asked, drawing herself up to her full height, about the size of a double decker bus.

Rosemary cowered, feeling very tiny, as she gave her a much abridged version of the story, careful to stick to the bare bones of what needed to be said.

"And what is it you'd have me do?" Cerridwen asked.

Rosemary sensed this to be a trick question. She knew better than to command or make demands from a goddess such as this. She returned to her own purpose. "I need to find my daughter... and then we're going to try to help her friend and get back to the earth realm, preferably in one piece."

Cerridwen threw back her head and laughed, a raucous cackle.

"It wasn't a joke," said Rosemary flatly.

"Not yet," said Cerridwen. "But you'll find laughter is often the best medicine."

She clapped her hands and the room transformed. It was like lifting a veil. Instead of the grey, sterile space that Rosemary had entered into, the room was glowing in warm light, enhanced by wooden walls, a hardwood floor, lovely mahogany cabinets, and a large oak table. There were dozens of plants hanging from the ceiling and trailing along shelves full of old books and hundreds of bottles of herbs.

"Take a seat," said Cerridwen. She herself looked younger and more full of life, her scraggly hair swept back under a scarf and her black clothing had turned a deep dark purple.

Rosemary stepped towards the table, unsure of whether to trust her own senses. It was too high for her to easily reach, though the goddesses' magic quickly scooped her up onto one of the chairs, which grew taller before her eyes as they came to rest on it, at about the right height to sit at the table.

She took a seat on one of the benches.

"You'll be having tea then," said Cerridwen, in a way that reminded Rosemary of Marjie, bringing with it a wave of home-sickness for Myrtlewood.

Rosemary merely nodded. This did not seem like the time to refuse hospitality from a goddess.

An earthenware cup appeared in front of her. It sat on the table, only slightly too big for Rosemary, more like a soup bowl. She admired its pale blue and deep brown glaze. Inside was a liquid that looked a lot like water but had a slightly silky sheen on top.

"Thank you." Rosemary took the cup, letting it warm her before taking a small sip.

The brew was soothing and tasted of familiar things, mint and lavender, sage and borage. It was reminiscent of something her grandmother might have served in her own kitchen.

The thought made Rosemary ache to find Athena even more.

"Just in time." Cerridwen raised her head towards the door.

A moment later a knock sounded and Rosemary's eyes widened as the Crone Goddess announced, "My other guests have arrived."

Twenty-Eight

Athena opened her eyes, groggy and woozy.

She was in what appeared to be a red, velvet room, only beneath her the bench seat was made of stone, not upholstery.

It was odd.

At first, she couldn't remember where she was, but then the recent events flooded back to her and with a sinking sensation she figured she must have woken up in the earth realm.

But what a strange place to be in! Where was her mother? And where was Elise?

Had all their efforts been for nought?

As Athena continued to adjust, she realised she wasn't completely in her physical form.

She reached out her arm to examine it.

Her body lacked definition that it would normally have.

She still held the glowing fae stone, which was illuminating the room surrounding her, just as it had when she had been walking through the darkness.

"I must still be in the Underworld," Athena muttered to herself.

This was both a blessing and a curse. It was good that she wasn't back to square one with no hope of rescuing Elise, but where was Rosemary? *And where am I?*

The room had no windows or doors.

"How did I even get in here?"

She hammered against the side of the wall. "Let me out!" she yelled.

She tried to use magic to blast her way through the velvety rock, but her powers were no good. All she could manage was a puff of smoke.

It makes no sense that the Oak King needed us here when our witch powers are all but useless...We must have simply been an ingredient required for his own purposes.

Being alone and relatively powerless in this realm was terrifying. Perhaps they'd just exhausted themselves in the battle. Had the summer god depleted their magic? Would they ever get it back? There were so many questions left unanswered.

Athena hammered on the wall again, getting angry this time. "Let me out right now!" she yelled. "Or else!"

She tumbled backwards onto the bench and slumped there, defeated.

A cracking sound caught her attention and the wall opened up, revealing a door on the side that had previously been solid stone.

Athena braced herself, anticipating some kind of monstrous

creature. After all, this was where the Underworld beasts had emerged from on Halloween and they were terrifying.

A loud, booming voice called out, "Athena Thorn, you have been summoned."

Athena wasn't sure who was summoning her, but whoever it was, they knew her name and who she was.

"Who is it?" Athena asked.

The door opened a little wider.

Athena expected to see an enormous beast, but instead, a tiny being with little black horns and feathery hair, and a red face that looked almost like a kitten, poked his head around from the bottom of the doorway.

"Oh my goodness, you're cute as a button!" said Athena.

The creature narrowed its eyes at her. In a loud and ominous voice, it declared, "I am not cute! I am a fierce demon of the Underworld. Tremble in fear in my presence!"

Athena pursed her lips, trying not to laugh out of respect. "Alright then. Just take it as read that I'm trembling in fear," she said flatly.

"Very well," the demon boomed. "You are being summoned. Come this way."

With some trepidation, Athena did as she was told. After all, fearsome or not, what choice did she have but to follow the little demon?

Twenty-Nine

R osemary trembled as she sat in Cerridwen's house. She was one hundred per cent sure that whoever was on the other side of that door wasn't someone she wanted to see. The knock sounded again.

"Hold your horses!" Cerridwen said. With a flick of her wrist, the door flew open before Rosemary could do anything to stop it, and in stomped none other than the Morrigan, only about ten times bigger than when Rosemary had seen her in the earth realm.

"You!" she said, pointing a long bony finger at Rosemary. "What are you doing here?"

Rosemary wished she could crawl under the table.

The Morrigan was a formidable figure at the best of times, but having the full force of her attention staring down on her was something else. Rosemary mumbled, "Mffmff...umm, why are you so big?"

The Morrigan narrowed her eyes. "I was trying not to scare anyone!"

"Out of the way," said a creaky voice from behind the Morrigan. A hand reached around, pushing the Morrigan aside, and another terrifying goddess stepped forward.

It was the Cailleach, her piercing pale grey eyes staring right through Rosemary.

"You?" said Rosemary. "Are you still trying to bring about endless winter?"

"I don't know what she's on about," said the Cailleach before turning towards the Morrigan's mortified expression, which prompted her lips to curve into a grin. "What's the wee lassie done now?"

"I haven't done anything," Rosemary stammered. The whole situation was beyond perplexing, like a strange dream but much more dangerous.

Was the winter goddess really so disinterested in bringing about endless winter, and if so, why had the Oak King gone to such lengths to stop them? Could it be just another ploy in the centuries-old struggle against his brother? Worse still, Rosemary had somehow managed to offend the most terrifying goddess of them all, who continued to glare at her, a crow perched on her shoulder.

"Really," said Rosemary. "I didn't mean to..."

"That's the problem," said the Morrigan.

"Look, I'm sorry," said Rosemary. "I didn't realise that when I called on you to help us at Samhain, that you'd take Elise from us."

The Morrigan frowned and looked from Cerridwen to the Cailleach, confused. "Elise?"

Rosemary gulped. "You know, the girl who went down into the Underworld."

The Morrigan threw back her head and crowed with laughter. "Do you think that's got something to do with me?"

Rosemary looked around in puzzlement. "You mean you didn't take her? You didn't coerce her into going with you?"

The Morrigan put her hands on her hips. "That's not my style."

"So why are you angry with me?" Rosemary asked.

The Morrigan tapped her foot on the floor. "We had a deal, young lady. You were going to...invite me to things."

The Morrigan looked down at the ground, and Rosemary could have sworn she blushed a little.

"Now, now, sit down, you two," Cerridwen grumbled. Rosemary shuffled nervously as all three goddesses joined her around the table.

"I didn't think you were serious about that," said Rosemary.

"Really?" said the Morrigan, not sounding convinced at all.

"Well, to be quite frank, I was scared to invite you, so I conveniently believed that you didn't really want to come and that you were just tricking us, pretending to let us off easy, when really what you wanted was to take Elise."

The Morrigan took a long slow exhale, shaking her head sternly. "You humans are so frivolous, believing whatever it is you want to believe. And is that what you're doing here? Really? You're looking for some other lost human?"

"My daughter's girlfriend," said Rosemary.

"Ahh, that explains it," said the Cailleach, picking at her long, grubby fingernails that protruded like spikes from her bony hands. "There's always something with you lot. But I suppose a rescue mission is understandable."

"So you want to find this Elise?" said the Morrigan, looking at Rosemary with a raised eyebrow.

"Well, yes and no," said Rosemary. "I've lost my daughter."

The Cailleach chuckled. "What a funny thing to lose. You really are surprising beings."

"It's not funny," said Rosemary, feeling her voice crack with emotion. "She means everything to me. You...maybe you didn't mean to," she said, looking at the Cailleach, "but your battle blew us back in different directions, and now I don't know where she is."

The Cailleach cackled, her voice husky and knowing.

"Don't think she's finding this funny," said the Morrigan. "It's just a deep cosmic amusement."

"I don't see how that's any better," said Rosemary, looking grimly around the table. She still felt tiny, like a bug at risk of being squashed by these immensely powerful beings, but none of them seemed to want her dead, and she didn't have the luxury of shying away. The matters at hand were too crucial. "Can you do anything to help me? I mean, I should probably know better than to barter with gods, but I really have nothing else to lose. My Granny led me here."

"That Galderall Thorn," said the Cailleach, "always getting her nose into other people's business."

"Sometimes it's helpful to have her involved in mine," Rosemary said. "Sometimes..." she repeated solemnly.

"What you need, my dear," said Cerridwen, "is a deep transformation."

Rosemary shook her head. "I don't have time for a spiritual spa treatment or whatever you're referring to. I need to find Athena!"

"Aha!" said the Morrigan. "That is the problem. You can never find things when you're in a state of looking for them."

"That doesn't make any sense," said Rosemary. "How else am I supposed to find her?"

"You need to be in a state of finding them, dear," said the Cailleach.

"Of course, you make it sound so easy," said Rosemary bitterly.

"That is not part of the plan," said Cerridwen. "Easy doesn't come into it. Transformation is like having your skin ripped off and stuffed right back through you again. It's being reborn like a phoenix from the ashes."

"Sounds painful," said Rosemary, grimacing.

"No pain, no brains, isn't that what you humans say?" said the Morrigan.

Rosemary scrunched up her face. "Not quite, but...I suppose I'll face pain if it means getting Athena back."

"It doesn't have to all be unpleasant pain," said the Cailleach with a wry grin. "You know, death, birth, procreation, they're all the same thing, really."

Rosemary coughed out her tea. "Excuse me?"

"Transformation, dear," said Cerridwen.

"She's right, you know," said the Morrigan with a smirk. "Transformation can be the greatest release."

Rosemary took a nervous breath. "Just tell me what I need to do."

Cerridwen looked her in the eyes. "You need to be prepared to let go of everything you currently know, to let go of your attachments right now, in order to let the new come forth."

"I'll do it," said Rosemary. "Anything find Athena...to get her back, safely."

"There's nothing safe about transformation," said the Morrigan, tilting her head to the side.

Rosemary gritted her teeth and took a deep breath. "Can you tell me what it is I have to do?"

"Better than that," said Cerridwen. "I can show you."

With a wave of her hand, the wall of her house fell away. Another ridge emerged through the many layers of fog, revealing a hidden path winding down towards a dark cave with the sea crashing around it.

"We need to go down there," said Rosemary. It wasn't a question; she already knew.

"That's right," said Cerridwen. "Come with me. I'm going to show you my cauldron."

Thirty

"Come, now, child." It was Cerridwen's soothing voice, and Rosemary took a moment to appreciate how nurturing this goddess of transformation was.

They looked out over the narrow ridge, into the darkness.

Rosemary shivered. "Do you really think I can get down there, without falling?"

"I forget the vulnerability of mortals, sometimes," said the Cailleach.

"Let me help." With a wave of Cerridwen's hand, a bubble began to form from the ground around Rosemary. The energy was jet black, but transparent. It felt safe, protective, as it encased her form.

"Thank you," said Rosemary, still feeling impossibly tiny compared to the enormous goddesses around her.

Cerridwen nodded. "Let us leave."

The goddesses rose up, floating through the air, and Rosemary found herself lifting too, floating in the bubble through the air along with them as they began to descend down, over the ridge, towards the cave.

Rosemary felt herself being gently pulled along through the darkness. She could barely see the way in front of her but knew that she was still floating along with the goddesses, down, through the air, as they continued towards the cave.

Cerridwen's voice sounded through the air, "This is as far as we can take you; the rest of the way you must go yourself."

Rosemary felt herself gently alight on the ground; the protective bubble around her vanished, and she felt a chill, no longer protected by the energy of the goddesses. She took a deep breath.

She could no longer see much at all.

She was aware that she was balancing on a precarious ridge; down below, dark waters crashed.

Rosemary wished she could turn back to the relative safety of Cerridwen's house, but she knew she needed to make her way on her own towards the cave.

She took tentative steps, not wanting to slip. Again, the questions arose: what would happen to her if she did? Could she die in the realm of the dead? Was it possible that she'd never return to her body? Of course, that could happen anyway. She had no idea how much time had elapsed but had been told there were only five days where time stood still enough that she could be here in the Underworld at all.

"Just trust your intuition," Cerridwen's voice floated up from the darkness.

Rosemary took another deep breath and continued on, more sure of herself this time. If the great goddess of wisdom believed in her intuition, then surely she could trust it somewhat.

Though the ridge wound sharply, impossibly narrow, Rosemary found it strange that her feet seemed to fall one foot in front of the other, just like when she was walking back in the Earth realm, processing her Saturn transit or whatever it was that Athena kept talking about. She found now too that as she followed her intuition and walked a path almost exactly straight, the ridge itself adjusted to her gait, straightening out in front of her. Certainly, it was unusual, but by far it was the least of the unusual things that had happened to her recently.

Once more, she reached out emotionally for Athena, but she knew that it was no use. She had to be centred now. Wherever her daughter was, she vowed she would get her back soon.

We'll be fine, she reassured herself as she continued to walk.

Walking itself became a meditation.

"That's it, my dear," said Cerridwen's voice. "The more you connect with your centre, the faster you will get here."

With that, Rosemary connected deeply to her core and found herself instantly at the entrance of the cave.

"Step inside now," said the voice. "It won't hurt a bit."

Rosemary took a step into the dark, deep unknown, expecting to find some sort of ground beneath her. But her foot slipped into nothingness.

A falling sensation overwhelmed her as she was enveloped by darkness. It was almost like a slide. She wound around, and around, her heart leaping into her throat, but Cerridwen's reassurance helped her stay as centred as possible, given the circumstances.

Falling, falling down, down, down.

She wished that she would wake up from the falling dream and be at home in Thorn Manor. If only Athena was there too, and they could carry on with their lives. But that was clearly not to be her fate, at least not at this particular moment.

She landed with a soft thud on stones that should have been much harder.

"Finally," said the Morrigan's voice.

"Don't chide her," said the Cailleach. "She's doing exactly as she needs to do, just like we all are."

"Err, thanks," said Rosemary. She stood up, still feeling uncomfortably puny.

Cerridwen was leaning over an enormous cauldron, her long curly hair falling into it. The cauldron itself must have contained some sort of light, for the goddess's face was illuminated and looked impossibly young for one so ancient.

"Almost ready," Cerridwen said, picking up a handful of herbs and a small vial.

She sprinkled the herbs, which turned into sparks in her hands and fluttered into the cauldron.

The small vial contained something that looked silvery. Cerridwen tilted it over the cauldron, allowing a single drop to fall.

A bright light flashed through the room. Bubbles and smoke poured out of the cauldron.

Rosemary took a step back to avoid the deluge of potentially dangerous liquid.

"This is for you," said Cerridwen as she ladled the potion up to her mouth and sampled it.

"You want me to drink that?" Rosemary asked, mortified.

The Morrigan cackled, and even the Cailleach guffawed. The three goddesses all laughed together in a cacophony of amusement.

"What's so funny?" said Rosemary.

"You're not going to drink it," said the Morrigan. "You're going to get in."

"Get in?!" Rosemary was appalled. "You're serious?"

"What do you think? Transformation is supposed to be easy?" said Cailleach.

Rosemary gulped.

"Fear not, dear one," said Cerridwen. "You will emerge from this process, I can assure you."

"In one piece?" Rosemary asked.

The Morrigan cocked an eyebrow. "Just the one?" she asked and cackled again.

Rosemary glared at her. "And you really expect me to invite you over for cocktails?" she said before she could stop herself.

The Morrigan stared daggers back at Rosemary and then threw her head back and laughed, much to Rosemary's relief.

"Exactly! So amusing! This is why I want to socialise with you strange human creatures," the Morrigan said.

Rosemary shook her head, unbelieving.

"If you're quite ready," said Cerridwen.

"Err, you know I've actually..." said Rosemary, backing away.

The Cailleach harumphed. "We've got things to be getting on with!"

"This is important," Cerridwen interjected. "Rosemary must take her time. It is not just a small matter. My intuition tells me that this quest Rosemary is on is connected to a deeper mystery that ties all of our fates."

The Morrigan paled. "It's *my* prophecy," she said. "It's about *me*. I am fae and witch, after all."

*So is Athena...*Rosemary thought, but was wise enough to hold her tongue.

"That is what she always thought," said Cerridwen, addressing Rosemary. "However, prophecies are strange creatures. They hold power of their own, and we can only interpret them."

"A bunch of nonsense, if you ask me," said Cailleach.

"What are you talking about?" said Rosemary. "Not the same thing the queen of the fairies told me...about Athena?"

"That little runt of yours is not the focus of the prophecy. I'm sure of it," said the Morrigan. Rosemary was too surprised to be offended by her daughter being called a little runt.

"It doesn't make sense," Rosemary said. "We came here to rescue Elise, not because of a prophecy."

"That is often what we believe, isn't it? We come for one reason, and yet a deeper purpose is at work," said Cerridwen.

Rosemary shook her head in disbelief. "You're saying we're not here to rescue Elise at all?"

"Only time will tell," said Cerridwen. "But your role in this story of life is to follow your path. What is it telling you now?"

Rosemary sighed. "My intuition is telling me that I need to go through this." She waved her arm around, gesturing vaguely towards the cauldron. "Whatever it is, this transformation business. If you think it will help me find Athena, then I'll do it."

"It will help you find her, if she can be found," said Cerridwen. "I can assure you it will help you find what it is you seek."

"But that may surprise you," the Morrigan warned.

"I don't especially like surprises," said Rosemary. "But I don't think I have any choice now."

"There's always some kind of choice," said Cailleach. "That is part of free will."

Rosemary sighed. "When has my will ever been free?"

The Cailleach continued, "In every moment, there is free will. That is part of the triad."

Rosemary looked around, perplexed, but none of the three goddesses seemed prepared to give her any more information. "Very well then," said Rosemary, "let's just do this."

Cerridwen dried off her ladle on her apron and then dipped it down towards Rosemary. "I'll give you a lift," she said.

"You're serious?" Cerridwen nodded.

Rosemary, somewhat dismayed, had no choice but to clamber into the warm wooden ladle, holding on for dear life, as the ancient goddess swung her around to the cauldron, then dipped her down towards the bubbling liquid.

Thirty-One

Athena followed the tiny demon along tall, dark passageways through what felt like an endless maze. At first, she tried to count the different turns they took, right and then left, and left again, then the middle way in a forked path, and so on. Soon, she gave up.

It wasn't like she particularly wanted to get back to the room she had woken up in anyway. She needed to get out of here and find Elise.

"This way," the demon said for the fifth time, guiding Athena down yet another long stone hallway.

"Are we almost there?" said Athena. "Where are we going, anyway?"

"Oh, you'll see soon enough," the demon's voice boomed, and she cackled.

Athena sighed and continued following along. It was hard to

take the creature seriously despite its loud voice. Up ahead, it looked to be a dead end. The small demon stopped.

"What is it?" said Athena. "Did we go the wrong way?"

The creature turned and glared at her. "I never go the wrong way," she said. "How dare you!"

Athena raised her hands apologetically. "I'm sorry. I don't know anything about this place."

"I'll let you off this time," said the creature, snapping her fingers.

A stone wall in front of her trembled and then rose from the ground.

A red light beamed out from there.

"Are you coming with me?" Athena asked tentatively.

"I think not," said the demon.

"It's a shame," said Athena. "I'm starting to enjoy your company."

"Of course you do," sneered the demon, preening. "Who wouldn't?"

Athena took a deep breath and then slowly walked through the opening towards the ominous red glow.

"What are you doing here?" The voice was familiar but deeper, somehow stronger.

"Elise?" Athena turned.

As her eyes adjusted to the red light the scene became clearer. In front of her, atop a grandiose throne made of flaming skulls, sat none other than her girlfriend.

She looked almost to be sewn in, as there was no clear boundary between the throne and her body.

"Elise," said Athena, her eyes wide. "I came to save you. We've got to get out of here."

Elise's face remained impassive.

"Elise," said Athena. "Come on. We've got to go. Before whoever is keeping you here comes back."

Elise looked around, raising her hand and waving in a gesture around the room. "And who is keeping me here?" she said, folding her arms.

"Oh..." Athena started. It was slowly dawning on her. "Nobody is keeping you here...It's true then."

Athena fell to her knees on the hard ground. She felt no pain, perhaps because she didn't even have a real body here. What felt like her chin sunk into the area of her collarbone, and she closed her eyes.

"I didn't want to believe it," she said. "I didn't want to believe you would leave us, you would leave everything. You would leave me."

Elise shook her head. "Of course you don't," she said. "Because you're the main character, and I'm just the supporting act. And it's always your job to rescue me."

"That's not how it is," said Athena, tears welling up in her eyes.

"Then why? Why did you come all this way to rescue me?"

"Because I didn't believe that you could break my heart like that," Athena admitted. "I thought you must still be affected by her, by Grace. All that trauma that she went through, that you lived through in her body."

Elise gazed off into space for a moment. "That's true," she said

190

quietly. "I am still affected by her. But that doesn't mean that I can ever go back."

"What—"

"I can't just go back to my old life. I'm different."

"Did you have to come here?" said Athena. "It's horrible. It's dangerous and different, and so, so hard to get to. Do you hate me that much?"

Elise shook her head sadly. "When will you understand that this isn't about you at all? I don't hate you, Athena. I love you."

Athena looked up slowly. "Why?"

Elise continued, "I have to live my own life. It's just like I said in my note. I needed to do this."

"That means I can't see you," said Athena. "It means I have to go back to my old life. And you won't be there, but your Mum will be there. And we'll just have this gaping wound where you won't be."

Elise closed her eyes. A red tear ran down her pale cheeks. She pushed her black hair out of her face. "Athena, I don't mean to hurt you. And I don't mean to hurt Mum, at all. But I needed to do this. I needed to have my own journey."

"What *is* this journey?" Athena asked as tears streamed down her face. "What is so important that you can't be with us anymore? That you can't even be in the same realm?"

There was a cackling from the doorway.

"Widget," Elise grumbled. "Stop eavesdropping."

"Why is she laughing?"

Elise shrugged.

"Don't you know?" said the demon who was apparently called Widget. "Don't you know what she's becoming?"

191

Elise gazed off into space again.

"What? What is it?" said Athena.

"She's becoming a goddess," said Widget and laughed again.

"This can't be the way it is," Athena said, staring at the girl she loved.

Tendrils of flowery rocks grew like vines from the fiery skulls of the throne, creeping over Elise's body, trapping her to the throne on which she sat.

"No," said Athena, "I can't...I can't leave you here like this. Do you have any idea of all the effort we've been through just to find you? Mum and I, we risked everything."

"I never asked you to. I told you not to come," Elise shouted. Her voice was deep and resonant, echoing around the room.

Athena flinched.

"You're serious, then?" Athena said. "You really want to stay here, in this awful place, even though we've been through hell to find you?"

Elise took a deep breath. "I have no choice. This is part of my destiny."

"No," said Athena, hammering against the floor. "You always have a choice."

She crawled towards Elise and began to pull at the stony tendrils of the throne. "I need to get you out of here," said Athena. "You'll understand. You're not yourself. I need to rescue you."

"Stop!" said Elise.

Athena froze at the intensity of her gaze.

"Stop trying to save me, Athena. You can't...you can't always be the hero. You're so obsessed with saving me when what you really want is to be rescued, yourself."

Athena stepped back and folded her arms. "That doesn't make sense. *I* don't need to be rescued."

"Maybe not right now, although..." Elise looked around the room. "It's possible that you do."

Athena felt a chill. She'd been through so much, only to find out she wasn't needed at all. She wasn't even wanted.

"I don't need to be rescued," said Athena. "I'll find a way out."

"That's not what I mean," said Elise.

"What is it then?" Athena asked.

"When you were little, things were hard, weren't they?"

Athena nodded. "Quite a lot of the time, but I don't see what that has to do with anything."

"Don't you think it's possible that you keep trying to rescue other people because when you were little you were the one who wanted to be rescued? You wanted your dad to come and save you from poverty and misery. You wanted your mum to get her act together when for some reason she never could. You wanted to be saved so badly – to be rescued yourself – and at some point you turned all of that into needing to be the hero for other people."

"You're saying I have a saviour complex," said Athena flatly.

"It's just a theory," said Elise, raising an eyebrow.

Athena sighed in exasperation. "Oh come on! Are you serious? I've come all this way, and you're just accusing me of needing counselling."

Elise shook her head sadly. "Don't blame me for your choices. Mirror communication was probably not the best idea, I admit that. It takes such a long time to get a message through from the Underworld. I just wanted you to know that I still care."

"How can you say that?" Athena's voice quivered. "How can you say that you still care when you want to stay here, when we've gone through so much to try and get you back? You don't care about me, you don't care about your Mum, or our world, or anything. You're selfish."

Elise let out a sob. "Maybe I am," she said softly, her voice choked with tears, "but I don't think you understand where I'm coming from. I don't know if you want to. You might have been through a horrible ordeal to get here. So have I, not just in traversing the Underworld, but everything that came before. I re-lived Grace's trauma, all of that. I couldn't go back to being happy little Elise with perky blue hair. I couldn't go back to being your sidekick girlfriend. I killed people, Athena."

"It was Grace...It wasn't really you."

Elise shook her head. "That's not true. I enjoyed it. What does that make me? Some kind of monster? I belong here. I belong in the darkness."

Athena was taken aback by Elise's words. "No," she said firmly. "You don't belong here."

"You don't know that."

Athena wiped her eyes. "You remember that ancient myth, Inanna and Ereshkigal, the ancient Sumerian goddesses?"

Elise nodded.

Athena cleared her throat. "You know how Inanna goes into the Underworld, to rescue her sister, and on her way, everything is torn from her. Her sister repays her by brutally stabbing her..."

"I'm familiar," said Elise.

"Well, you might as well have just stabbed me in the heart, as melodramatic as that sounds...I don't know how to live without you. I don't know how to be without you in my life. I don't even know who I am without you."

"Don't be ridiculous," said Elise. "You're probably the most powerful fae witch on Earth for centuries. You're Athena Thorn. You're got everything going for you. You'll forget about me."

"I won't!" said Athena. "I've never found it easy to connect with people. I've always felt different."

"But you've always been special, haven't you?"

"And you are too!" said Athena. "You don't need all of this to show that you're special."

"It's not about that anymore," said Elise, her tone solemn. "I've sat at the foot of the Fates, and they've whispered to me about my purpose, my destiny."

Athena's mind swam with these words, along with everything else that had happened in the past few weeks. It was too much to process.

"And now," said Elise. "It's time for you to go."

Athena cried out, but it was too late. Black tendrils wrapped around her, dragging her back. She felt herself sailing backwards, moving through time and space.

She woke, coughing and sputtering, back in her physical body in the earth realm. She looked around, desperately reaching for her mother, but Rosemary was still fast asleep.

Thirty-Two

Athena groaned, rolling over onto her back. She lay there for a while, looking at the ornate ceiling mouldings of Thorn Manor, heart beating wildly in her chest. It was so odd to be back in her physical form, and even more unsettling knowing that her mother was still out of her own body.

"What do I do?" she mumbled to herself.

It was clear that Elise didn't want to be rescued. And yet, Athena couldn't just leave her there. She had to *do* something.

As for Rosemary, what if she couldn't get out alone? *It will be all my fault.*

She'd led her mother, who was determined not to leave her side, into the realm of the dead itself.

"Mum? What happened to you?" Athena asked, turning towards Rosemary.

She looked so peaceful, as if in a perfectly ordinary slumber, and yet unnaturally pale and still.

Athena put her hand on her mother's forehead; it was mildly warm. She felt for a pulse at her neck, which was still beating strong and reassuring.

"You're coming back, Mum. If you can hear me, try to follow my voice."

She reached out with her mind, trying to make contact with Rosemary in the usual way.

There was nothing to latch onto. Rosemary was far away.

Athena tried again several times, holding tight to Rosemary's hand, whispering in her ear, attempting to connect, but it was no use. Where her mother had gone, Athena couldn't reach her, at least for now.

"Just think," she said to herself, "think, think, who can help?" She immediately thought of calling Detective Neve, but surely, she'd be on parental leave and have other important things to occupy her.

Besides, this was probably no time for law enforcement; they were unlikely to have the answers. But who would?

The first person that came to mind was Marjie, not because Athena was sure she'd know what to do, but because she craved the nurturing comfort that her mother was in no fit state to provide.

She reached for her phone and tried dialling the shop to no avail. Desperate, she decided to dial the number of the mobile phone which Marjie seldom used.

Athena jolted in shock as a little ditty rang out from the kitchen.

"Athena!" a familiar voice called out. Moments later, there was the sound of footsteps. Athena tried getting up, though her body felt frail and she was struggling to regain full control of it. She'd managed to prop herself up against the sofa when Marjie bustled in, somehow already having a tray of tea and scones prepared.

"Oh, there you are, my dear," said Marjie, "you're back already. Tell me, how did it go?"

Athena couldn't help but burst into tears; the familiar, comforting presence was too much for her.

"Oh dear." Marjie put the tray down and rushed forward to wrap Athena in a warm hug, letting her sob for a while.

Athena cried onto the floral apron strap at Marjie's shoulder, releasing waves of fear and grief until she felt she had nothing left in her.

Marjie released her, and Athena sank back down, finding herself inexplicably on the sofa, wrapped in a warm, crocheted blanket with a cup of tea and a jam and cream scone on a plate on her lap. Marjie, herself, seemed different, more energetic and full of life than Athena remembered her being before. She had more presence, or perhaps that was just Athena's addled brain, distorted by her Underworld escapade.

"Now, when you're ready, you're going to tell me everything," said Marjie. And so, Athena did, recounting all the details she could recall of their Underworld journey, of coming across the winter gods, of being separated from Rosemary, and finally, of meeting up with Elise.

"It's all a disaster," Athena said. "If it wasn't for me, Mum would be back here safe. Elise didn't even want me there."

"She might not think so," said Marjie thoughtfully. "People don't always know what's good for them."

"You can say that again," said Athena with a sigh. "I still can't believe it. It's like she's being swallowed by the darkness, but she wants to be. She wants to stay there..."

"Well, we can't change other people's lives for them," said Marjie.

"But now, what if it's all for nothing? And I've lost Mum." Athena choked up again.

Marjie patted her hand. "There, there, sweetheart. I love you, my dear, and you will be fine, and so will your wonderful mother. I'm absolutely sure of it. She might come across as a bit hare-brained at times, but Rosemary is a smart woman, and she's capable of getting herself out of sticky situations just as much as she's capable of getting herself into them."

Athena giggled a little bit. "This time, it was my fault."

"Blaming yourself is absolutely no use," said Marjie. "Yes, it was you who led her down there, but Rosemary chose to go. Besides, I do truly believe that everything that happens to us does have a greater purpose. The Fates are weaving our lives along with us."

"How can you say that when there are so many atrocities in the world?" said Athena, feeling her burning outrage, not at Marjie per se, but at the thought that she'd proposed.

Marjie shook her head and sighed. "Look, my dear, I can't speak to all of that, not at all. And maybe some things happen for no good reason. Maybe fate is cruel. It's not really for us to understand it all. But I firmly believe that in my life, all the horrible things that I've faced have led me to a greater place, a deeper knowing. Believing that helps me get through."

Athena shrugged. "I suppose. But it sounds like wishful thinking, though."

"Wishful thinking can be important," said Marjie firmly. "If we don't have faith, we're not going to get anything done. Now, drink your tea and eat up because we have work to do. We're not going to stop until we have your mother back, safe and sound."

Athena nodded firmly and gulped down her tea. She could definitely agree with Marjie on that point.

Thirty-Three

As Rosemary stepped into Cerridwen's cauldron, she felt an immediate pull. Her sense of her own physical form, which was only an illusion in this realm anyway, began to dissolve and her awareness raced like a running film, taking her on a journey back through her life, right back to her earliest childhood memories, through all the triumphs, hardships, and lessons of her life. It was as if she could physically feel the tensions that had shaped her, as well as the joys, the changes, the dissolution, and the reforming. She was back in the womb, safe and cocooned. Rosemary, or the being that was formerly Rosemary, winced as an uncomfortable wrenching sensation gripped her. It was as if she was yanked through her own belly button by a crochet hook, flipped inside out and ground down by the mortar of the great goddess, then carried by the winds to the farthest corners of the universe.

Even as she disintegrated and became one with everything, she felt a profound sense of safety.

She knew there was always eternity, always expansion.

She knew her love for Athena transcended time and space, just like her love for others in her life, special people like Burk and Marjie, along with all her other friends and family.

The sensation of love was interrupted by pain.

Crashing down on her.

Crushing her.

It was a crucible of pain.

The consciousness of Rosemary found herself re-forming in the darkest of dark nights. She began a slow journey. One foot in front of the other. Walking like she had, not so long ago in the earth realm.

After a long time in the darkness a light began to grow in the distance.

The white light she was walking towards seemed like a journey towards joy...finding the joy in celebrating life, even though there was so much pain.

The understanding began to dawn inside Rosemary that her purpose was more than just creating delicious chocolates. She had a deeper purpose, to create and spread joy, whether with close friends and family or all her customers whose lives she had touched. A warmth flooded in, like sunlight, and she knew she didn't need any grander purpose, she didn't even need the three goddesses of transformation. Not now. Not here in this weightless, flightless, floating spaciousness.

All she needed was her sense of self and divine purpose.

She had to surrender everything, including her fears and

worries about Athena, because she knew it was the only thing to do.

The process of transformation required surrender, letting go, and allowing.

The goddesses had revealed to her that she couldn't find fulfilment if she was only seeking it.

The state of looking was not anywhere near the state of finding.

To be united with her daughter, she needed to ascend to that state of reuniting with her.

Ascend! she instructed herself.

Rosemary felt herself rising up. As she floated in this wide open space which was not darkness or light but shades of grey, ripples like water appeared around her and then clouds formed.

She rose up through the clouds, a soft pink light illuminating them. She wondered briefly if this was heaven. A platform appeared before her with steps leading up to it. It looked to be made of marble, yet it was floating in the air. She ascended the steps and found herself in an ancient, sacred temple, not even of the Earth itself, but something deeper, older, and more universal.

She walked through a giant archway into the temple.

If she'd felt tiny in Cerridwen's house, Rosemary had the sensation of being positively microscopic now, in this enormous marble building. Somehow, she managed to climb up enormous steps. Another doorway towered above her.

As she approached, it began to open, revealing a brilliant bright light.

She walked through only to find another door, and then another, each bearing different engravings of flowers, animals, and what appeared to be mythological figures, each one leading her deeper into the mystery of life itself.

Finally, the last door opened – into darkness. Stars speckled the space in front of Rosemary.

As her sight adjusted to the darkness she instinctually recognised what it was she was looking at. The twinkling lights were merely part of a vast and ever expanding tapestry of destiny, woven by the Fates.

Rosemary looked up to see three figures looming above, floating in the air.

They were both a part of their tapestry, and standing out from it, with piles and piles of dark, sparkly wool which glistened, iridescent, in all the colours of the rainbow, yet somehow also black.

Though Rosemary felt about the size of an ant, the Fates themselves regarded her and somehow she recognised them.

The old one embodied determination – that which is set in stone.

The middle-aged one was the essence of free-will – that which we can choose ourselves.

The young one was simply chaos – that which defies all other rules and simply sparks in brilliant and surprising randomness.

They had many names in many cultures, but Rosemary decided to refer to them in her mind as she saw them: Determinism, Free-will, and Chaos.

"Who seeks wisdom from fate itself?" they asked.

"I know, for it is foretold," replied the old one. "Back again so soon?"

"What are you talking about?" said Rosemary. "I've never been here before."

The old one, Determinism, looked at Rosemary more closely. "Not you, but your lineage. For it was an ancestor of yours made her way to our doorstep."

"I don't understand." Rosemary said.

"Yes, you will. And we, the Fates may guide you," said Determinism.

"Is this about that prophecy?" Rosemary asked. "Is it really about my daughter or is it just made up?"

"Only we can create prophecies and send them down to earth to be shared by prophets, although they never come out quite right," explained Free-will.

"Aye, they are woven into the tapestry in some way, shape, or form," said Determinism.

Rosemary examined the tapestry, but it was no use – the thing was too complex.

"How can I find my daughter?" she asked.

"You have already found her," said Chaos, laughing with a maniacal gleam in her eyes.

"That's true. She's with you right now," Free-will added.

Rosemary looked around. "No, she's not."

"She's with your physical form, dear. She's returned to your old realm," said Determinism. "Just as I foretold."

Rosemary felt a wrenching sensation in her chest. "But what about me? Am I stuck here?"

"You have a role to play. And then you can return if that's what you choose," Free-will assured her.

Determination shook her head. "You always think that, even if it's not true."

"We are all truths in our own way," Chaos interjected, "even if it's a banana."

Rosemary gave Chaos an odd look.

"Right!" said Chaos. "And don't ever fall into the wrong kind of trap. You know, it could be quite bizarre." She giggled, "Much like a snail, don't you think?"

"Ignore her," said Determination. "She's always on like that. And we love her dearly for it. But sometimes, it would be nice to have a bit of peace and quiet after an eternity."

"You have plenty of that," Free-will retorted. "Besides, you could choose it."

"I have no choice at all," said Determination. "You know that. I simply am as I am."

"What am I doing here?" asked Rosemary.

"Your magic holds the key," responded Determination.

"To the prophecy? Is this all about that?" asked Rosemary.

"The prophecy isn't about you at all." A gleam appeared in Determination's eyes.

Rosemary gulped. "Enough with the cryptic words," she said. "I'm just going to sit here and listen. That's what I don't do enough of, and I'm pretty sure if you have anything useful to say, you will say it in my presence. And then maybe I can leave this place and get on with my life and find Athena again."

"I knew she'd say that," said Determinism.

Chaos responded with a giggle, "Such a know-it-all. Know-it-all. I know nothing at all. Only that change is coming, right now!" she shrieked.

Suddenly, the floor of the temple cracked open and Rosemary found herself falling through time and space, right back to her old self, back to her young self, then her baby self, aging backwards and then being reborn yet again as the person she always was in essence, but somehow stripped bare, cleared of so many of her previous emotional burdens.

The three faces of the goddesses peered down into the cauldron at her, which was now bone dry.

"And?" said the Morrigan.

Rosemary coughed. "That was some journey."

"Now what?" Cerridwen asked her.

"I'm still determined to find Athena, but now I understand that I need to get into the emotions of seeing her again, not of looking for her."

The Cailleach scowled. "I'm sure I told you that before."

Cerridwen regarded Rosemary fondly. "Very good, dear." She turned her head to the Cailleach. "And you know as well as I do that being told something or even knowing it in theory is worlds apart from actually understanding it deeply. That's why transformation is always required."

The Cailleach threw back her head and cackled again.

"Erm, there's something else you might want to know," Rosemary said before describing what she'd witnessed – the cracking of the temple of the Fates.

The goddesses looked grave.

"Is it something I did?" Rosemary asked.

"No, no, it's not you. It's a power far greater," said the Cailleach darkly.

"They weren't surprised when it happened," said Rosemary.

"They're the Fates," said the Morrigan. "They know what's coming, they know that time has been unbalanced here and in your world, and that time connects to all worlds."

"This could mean the end of everything," said Cerridwen, her voice steady and serious.

"They knew it was coming, so why didn't they stop it?" Rosemary asked in desperation.

"That is not their role," replied the Cailleach.

"Are you saying it's mine?" Rosemary questioned, her voice barely a whisper.

"We all have a part to play in the unfolding of the universe, dear. It is your role now to figure out exactly what that part is," said Cerridwen.

Beginning to understand the gravity of the situation, Rosemary fell silent, considering the weight of her destiny. The three goddesses watched her, their ancient eyes filled with a wisdom that spanned many lifetimes.

Thirty-Four

"I can't believe it's only been three days," said Athena. "How's that even possible? It felt like weeks at least."

Marjie shrugged, pouring another cup of tea. "They say time works differently outside of the physical realms," she said.

"Differently how?"

"That's more of a question for Agatha," said Marjie, tilting her head towards the aged historian who was sitting in the lounge across from them, having been called by Marjie almost immediately after Athena had woken up without her mother.

Agatha Twigg took a sip of her tea and raised an eyebrow. "You really want to know about time?"

"It's one of her favourite topics," Marjie said.

"Go on," said Athena. "I can't see us doing anything much more useful right now."

"There, there." Marjie patted Athena's hand.

"Humans have a most erroneous perception of time. Many

believe that time simply marches on, regardless of what we do. But we are interacting with it all the time. It is a sort of magic, you see, and even mundane people go in and out of different states of time. Time stretches, becomes longer, shrinks, and speeds up..."

"Oh yes. I'm vaguely familiar with the concept," said Athena. "You mean like when I'm doing something I love and time seems to pass so quickly? And when I'm waiting for Mum to get out of the bathroom so we can get going, it seems to take forever."

"Precisely," Agatha said.

"But how does that explain time in other realms, like the Fae realm?" Athena asked. "There are currents of time there."

Agatha took another sip of tea and paused, as if for dramatic effect. "Time can pass more quickly or slowly in other realms, and the fae realm has time currents, which can have dire consequences of coming back too old or too young if not navigated properly."

"Sure," said Athena. "I know that much, but I don't completely understand how that stuff works either, despite having spent a lot of time there."

Agatha nodded. "So I gather. However, in the divine realm and the Underworld itself, I understand that time functions even more differently. Scholars talk about it as being 'outside of time', but I don't think that's quite right. It's not that things don't progress; it's that they progress at their own rates. Time is not a linear unfolding the way we often experience here, where we can agree based on our timekeeping system that it is eleven o'clock," Agatha explained.

"Eleven fifteen," said Marjie, looking at her watch.

Agatha raised an eyebrow.

"Carry on," said Marjie.

"There's something innately mysterious about that realm, which is sometimes called the spirit world, but it's so much more. I understand time there to progress in terms of developmental time, not linear time. There is no clock, and a clock would not work. Things do not go faster there than they do here, as they might in the Fae realm or some other place..."

"How many realms are there?" Athena asked.

"That is still unknown," said Agatha. "However, to continue with your earlier question, this particular time of year, time is said to stand still."

"Of course," said Athena. "Which is why we were able to go to the end of the world at all. Does that mean Mum might be stuck there indefinitely?"

"These things do happen, you know. However it won't be indefinite as her body can't go on for weeks on end without a spirit."

Athena sighed. She made a mental note never to go to Agatha Twigg for comfort.

"Don't fret, dear," said Marjie. "Agatha, if you're not going to be any use, you might as well go home."

"Well, why did you call me over then?" Agatha asked with what resembled a slight pout, but Agatha would have insisted it was only a subtle frown as she firmly believed she did not pout.

"Because you know more than anyone else about that dratted realm," said Marjie. "We need to get Rosemary out!"

Agatha turned her head with a puzzled expression. "I daresay, is that birdsong? It can't possibly be a cuckoo at this time of year."

"Don't change the subject," Marjie grumbled.

"I'm not," Agatha insisted. "Something is going dreadfully wrong."

Just then, the house trembled.

Athena stood and pulled back the curtains to look outside. The snow had melted. Previously it had blanketed the lawn outside Thorn Manor, but now it had thawed all of a sudden, revealing bright green grass poking through.

"What's going on?" said Athena.

The house trembled again.

"You mentioned something about the seasons, the Oak and the Holly King," Agatha said, her voice deathly serious.

"I don't really get it," said Athena. "I know they're always supposed to be fighting, but the Oak King says it's till the death this time. He accuses his brother of wanting to create eternal winter, but maybe killing the Holly King will only do the opposite."

"What does that show you?" Agatha pointed outside the window.

Athena observed as the ice melted further before their very eyes, and more plants peeked through as though they'd merely been hiding rather than killed off by the freezing cold.

"Something is messing with the balance of the seasons and, therefore, I wouldn't be surprised if it's those rascal gods," Agatha grumbled.

Marjie and Athena exchanged looks of concern.

Athena felt a wave of dizziness wash over her. She feared she might faint.

"Sit down, dear," said Marjie.

"How can you say that when something terribly wrong is

happening out there?" Athena protested, but Marjie urged her again to take a seat.

The house shuddered again, though for some reason, there was an eerie stillness within. "What's wrong with my house?" Athena questioned with a mix of worry and frustration.

"Do you mind if I take a look around?" Agatha asked. "I've long been curious about this house."

"You want to look at our house?!" Athena asked.

Agatha frowned. "No, actually, I just need to freshen up. Do you mind if I go to the powder room?"

"Do whatever you like," Athena replied dismissively. "I don't care. Just if there's anything that anyone can tell me of any use, please..."

Overwhelmed, she dove into the couch, covering her head with a cushion, desperately trying to calm herself and stop from hyperventilating. Her racing mind struggled to focus on what could possibly be done at this point.

"Call Burk," said Athena.

"I just did," said Marjie. "When I put the tea on."

"And?"

"He said he'll be over," Marjie reassured her.

"I'm right here," said Burk's voice as the door swung open, and in walked Perseus Burk without bothering to knock. "My apologies for the intrusion," he said.

Athena, emerging from her cushion fortress, responded, "This is not the time for apologies."

Burk took the armchair next to her. "Tell me everything," he said.

Athena reached for her cup, took a long swig of tea, and then began to recount the tale yet again.

Thirty-Five

"I'm going down," said Burk.

Marjie raised an eyebrow. "I beg your pardon?"

Athena looked at her mother's vampire boyfriend. He was deathly pale. If he could perspire, she was sure he would be sweating buckets. There was a tremble throughout his very being.

"What are you talking about?" Athena asked.

"I can't just leave Rosemary there. I have to go down to the Underworld," Burk explained urgently.

"You can do that?" Athena said flatly.

Burk breathed a sigh. "There must be a way. Vampires are Underworld creatures, you see. Though we're born on the surface, our nature, our very condition, comes from beyond that veil."

"You're serious? You can enter the Underworld like there's some kind of doorway?" Athena frowned. "Why didn't you say anything before?"

"It is a secret so closely guarded by my kind that even I barely know anything about it. My father, who's on the council, has only dropped small clues. But I do believe that there is a door fiercely guarded by the council, that allows our leaders passage to the Underworld. I'm not sure what kind of shady business they conduct there, whether it's linked to our existence as vampires or some kind of trade. But there might be a way that I can get through the layers of secrecy and bureaucracy and find my way to Rosemary. We can't just leave her down there."

"No, we can't," agreed Athena. "I'll come with you."

"Impossible," said Burk, shaking his head. "It's likely that you're only able to pass into the Underworld through your dreams, not in your physical form. You are living, I—" He looked down at himself, brushing a speck of dust off his expensive shirt-sleeve. "I'm technically not."

"It's not fair," said Athena, her eyes clouded with angry tears. Marjie comforted her for a few moments as Athena's mind raced.

If I can't go to the Underworld as a mortal then maybe there's no other option but to become a vampire.

She'd never thought much about the possibility before, though she'd wondered if Rosemary herself would want to be turned to live an endless night with her charming boyfriend. Rosemary had to live. Athena was sure of that. Perhaps the only way she could get to her to save her was to be turned into a being of the Underworld, herself.

"Then turn me," she said, staring Burk in the eyes.

"Excuse me?"

"If I have to be a vampire to get to my mother, then make me a vampire. I don't care."

"I can't do that," said Burk firmly.

"And you certainly shouldn't," Marjie added. "Imagine what Rosemary would think!"

"That is my primary concern," said Burk. "Aside from the fact that you're underage."

"I'm older than Geneviève or Dora must have been," said Athena, folding her arms.

"Times have changed," said Burk. "We no longer accept applications for vampire conversion until someone's at least twenty-five. We've learned that the hard way. Brains are not fully developed until that age."

"Explains a few things," Athena muttered, thinking of Dora and Geneviève. "Not about me, of course."

Marjie smirked.

"But you must be able to do it even without permission," said Athena. "I can't just leave Mum down there. I have to do everything I can to help her. It's my fault." Her voice was trembling.

Burk shook his head. "Don't blame yourself, Athena. But I certainly know I could not withstand your mother's wrath if I were to make her daughter a vampire. Besides, it's something I vowed never to do." There was a darkness in his eyes, and Athena guessed there must be a story there, at least one, possibly several; some kind of tortured past befitting a broody vampire.

She sighed. "Very well then. If you think you can get to her and help, then do that. But please, if you have any information at all..."

"I'll let you know," said Burk, then he disappeared so quickly that he might as well have vanished into thin air, leaving behind only a gust of wind and the lingering scent of his expensive cologne.

Athena slumped down onto the window seat. "Do you think it's hopeless?" she asked Marjie.

"Of course not, dear. What have I been telling you? There is always hope. We need light to lead the way in the darkness."

"What nonsense," said Agatha, coming back from the bathroom where she had been for quite some time.

Athena wondered whether the old historian had actually wandered off to inspect and perhaps pilfer things from the house, but she had more important things to worry about.

"What do you know?" Athena asked Agatha. "I mean about what's going on with the house. Have you figured it out?"

"I have a theory," Agatha said, raising an eyebrow.

"Tell us then," Marjie urged.

"It's not exactly a fully thought-out theory, more of an inkling. And I don't trust inklings," said Agatha.

"Whatever it is, please tell us," Athena said.

"Very well," Agatha said, pouring herself another cup of tea from the pot that Marjie was perennially replenishing. "This house is not just a house."

"No, it's a home," said Marjie.

"More than that," Agatha continued sternly. "Your ancestors were involved in very powerful magic, my dear."

It was the first time that Agatha had referred to Athena with such a term of endearment. Athena almost fell off her seat.

"What do you mean?" Marjie asked. "The Thorn magic is powerful. We all know that."

"But it's not just powerful," Agatha replied. Looking around, she reached out to touch one of the wood panels of the old manor house, which quivered ever so slightly.

"I've always felt as if this house was alive," said Athena, "like a friend. Sometimes, a very helpful one." She thought back to the time when Thorn Manor had conveniently created her balcony and stairs leading down to the garden when she had wanted to escape into another realm – a misguided adventure to get away from her mother. She felt another pang of guilt; after all she'd put Rosemary through...now she had somehow abandoned her in the darkness of the realm of the dead.

"Yes, it is rather lively," said Agatha, giving the panel a tap. "But not only that. The magic goes deep, deeper than anything else I've encountered. It's not just old magic; it's ancient magic."

"Oh..." said Athena, feeling as if puzzle pieces were starting to form in her mind. Not quite fitting together yet, but swirling around as if they might just find the right place to slot in.

"This is a special house," Marjie interjected. "But I don't see what this has to do with anything. It's rather hot in here, though," she added, fanning herself. "Do you think the house has gone and lit the fire for us?"

"I don't think so," said Athena. "It wouldn't need to." She gestured towards the window where bright sunlight streamed into the garden. The once icy garden was now glowing and blooming as if it were full summer.

"This isn't good at all," Agatha muttered. "Time and the seasons are connected."

"You're saying the reason the house is shuddering is something to do with time being disrupted and the seasons?" Athena asked.

"That's as far as I've gotten with my theory," Agatha said glumly. She gulped back her tea and then set the cup down rather quickly, making a sharp clink. "We're going to need a lot of power if we're going to do anything about this," she declared.

"What are you suggesting?" Marjie asked, her mouth curling into a slight smile.

"Well, as much as I hate to say it," Agatha said bitterly, "this might be an occasion that calls for community involvement."

She uttered the words as if they were dirty, filthy, something she disapproved of.

Marjie beamed. "What a fabulous idea. I'll get my phone tree." She bustled off to the telephone.

Agatha stood up, raising an eyebrow slowly. "Well, I'll be off, then."

"What do you mean?" Athena asked. "I thought you said this called for community involvement."

"Exactly," replied Agatha. "But that doesn't mean that I have to be here."

"You're part of this community, you know," Athena insisted.

"No," said Agatha defiantly. "Not if I have any choice in the matter."

"Oh, come on," said Athena. "The last thing we need is for you to disappear now. You might not enjoy being around people all that much, but you must like it at least a little bit. You spend all that time at the pub."

"They have good sherry...and peppermint schnapps."

"Well, so do we," said Athena. "There's a nice bottle of sherry in the pantry."

Agatha raised an eyebrow slowly. "Now you're talking!"

Athena couldn't help but smile a little. "Alright, sit tight. We're going to need your wisdom."

"For what it's worth," Agatha said, with a sigh. She folded her arms and sat back down on the kitchen chair. "Make that a double sherry."

Thirty-Six

"Aren't you going to help me get out of here?" Rosemary asked, looking at the three goddesses. They glanced at each other.

Cerridwen reached down towards Rosemary in the cauldron, offering her an arm. But just then, the cauldron itself began to crack.

"Oh no, it's happening again," sighed the Morrigan.

The Cailleach tutted.

"You mean, this isn't a normal part of the process?"

"There's nothing normal about transformation," said the Morrigan. "But this...this is much bigger."

The cauldron cracked further, and the goddesses stumbled back.

The solid foundation beneath Rosemary gave way, and once again, she was falling – though, no longer through the magical working, but through time and space itself.

Her heart leapt to her throat as panic took over.

I'm going to die here, and nobody will truly know what happened. Maybe this is the end of everything anyway...

But Athena...

Rosemary reached out once more, her mind grasping at anything but finding only the void itself.

However, the void seemed somehow conscious.

"Who are you?" Rosemary asked, desperately seeking answers. "What are you? What am I doing here? What's going on?"

The void did not answer in words, but it shimmered with awareness of her and her concern, offering a consoling warmth. Rosemary took it to mean "you are a part of everything, and I am all that is."

"Then stop me from falling," said Rosemary.

Rosemary found herself suspended in mid-air. The void flowed around her, observing her and whispering strange words she couldn't comprehend – words that sounded like magic.

"What's happening?" Rosemary asked. "I just need to get back to my daughter, to get home safely. I need both of us to be okay."

"The collapse of time is upon us," echoed the void. "There's no safety here."

"Then why are you trying to reassure me?" Rosemary yelled. "Show me! Show me what's happening. Show me what I can do to help."

In her desperation, she cried out, and the void trembled as her terror tore through it. Rosemary felt herself spiralling into another time entirely, returning to herself, shrinking down into her own cells, into her very DNA. She travelled back through her lineage until she came to rest on the ground.

She was flung across the vastness of time and space. As she spiralled through the swirling mists, her surroundings transformed from a realm of magical energy to an ancient forest. The air grew thick with the scent of moss and damp earth.

With a jolt, Rosemary landed on the ground, her limbs tangled and disoriented. She staggered to her feet. As her eyes adjusted to the dim light filtering through the dense canopy, she realised she was no longer in the present.

It seemed she was sitting in a small mud hut with a thatched roof. Inside sat a woman – small yet powerful. Her long, tangled hair glistened with stones, shells, and bones knotted into it.

"You," she said, looking at Rosemary.

"Where am I?" Rosemary asked, bewildered. "What's happening?"

"You are the future," the woman answered. "And to you, I am the past."

She raised her hand. The air shimmered around them. Rosemary became aware that this woman was indeed her ancestor, from long before Granny, long even before Elzarie Thorn.

"Time has a way of repeating itself, doesn't it?" said the woman.

Rosemary nodded, somehow understanding, even though the ancestor spoke in what was clearly a different tongue. "It was I who sought the gift of the gods," she whispered.

The hut and everything else around Rosemary dissolved. She found herself watching as her ancestor, much younger now, embarked on a quest through the depths of darkness, descending into the Underworld on the Samhain, descending into the Underworld by Winter Solstice.

Through many dangers, she fought until she reached a sacred goddess, Cerridwen. She pleaded for protection, for her village was under threat. They had endured a long, cold winter the previous year, followed by a dry summer in which the crops could not grow. Famine and diseases plagued them.

"I need the power, the understanding, the wisdom. I need the magic to protect my village," she implored.

The goddess, with a stern expression, responded, "And I need somebody to stir my cauldron."

It was just like the story of Taliesin, performed as part of the Yule fair.

The woman did as she was asked and continued to tend to Cerridwen's cauldron, stirring it for what felt like an eternity until it finally had cracked. Wisdom sprang from the cracks, three drops of awen, landing like ambrosia on her tongue.

In that moment, Rosemary could tell an awakening had taken place. The ancestor had understood then, the deep interconnectedness of time and space, the inherent presence and essence within all things.

She awakened in her hut, possessing strong connections to the seasons and the fabric of time itself. She restored the disrupted balance, bringing a bountiful harvest the following year. And thus, passed down through her ancestral line, that power, sometimes referred to as automancy – the power to connect profoundly with a thing itself, to understand its essence and purpose, while maintaining harmony within the universe, avoiding utter chaos in its wake.

"You have shown me where our power comes from," Rosemary acknowledged, looking back across the hut at the ancestor. "But how does this help me? Where will it get me? Understanding is no good if it cannot be used for anything."

The ancestor faded away before her eyes and Rosemary was returned to the void.

She screamed, releasing her anguish – the potential loss of her own life, her daughter, and everything she held dear in the imminent demise of the world she knew.

"Someone has disturbed the balance," the ancestor's voice said. "It is your duty to restore it."

Rosemary took a deep breath. "This is just like that stupid prophecy," she muttered, staring out at the infinite void once again, feeling no wiser.

Thirty-Seven

The mayor, His Majestic Excellency Ferg, was the first to arrive following Marjie's phone tree activities. He didn't come empty-handed; in fact, he came with an entire entourage, carrying many cases and boxes full of magical implements. Athena had no idea what he planned to do with them all.

"It's simply not proper," said Ferg. "This is winter; we should be having wintry weather. None of this ridiculous summerishness. Everything's out of balance. Today I saw a duck making eyes at a squirrel!"

Athena shot him a concerned look.

"Exactly," said Ferg. "For some reason, this house"—he looked around sternly—"is the epicentre of the disturbance. We must contain it, or perhaps demolish it."

Athena was mortified at the suggestion.

"Nonsense," said Marjie, crossing her arms. "It's not the house's fault, and destroying it would only make matters worse."

"She's right," said Agatha Twigg from her rather regal position. She was raised up high on a pile of cushions on a large armchair in the centre of the living room, with a tray of sherry and peppermint schnapps, as she'd requested. "We must be careful of the house," she said.

"I can feel it trying to hold on," said Marjie.

"If only we had the four elemental crones," said Agatha. "None of this would ever have happened."

Athena gave a guilty shrug. She couldn't help but worry that it was her doing. Leading her mother into the Underworld and somehow giving their power to the Oak King may have had some effect. The skirmish, or perhaps all-out war, waging between him and the Holly King must have something to do with all this. And the summer god had been determined to lead them there. Something was definitely wrong with his story, even though he'd seemed like a perfectly nice guy to begin with.

"It's funny, or perhaps not funny at all," said Neve, who had just arrived after Ferg's entourage. "Only a few days ago we were preoccupied with trying to figure out what was causing a handful of deaths."

"Winter-related deaths," said Athena.

Neve shrugged. "There must be some connection, you're right. That's what I've been thinking about, but I can't figure out exactly what it is."

"I think it's part of the ongoing battle between those gods," said Athena. "I wish they would just sort it out and have a cup of tea."

"It's bigger than that, I guess," Agatha said sternly. "This is no mere battle of gods. It goes deeper."

Athena felt a chill, despite the unseasonably warm weather they were having. "Do you think the Holly King went about murdering people, and then the Oak King retaliated by taking away the winter?"

"It's possible," said Agatha, "but he shouldn't be able to do that; it goes against the very laws of nature itself."

"Then why even bother to fight about the seasons?" Athena asked. "Haven't the Oak and Holly Kings been fighting for millennia?"

"Tensions hold us all together," said Agatha. "It is through the fight that we learn who we are."

"It's a great metaphor," said Athena. "But I'd rather not be in a state of global collapse, personally."

"Wouldn't we all, dear," said Marjie, patting Athena on the shoulder.

Liam arrived next, bringing with him a whole group of rather hairy individuals. Athena gave him a questioning look.

"We were having a meeting," Liam explained.

"A werewolf meeting?" Athena asked.

"Well, more of a gathering, a get-together if you will."

"Don't tell me there were drumming circles." Athena grinned at him.

"I cannot confirm or deny," said Liam with a smirk.

"Over there," said Agatha, pointing out to the garden.

Liam gave her an unimpressed look. "You're sending us outside like dogs?"

"I'm merely conducting this operation much like a maestro would conduct an orchestra," said Agatha. "I'm not sure exactly how werewolf magic works, but I have a theory that it relates to nature. And so, I would like for you to guard the perimeter."

"Guard the perimeter?" said Liam. "Are you worried about some sort of attack from people? Other beings?"

Agatha shrugged. "I suspect that whoever's orchestrated this situation may have allies."

Liam and Athena looked at each other quizzically, and then Liam shrugged. "Right then." He strode across the room and out through the French doors to the lawn, leading his werewolf buddies with him.

Una, Ashwin, and Tamsyn arrived shortly after, bearing what appeared to be the entire contents of Marjie's tea shop. They set up tables in the lounge and garden, laden with baked goods and pots of tea.

Agatha wrinkled her nose. "I'm conducting a serious operation here, not a tea party!"

"People need to eat," Marjie argued.

"Oh very well. More sherry, please," Agatha said, raising her finger.

Athena sighed and passed her the bottle.

The group of children who'd arrived with Una, Ashwin, and Tamsin, ran around the garden playing games with the werewolves.

"Are you sure it's safe?" said Agatha. "The children, I mean."

"Liam wouldn't hurt a fly," said Athena. "And besides, he told me how the werewolf community is really blossoming lately now that he's shared all of his special protective enchantments with his friends, meaning they're no longer a danger to society. They're not going to accidentally scratch and infect the children, don't worry."

Agatha harrumphed. "Very well," she said.

"What exactly is this operation you're directing?" Athena asked as she watched Ferg and his entourage assembling the mysterious magical paraphernalia in the corner of the living room next to the bed where Rosemary still lay sleeping, at least in her physical form, while in spirit she was still somewhere in the depths of the Underworld. Athena tried to push away her dreadful fear for her mother's safety. Fear would only addle her brain and make it difficult to focus when she needed all her wits about her right now.

"That is yet to be determined," said Agatha. "But we have strength in numbers. Once everyone arrives..." She looked at her watch, which was, of course, a large silver pocket watch, and then tapped it. "Blasted thing's stopped. I'm sure I wound it this morning."

Athena had an uneasy sensation. She glanced at the grandfather clock in the corner of the room, only to see that it, too, had stopped ticking.

"Odd," she said.

"What is it?" Marjie asked.

"Something is wrong with all the clocks," said Athena.

"It's as I suspected," said Agatha Twigg. "Time. I told you it was time, and I was right."

"You're always right, aren't you, Agatha?" said Marjie, rolling her eyes.

Athena couldn't help but giggle. Marjie was normally the most tolerant person on Earth, with a few exceptions involving past werewolf prejudices no longer to be discussed. However, she was clearly at her wit's end when it came to Agatha Twigg. And yet, something about the combination of the two older women was incredibly amusing.

Over the next twenty minutes, it seemed the whole town had descended on Thorn Manor. Papa Jack and his family were there, along with Covvey and Athena's school friends, who were happy to see her but also bereft to hear about Elise. Even Ursula, Rowan, and Hazel arrived with their house truck.

"You were on the phone tree too?" Athena asked, puzzled.

"Phone tree?" said Rowan, questioning.

"No, I'm afraid we're uninvited," said Hazel with a delightful cackle. "Something very strange is going on. At first, I thought Ursula's powers had gone haywire because everything was bursting into life in the dead of winter. Then we figured it was something else, something stronger that had gone dreadfully wrong, and we thought we'd come and ask you about it."

"I wish I knew more," said Athena. She felt as if she'd recounted the story of her recent failed journey so many times now that she couldn't bear to do it again. Instead, Marjie took the new guests aside as they arrived and gave them the basics while Athena went upstairs for a little nap.

Of course, she couldn't sleep. Her mind was racing. But as an introvert, it was a welcome relief not to have to talk to anyone for a few minutes. She closed her eyes and tried again to reach out to Rosemary, or Elise, or anyone – even Burk, who she'd never once made any kind of telepathic connection with and doubted whether she could, considering that he was undead and perhaps didn't have the same kind of psychic brainwaves as living people.

Nothing worked. She rolled over onto her front and buried her face in the pillow. *It's no time to give up hope*, as Marjie had said. After a few deep breaths, a couple of attempts at calming spells, and a swig of several of Una's nerve tonics suitable for those with fae heritage, she felt a little better. Athena dragged herself to the bathroom to have a quick shower, washing away some of the emotional dregs from the roller coaster of the past day or so, which felt more like a lifetime. She emerged more determined than ever to get her mother back – and Elise, only if she would consent to such a thing.

"Put her out of your mind, dear," said Marjie as Athena made her way back to her room, clearly looking bereft at she met Marjie on the landing with a tea tray with a pot of her favourite strawberry and cream tea.

"I don't know how to," said Athena.

"People have to live their own lives," said Marjie. "As much as we might despair at their choices."

"But it's not right," said Athena. "She's lost to the darkness. I wish I could have done more to save her."

Marjie gave Athena a stern look. "Wasn't that what she accused you of doing, trying to save her all the time?"

Athena sighed deeply. "Yes. What else am I supposed to do?"

"Well, in my experience of being a chronic rescuer," said Marjie, "when all else fails, I have a cup of tea and I centre myself."

Athena smiled slightly despite the heaviness of the situation. "I think I might just do that," she said gratefully, accepting the tea tray.

By the time she made her way back downstairs, the entire town seemed to have gathered, even the Flarguans and several teachers from

233

Myrtlewood Academy. Burk's family were nowhere in sight. Then again, it was the middle of the day, and a very summery day at that.

Sherry was there, seeming to offer several additional bottles of her namesake beverage to Agatha Twigg, something Athena was slightly relieved about, having almost been drunk dry already. Amazingly, Agatha seemed completely sober. Athena briefly wondered whether she had a totally different metabolism through which sweet alcohol was merely fuel to her.

"There are a lot of magical people in this room," said Marjie as Athena approached.

"Hopefully it will help," said Athena.

Marjie gave her a warm hug. "Feeling a little better?"

"Slightly," said Athena. "Given the circumstances, I'm doing wonderfully."

"That's the spirit, dear," said Marjie.

"What are we going to do?"

"Agatha has a theory," said Marjie, drawing out the word into a kind of verbal eye-roll.

"And the theory is?" Athena prompted.

"Why don't you ask her yourself?" said Agatha grumpily.

"Okay, then. What is your theory, Agatha?" Athena asked as politely as possible.

"It's actually not much of a theory," Agatha conceded. "We need power, and the most powerful thing in town, aside from perhaps this house, is all of us combined."

Athena looked around the room. All of the teachers she knew from school were there, along with quite a few of the oldest students and many other magical people. Van-loads of druids had pulled up to support and were now mingling with the locals outside on the lawn.

"You're right," said Athena. "There's a lot of power in this room. But what do we do with the power in this situation?"

"I think the house is somehow connected to time and deep ancient magic – your family's magic."

"Automancy," said Mr Aventurine, Athena's heavily bearded teacher who'd shown up with a van load of others from the school. "That's right. Of course. That explains it."

Athena shook her head. "Explains what?"

"What we need to do is combine our collective powers," said Agatha. "And then you"—she pointed her bony finger angling at Athena's head—"young girl, you must commune with the house."

"Commune with the house?" asked Athena.

"With the season," corrected Agatha. "Commune with winter."

"Sounds rather abstract," Athena said.

"Indeed," said Dr Ceres, Athena's astrology teacher. "Perhaps it would help for you to think of it in terms of the planets. Saturn is the lord of time and often connected to winter."

"I'm not sure I'm qualified to give Saturn a call," said Athena. "Besides, that sounds terrifying."

Just then, the house shook and the teacups trembled in their saucers on the tables nearby.

Marjie shook her head. "This is all wrong."

"What are you talking about?" Agatha asked.

"The atmosphere," said Marjie. "It's far too much like a

summer tea party. If we want to invoke the spirit of winter, then we must decorate for it."

With several waves of her arms, wreaths of holly appeared around the room. She picked up a teaspoon and pointed it at seemingly random places. Enormous snowflakes burst into the air and hung there, glistening.

Athena watched transfixed as Marjie transformed the summer atmosphere into something much more akin to Yule. Something was definitely different about Marjie. She was more confident and much more powerful, even in her usual kinds of food-related magic.

Moments later, Marjie stood over the tea table holding two teaspoons this time and somehow managed to transmute several cakes into a convincing-looking yule log and a bunch of figgy puddings.

"Amazing," said Athena.

Agatha shook her head. "Trivial is what it is."

Athena shot her such a bitter look that Agatha recoiled. "What I mean is you should be focusing on the working," Agatha continued. "It must start." She tapped her pocket watch, which still didn't appear to be moving. "Time is of the essence."

The house trembled again.

Agatha cupped her hands around her mouth and her voice boomed out across the grounds. The Myrtlewood village people, who were assembled, all stood to attention as she commanded them to hold hands around the perimeter of the lawn and circle the house.

"Room for one more?" said a voice at Athena's side. She

turned to see Nesta there, holding a still-glowing and gorgeous cherubic baby.

"I told you to stay home," said Neve, her voice laden with worry.

"Something told me I needed to be here though," Nesta replied, giving her wife a peck on the cheek.

"There is no time for kisses!" Agatha said. "Everyone take your places."

"You stay in here," Neve told Nesta.

"I don't think it's much safer," Athena muttered under her breath, but it was too late. Nesta took a seat next to Marjie on the couch, who immediately began swaddling the baby and cooing.

"Right," Agatha said. "I have constructed a chant. The purpose of which is to concentrate everyone's attention on the matter at hand. *Father Time and Mother Winter. Come to us at our hour of need.*"

And so the chant began, a low murmur that rang out across Thorn Manor.

"Now, close your eyes and concentrate," Agatha said to Athena, who did as she was told.

Thirty-Eight

Athena tried to concentrate, as Agatha had instructed, but something seemed wrong. She looked out through the window. The citizens of Myrtlewood were gathered outside Thorn Manor with joined hands, reciting the chant.

"Now, we must do the same," said Agatha. "Join in with the chant."

Just then, a loud knock resounded from the door.

Marjie and Athena looked at each other. "More recruits?" said Marjie hopefully.

"No time, so we must continue," said Agatha.

"Wait!" A loud voice interrupted them. It was the Arch Magistrate herself, entering the living room. She looked around. "What is this chaos?" she asked.

"Err...What are you doing here?" Athena said rather brusquely.

The Arch Magistrate raised an eyebrow. "For your information, some of my agents were in your little township investigating a series of mysterious magical deaths. They notified me of the most uncouth disturbance in the weather. I decided to make my way here forthwith to see what all the fuss was about."

"Okay," said Athena. "So you're here to help us?"

"Help you with what exactly? Tell me, what is the meaning of this? You Thorns seem to always be getting yourselves into trouble."

"It's not our fault," said Athena, though she wasn't entirely convinced by her own words. "It's something to do with the Oak and Holly Kings, we think, disrupting the seasons."

"This is most irregular," said the Arch Magistrate. "However, there's no time for complaining. I will be back presently with reinforcements."

She disappeared in a puff of purple smoke, leaving behind the distinct scent of lavender.

Athena sighed in relief that she wasn't being arrested, because it would be rather inconvenient timing. However, before they could resume the magical working as conducted by Agatha, more new arrivals graced Thorn Manor with their presence. Dain pranced in, with Finnegan and Cedric in tow.

"Let me guess," said Athena. "You heard there was some kind of magical disturbance and you're here to help."

Dain raised a finger and then, after a moment of considering Athena's words, he merely nodded. "Where do you want us?"

"Make another circle around the perimeter," said Agatha.

"There's only three of them," said Athena.

Agatha pointed outside, where an enormous troop of fae

soldiers dressed for very cold weather indeed had assembled on the lawn in tight formation.

"How did you know?" Athena asked Dain.

"My mother knows far too much for her own good," said Dain. "We brought some fae magic with us. It should resemble winter, or near enough to it in this world, alright?"

"Thanks. I really appreciate it," said Athena.

"You can thank us later," said Finnegan. "Let's go, Pops." He grabbed Dain by the sleeve and they trooped back outside to join the fun.

Athena sighed. "This is all quite a lot for one day. And we're only just getting started. Any more uninvited guests?"

"Actually," said a calm and wavery voice, "we thought we would come to help too. My name is Ariadne..." Athena turned to see none other than the Oak King's disciples, dressed in bright yellow. She hadn't met them herself, but she recalled Rosemary's vivid and hilarious description.

Athena narrowed her eyes at them. "Why would you want to help?"

"The Children of the Sun seek harmony," said Ariadne, who was clearly the leader of the bright-yellow dressed group. "We understand now that the seasons must be restored to their proper balance."

"We don't have time to dilly dally. Outside with you!" Agatha ordered.

Athena had an uneasy feeling as she watched the Children of the Sun wander out through the French doors. "Maybe they should stay inside and we can keep an eye on them so that they don't cause any trouble, or they could just go away altogether."

"We don't have any time to dawdle," Agatha said as the house trembled again, as if in agreement with her words.

"That's the problem," Athena said, glancing towards the stuck grandfather clock. "Okay, fine. Let's get on with it."

Just then, the Arch Magistrate reappeared in front of them, surrounded by a circle of MIB agents and witching authority figures, including cousin Elamina.

Each agent seemed to be paired with none other than members of the Bloodstone Society, including Geneviève herself, who sneered at Athena.

Athena gasped in outrage. "What on earth are you doing?"

"They want to help, dear cousin," said Elamina, who was dressed in a silver pant suit, with her white blonde hair quaffed back. "And quite frankly, you need all the help you can get right now."

"How can they possibly help?" Athena asked.

"Look," Elamina said, "whatever you think about the Bloodstone Society, they are experts in ancient magic, which is what this is, or at least this is definitely a disturbance in something incredibly ancient."

"But they'll sabotage us," Athena protested.

"Why would we do that?" said Geneviève.

"We don't want the world to end any more than you do. It would make our quest for power fruitless and much less fun," said Despina.

Geneviève shot her a disapproving look.

Athena sighed and gave her cousin a warning look. "If you really think they can help, it's your job to make sure they don't get up to any mischief."

"Oh, don't worry," said Elamina. "I've already enchanted them for the next twenty-four hours. They can do nothing but what I have approved. It's quite hefty magic to wield and mostly illegal."

"But I have approved it," said the Arch Magistrate. "Now, everyone assemble on the lawn."

"*I* am running this operation," said Agatha haughtily.

"Very well. Where do you want us?" asked the Arch Magistrate.

Athena jolted in surprise as Agatha directed the leader of the witching world, along with a gaggle of their sworn enemies, out to the lawn.

Athena shook her head in bewilderment as MIB agents opened large umbrellas to shield the vampires among the Bloodstones from the sun.

They headed outside in single-file where they collided with none other than the Children of the Sun.

Athena couldn't tell if it was by accident or design, but Geneviève's foot stuck out at an odd angle in front of Ariadne. The chaos unfolded as if in slow motion. The yellow-clad follower of the Oak King cried out as she tripped and spun as she tumbled to the ground. Her satchel was flung into the air, opening and sending wintry magic spiralling out onto the lawn.

"What's this?" Ferg asked. "You came prepared!"

"Let us take a closer look at that," said the Arch Magistrate, raising an eyebrow.

Moments later, MIB agents stood over the scene with clipboards and then whispered in the Arch Magistrate's ear. "Oh, I see..."

"We don't have time for this right now," Agatha bellowed from the house.

"What is it?" said Athena, approaching the disturbance.

"It seems these strangely dressed hippies are the ones responsible for the wintery deaths in Myrtlewood," said the Arch Magistrate.

Athena sighed deeply. "Really?"

"My agents recognise their signature," the Arch Magistrate explained.

"We're a bit busy at the moment," said Athena. "Can you arrest them later?"

"No!" cried Ariadne, holding her arms up. She began to weave a complex spell like a spiderweb of light in the air in front of her. "We must protect the Great King's wishes. We are here to disrupt you!"

"We do not have time for this," said Agatha sternly.

"Indeed," agreed the Arch Magistrate. With a nod of her head, a large dome of energy emerged, wrapping around the Children of the Sun and trapping them in what appeared to be a stainless steel prison. "We'll deal with them later."

"Thank you," said Athena with a sigh. "Now what?" She turned back to Agatha.

"Now, my dear, you must commune with the spirit of winter."

"Why me?"

"Because you are the most connected with this magic in this house, which is also connected with whatever is going on here."

"Okay," Athena agreed.

At Agatha's direction, the chanting started up again, making a waterfall of sound as it rushed through, from the fae guards who'd only learned the words just now, bringing their own particular flavour of wintry magic, through to the townspeople of Myrtlewood and their werewolf and druid acquaintances, alongside the Arch Magistrate, her agents, and their sworn enemies, the Bloodstone Society, as they all took part in the magical ritual.

"Take a seat, dear," said Marjie, pushing a nearby chair underneath Athena with a wave of her hand.

Athena did as she was told.

In the inner sanctum of Thorn Manor's living room, she, Marjie, Agatha Twigg, and Nesta all joined in on the chant.

Athena closed her eyes and did her best to relax and focus, connecting with the magic of winter: the cold, the storms, and what she knew of the Cailleach and the Holly King themselves.

This was not energy to be trifled with; winter was a powerful force, a time of scarcity, of turning inwards, hardship for many, but also a time for peace and rest for the earth itself.

She could feel the earth beneath, now stripped of its snowy blanket, aching for rest. She could sense the imbalance and the dire consequences that would be reaped if that balance wasn't restored.

She could also sense the great power among them: the fae, the witches and druids and other magical folk, the amplification provided by Rowan's newfound power to amplify the forces around him, and something even stronger, much closer by. She looked up; the baby in Neve's arms was glowing even brighter. The miracle child's magic was a force so incredible that Athena, who had been in the presence of quite a few gods, shivered in awe.

She inhaled deeply, drawing the power into herself. As she did, the house began to shake in spite of, or perhaps because of, all the magic, its beams groaning under the weight of all the power.

It's not safe in here...

"Get out!" Athena cried, flinging her arms wide. With a big burst of her magic, she sent those closest to her spinning out through the French doors and onto the lawn as the windows of Thorn Manor cracked and then smashed. The wood groaned in its joints and then, too, began to splinter, snap, crack, and then disintegrate before her very eyes. The house itself collapsed on top of Athena, who ducked, protected only by a bubble of her own magic.

As the dust cleared, a great vortex emerged right in front of Athena, its dark insides resembling what she thought a black hole might look like. And yet her intuition told her there was only one way through this.

She took another deep breath and stepped towards the vortex, feeling its pull. She allowed it to suck her right inside and down into its depths, into the unknown, silently willing that it would lead her back to her mother.

Thirty-Nine

Perseus Burk wasted no time, moving as quickly as his vampire strength could carry him. He was considerably faster than any vehicle, and he swiftly returned to his imposing family castle. He interrupted his parents, who were engrossed in a heated fencing duel in the ballroom.

"What is it, son?" said Azalea with a somewhat disapproving look as Burk came within an inch of her blade.

"It's time," he said to Charles. "I need to know how to get to the Underworld."

Azalea smiled, a glint of delight in her eyes. "This is for your human, isn't it? You intend a rescue mission?"

Burk kept his expression as grim as possible, as he tried to impress upon his parents the gravity of the situation. Yet, they both beamed back at him as if he had proposed a trip to the seaside.

"This is serious," he said. "Rosemary is in terrible danger."

"How exciting," Azalea replied, brushing a bit of lint from Burk's collar.

"Thrilling!" said Charles. "But you don't mean the actual Underworld, do you?"

"I'm afraid so," Burk replied. "You've told me before that there's some kind of door."

"Ah," said Charles, his expression becoming more serious.

Azalea looked at him quizzically. "You mean you're going to hell? How poetic!"

Charles stiffened. "The door is guarded most fiercely by the inner depths of the Vampire Council."

"I'm willing to risk it," Burk said. "I have to. I can't just leave Rosemary down there." His parents exchanged a glance before looking back at him.

"It would be very dangerous," Azalea warned.

"Almost certainly," Charles agreed. "We're not entirely immortal, you know. You're risking life and limb, and even after-life. Besides, even if we make it past the council guards, there's no guarantee we would survive the Underworld, let alone return."

Burk nodded. "I know. There's no other way. I have to go." He pressed his lips into a fine line as he waited with anticipation for his parents' disapproval. "Wait a minute. You said 'we.' Would you come with me?"

Charles raised his sword in the air. "Sounds like a rollicking adventure!"

Azalea crowed with laughter. "Of course we'll come with you. After all, what's eternal life without a bit of risk?"

Burk eyed them uncertainly, unsure whether they would make

good and useful companions or if their 'help' would only get in his way.

However, after weighing the situation for a mere five seconds – time that seemed far too long for him despite his millennia on the planet – he decided it would be more work to try to stop his parents from helping than to just let them.

"Alright," Burk said. "There's no time to spare."

"Shall we take the Bentley, dear?" said Azalea.

"Oh no," said Charles. "To do this, we'll need the private jet, or perhaps the submarine. Or both!" He raised a finger in the air triumphantly.

"We have a submarine?" Burk asked.

"Of course we do, darling," Azalea interrupted. "Where do you think we go in the middle of summer for two weeks every year?"

Burk shrugged. "I've always been too scared to ask."

Charles and Azalea looked at each other adoringly. Before they could launch into any further affections, Burk moved towards the door.

"I hope you know where we're going," he called out to his father over his shoulder.

"I have a vague idea," Charles replied. "And no doubt we'll figure it out along the way."

They quickly prepared, packing their bags and dressing in suitable clothing, which Azalea assured them was to be clad entirely black leather. Burk felt somewhat uncomfortable in his tight shiny pants, but again, he didn't have the time to waste arguing with his mother, who had very specific opinions about attire.

"Don't worry, I have outfit changes in here," she said, patting an enormous suitcase.

"That is a rather large trunk you have, my love," said Charles with a grin.

"I beg your pardon," said Azalea.

"But it's not as large as mine." Charles returned momentarily with an even larger suitcase, which he trundled into the living room.

"Trapdoor, I think," said Charles. They made their way to the square of floor normally hidden beneath an enormous Turkish rug.

Azalea tapped the floor in a precise rhythm, and the floor gave way below them, sending them down into the labyrinthine tunnels beneath the castle where Charles liked to hoard his gold in a most dragon-like fashion. Azalea preferred banks, mostly because she enjoyed awkward social interactions with the people who worked in them.

Navigating between several piles of gold while Azalea made disapproving noises about the mess, they found themselves on the underground part of their private runway, standing in front of the family jet.

They quickly boarded and launched the plane faster than any human could have, protected from the sun by extra thick UV-resistant glass.

Within half an hour, they were flying somewhere over the Atlantic Ocean.

"Are you sure this is the right way?" Burk asked.

"Why do you keep asking me that?" Charles replied from the cockpit. "I've assured you that I'm not sure of anything."

"That's not very reassuring," Burk said.

Charles shrugged. "If we knew exactly what we were doing, it wouldn't be an adventure."

Burk sighed and reclined on a chaise lounge, for of course, the interior of the plane was quite as luxurious as Azalea's private parlour happened to be, given that she had them both decorated at the same time when she'd developed a proclivity for gold velvet.

As the plane began to descend, Burk asked, "Are you sure this is right?"

"Stop asking that," Charles said as they hurtled down towards the ocean.

An island came into view. It was rather small and likely uninhabited. Burk felt some relief as they neared, when he noticed a long, flat space that could serve as a runway.

"Tally ho!" Charles called, before making an abrupt but skilled landing. "Now, to the submarine."

Azalea raised an eyebrow and Burk shrugged, resigned as he was to go along with his father's bizarre adventure scheme.

The submarine, it turned out, was a former World War II vessel that had been artfully and lavishly, and possibly somewhat tastelessly, decorated with a copious amount of gold, presumably in the same era as the parlour and the jet.

Burk shook his head in wonderment, trying to stop himself from thinking about Rosemary and the imminent danger she no-doubt faced. He'd been trying to avoid thinking about her in order to preserve his sanity, although he couldn't help but wonder about her reaction to this entirely ludicrous situation.

Catching his unintentional glance, Azalea winked. "When you get her back, be sure to take the sub for a spin sometime."

Despite the circumstances, Burk couldn't help but smile, vowing again to himself that he would indeed get Rosemary back. He looked forward to the day he could enjoy watching her wonder and amusement over the absurd decor.

"So, explain again," said Burk as the submarine descended deeper and deeper into the ocean. "Why a submarine? And where exactly are we going?"

Charles, who was observing the surroundings through the viewing screens as Azalea navigated the vessel, chuckled lightly. "Always so many questions, son," he said, grinning.

"Well, it's not an ordinary day when I find myself completely dressed in black leather, reclining on a gold velvet sofa in a submarine, deep below the Atlantic Ocean," Burk retorted.

"Doesn't it sound fun?" Azalea chimed in. "Are you having fun?"

"Of course not," Burk snapped back. "How could I have fun when Rosemary is in imminent danger?"

"That's the point," said Charles. "It really gets the blood pumping – danger." Sensing perhaps that her son was at the end of his tether, Azalea nudged Charles, whose expression became more sombre.

"Okay, Perseus," he began, "here's the thing. You know about the underground labyrinth tunnels? The ones that vampires use regularly?"

"Of course I do. I use them myself quite often."

Charles nodded. "Well, they go a lot further than most people think."

Burk was startled. "You mean the tunnels go all the way under the ocean?"

"Of course they do, dear," Azalea interjected.

"Only the Council keeps it very secret," said Charles. "We wouldn't want day-walkers running amok."

"No, we couldn't have that," said Burk, glaring at his rather "amok" parents. "I take it that the entrance is somewhere around here then?"

"That's right, as far as I know," Charles said. "I've never been there myself. I've always thought I might take a trip..."

"It sounds so endearing, doesn't it?" said Azalea. "The realm of the dead!"

"So romantic," Burk said cynically.

"It would have taken us a lot longer," said Charles. "But we could have gotten there directly from Myrtlewood without having to go by air or sea."

"I appreciate taking the shorter route," Burk conceded, "but do you think we'll be able to get through?"

"Oh, that's a question, isn't it?" said Charles.

"You mean you've never been down here at all?"

"It wouldn't be an adventure if I had, would it?" Charles replied.

Burk sighed.

"Fear not, my boy," said Azalea, "it's going to be a rollicking time, as your father said, and we'll get your human back in no time."

It wasn't long before the submarine docked at a deep-sea port. The two sets of doors opened and closed in turn, allowing the vampires to exit. Not needing to breathe air meant that they could simply walk along the bottom of the ocean, weighed down with special backpacks that Azalea had prepared earlier, which Burk assumed contained costume changes.

"It's around here somewhere," Charles mumbled, peering into the ocean depths. "Aha!" He held up a hand and pointed to what looked like an innocuous enough boulder on the sea floor. As they watched the deep-sea fish swim past producing strange glowing lights, he helped his parents move the boulder. They clambered into a tunnel, quickly sealing themselves in by putting the boulder back in place.

All around them were pathways leading in different directions.

"This way," said Charles, leading them with vampire speed down one of the tunnels – the largest one.

They were so deep in the earth now that Burk experienced a strange sensation. Vampires were not affected by the same kind of pressure as a human body would be. Coming down here would have been impossible for most mortals without a huge amount of technological intervention or perhaps magical support.

"Surely nobody comes this far out?" said Burk.

"You'd be surprised," Azalea replied just as vampire guards appeared, clad in rather old-fashioned capes. Charles and Azalea quickly subdued them, leaving them seemingly unconscious on the floor.

"What are they guarding?" Burk asked.

"The gateway, of course," said Charles. "We can't have people wandering willy-nilly into the Underworld now, can we?"

Burk frowned. "Do you think people would just casually wander into the deepest ocean? What's down there that's worth protecting?"

"Secrets, of course," whispered Azalea. "And I fear that these guards have alerted the Council. You must be quick, dearest. Through this way. Charles and I will create...a distraction, won't we?" She grinned playfully at her husband.

"Just leave me out of it," said Burk. He thanked his parents for their help and then got out of eyeshot as quickly as possible.

He hurried along the tunnel, delving deeper and deeper into the earth.

There was very little lighting and then none at all. Even with his vampire sight, which allowed him to see reasonably well in the dark, it was hard to make out what lay ahead of him. The darkness here was different, almost as if it consumed everything it came into contact with. But he had no time to worry about that.

As quickly as he could, he moved along the tunnel until he came to a large, ornate door, flanked by flaming torches of an undoubtedly magical nature, given they were producing bright purple fire.

The door, at least twelve feet tall, seemed to be engraved with some kind of story. Burk had no time to study it. However, he did his best to capture it with his photographic memory so that he could return to what appeared to be a tale of vampire origins at a later date.

He tried to open the door, straining against it, but nothing happened. He stood back, breathless, though he didn't really need to breathe at all.

"I've got to get through," he muttered to himself.

He hammered against the door. "Let me through!" he cried, although he wasn't sure if he was speaking to the door itself or some more ancient magical power.

As if in answer to his command, or perhaps in response to the small blood sacrifice he'd inadvertently made through hitting the door with his fists, a knocker appeared, manifesting out of the air in front of him. It was a black, grotesque gargoyle, holding onto a ring about the size of a large pumpkin.

He grasped the handle, though it burned him to do so, and knocked three times.

The doors began to crack open, revealing what lay beyond.

With a sense of awe, Burk found himself standing on the precipice of the Underworld.

Forty

R osemary struggled against the oppressive darkness.
She could not speak.

No sound here was possible.

Cocooned in the void, as she was, the absence of sensation
was so extreme that she struggled to discern where she ended
and the outside began. It felt as if an eternity had passed, and
perhaps everything had been lost. She didn't know whether the
world had ended or simply continued to unfurl without her,
while she remained trapped in an endless cycle of darkness and
longing.

But she was more determined than ever to escape, to return to
Athena and Burk, though even her memories of them seemed to
be fading, becoming fainter, more distant, as if the void was
devouring her mind.

Perhaps she could not speak, but some magic surely must be
unspeakable...she had no voice, but she could still think, and

beyond the panic of her racing thoughts, she could listen to intuition.

Sometimes you just have to go through. Cerridwen's voice floated, ethereal, through her mind.

Rosemary was unsure if it was a memory dislodged from her degrading psyche or if the goddess was communicating with her on some deeper level.

Go through? Rosemary wondered. *Do you mean to turn myself inside out?*

Her own thoughts faded into the void as if they too were being consumed by the nothingness.

Then, with her last ray of hope, she began to push, to struggle, to fight.

The void clamped down on her like a vice.

Rosemary wanted to surrender, to give up.

She was exhausted, and as far as she'd come, she felt as if she had nothing left to give. But something – perhaps intuition, perhaps ancestral wisdom, perhaps the goddesses themselves – urged her to keep going just like when she was walking around Myrtlewood, putting one foot in front of the other.

Work with the tensions, came whispered guidance from within.

Rosemary let go of the fight. She needed to work *with* the powerful forces, not against them.

The void itself was unfathomable, but there were tense forces, present within Rosemary herself.

The inner and the outer reflect. Elzarie Thorn's voice echoed in her mind.

As her ancestor had once told her to do, Rosemary began to

work more deliberately with the tensions, reaching into the darkness for her own taut inner feelings and pulling them towards her. It felt like she was seizing the reins of a horse, directing her own fate.

Suddenly, there was a cry, and something heavy fell from above, landing on her. It cast her out of the void, and she tumbled to the ground.

Something hard fell on top of her.

Instinct took over, and Rosemary began to curse. "Get your feckin' arse off me!"

As relieved as she was to be out of the void, she now needed to defend herself against this new assailant, whatever it was.

"Rosemary?"

"Burk?"

"Thank goodness I found you," his familiar voice said. "It felt like I was falling forever. I just had you in my mind..."

"And how the hell did you get here?" Rosemary asked, both pleased and suddenly angry.

"I guess...this," he began, but his words seemed to fail him.

"You've known about a way into the Underworld all this time, and you didn't tell me?"

"Well, not exactly. There were rumours. But mortals couldn't possibly travel this way. I'm here in my physical form, you see, and—"

"Oh, never mind. We can argue about it later," said Rosemary. "We've got to find Athena and get out of here. As soon as we can."

"Athena's home," said Burk. "She's back at Thorn Manor."

"So it's just me who's lost then?" Rosemary asked, feeling rather put out.

"Something like that."

"What about Elise?" Rosemary asked.

"I'll let Athena tell you about that," Burk replied.

"It feels like this whole mission was pointless," Rosemary grumbled.

"Why would you say a thing like that?" Another voice chimed in, jolly and cheerful. A light shone in the darkness, illuminating both of them as they sat on the rocky earth.

As Rosemary's eyes adjusted, she recognised the figure before her – it was the Oak King, huge and resplendent in garments made of sunflowers and oak leaves.

"What's going on?" Rosemary asked suspiciously as the earth trembled beneath them.

"It is all as I planned," said the Oak King, a note of triumph in his voice. "The great unravelling has begun. We will have an eternal paradise."

"What are you talking about?" Rosemary retorted. "Was this really your plan? Did you want to create total chaos and destroy the earth?"

The Oak King laughed his jolly laugh. "No, not destroy the Earth. Rebuild the earth in my image, where there will be no suffering. A place where people can simply revel in the lavishness of summer. A place without the bane of winter!"

"Uhh...did it not occur to you that it's a terrible thing to do?" Rosemary asked. "Winter is a season, just like the others...We need all seasons. Wait a minute. It was you wasn't it? You went around killing those people in Myrtlewood and set it up so that we'd blame your brother and let you use our magic!"

"Don't be ridiculous," said the Oak King. "Of course the deaths were caused by the winter gods."

Rosemary glared at him.

The Oak King belted out a laugh. "Oh well, I suppose the ruse is up, but I did need your magic in order to get the upper hand, you see. It's all for the greater good. Your family has the fabled awen. It runs strong through your bloodline and it was essential to my plan, you'll understand."

"I don't take kindly to being treated as an ingredient," Rosemary grumbled. She might be tiny and powerless compared to this god, but after going through so much already, she felt stronger in herself than ever, and instead of her usual rambling she was saying exactly what she thought. "And like I said before, your plan is terrible."

The Oak King laughed again and then broke into a jaunty tune.

Oh summer of warmth, hear my joyous refrain,
Dancing with the flowers over the endless golden grain,
Through the hills and the verdant, emerald plain,
An ode to a summer, in my reign, shall always remain.

Rivers under my watch run free, glisten under the sun,
In my world, winter's chill is outdone,
Laughter and merriment have only begun,
Under my watchful eye, the jovial one.

. . .

No frost to mar, no winter to blight,
  Just fields of gold bathed in gentle light,
  My domain, a testament to summer's might,
  Where I reign supreme with an eternal right.

Rosemary stared in awe and horror. The Oak King was so proud of his awful plan to disrupt the seasons he was practically crowing about it.

"You've done it then," Rosemary said, a note of defeat in her voice. "What about the Holly King?"

"He's been taken care of," the Oak King smugly stated.

"I most certainly have not!" a booming voice echoed. Rosemary turned towards the voice, and in the distance, she could make out a figure, hunched and restrained. It was the Holly King, who surely should be at his strongest at this time of year, defeated and bound.

"You've been plotting this for millennia," Rosemary said. "Why now? Why would you do this?"

"Ah, the people of the Earth called out to me," the Oak King said, dramatically sighing and placing a hand on his brow. "And I, like a faithful golden God, answered them. They wanted only success and goodness. They desired to win all the time."

"All light and no shadow," interjected a stern and powerful voice. Cerridwen was there, standing behind Rosemary. "You know no good will come from this."

"I beg to disagree," said the Oak King. "Only good will come from this."

"He's been corrupted," the Morrigan stated, stepping forward.

"Of course he has," replied the Cailleach. "Just as humanity is corrupted, just as men – predominantly men and also some women – seek more power at the expense of the whole, just as they ignore their own shadows, so too has Diggly leaned too far into the light."

"Diggly?" said Rosemary, amused.

The Oak King blushed bright red. "It's a perfectly good name!"

A bright light appeared above them. As Rosemary looked up, it appeared as though the sun was shining down. The golden orb began descending towards them.

"Here it is, the eternal summer!" cried the Oak King.

"No!" said Rosemary. "This is not how it goes. Time is unravelling...I saw the Three Fates. They said—"

"They have the old paradigm!" the Oak King cried. "I, as the new all-powerful god – one God – shall rise and rule over all. It will be a wonderful and benevolent dictatorship."

"I don't think so," Rosemary countered.

"But see, I command the sun and the light of the universe." He waved his hand towards the golden glow.

"I don't think that is what you think it is," the Cailleach chimed in.

"You silly old woman! What would you know?" the Oak King retorted.

"There it is," Morrigan quipped. "The patriarchy, right there."

"It's time," Cerridwen announced. "Summon the old ones."

The sound of a drumbeat echoed in the distance, growing closer and closer through the darkness.

"No!" cried the Oak King. "This is not the time for the old. This is the time for the new. The time for success! The beginning of eternal summer!"

Rosemary looked towards the glowing ball of light. She felt herself fading, but as she recognised her daughter's face her energy rejuvenated.

Athena glided down in the golden ball of her own magic, towards her mother, wrapping her magic around Rosemary, fortifying her.

"No, this can't be!" the Oak King bellowed. "You are not the Sun..."

"I'm the daughter," said Athena. "And you shouldn't have messed with our magic. It is old, learned and used with respect for time itself."

Thunder and lightning crashed through the Underworld skies.

The Three Fates appeared in the clouds above, enormous and bearing down upon them. "He who seeks the unravelling of the known world does not understand its true nature," the three entities spoke together as one.

"Now," Cerridwen said, "it is time to restore the balance."

"You cannot fight me, for I have all the power!" cried the Oak King. "I have taken what is rightfully mine."

"No," Rosemary countered, "it's not yours at all."

"I have the power of the sun itself – of light, of success, of gold." Sunlight beamed out from him, shaking the very foundations of the Underworld.

"He shouldn't do that in here," the Cailleach said. "It's improper. The Underworld isn't supposed to be exposed to sunlight."

"Ah!" said the Oak King. "But this is how the world, as you know it, ends and the new world forms. I believe in utopia!" he crowed as the sound of drums grew louder and louder.

Suddenly, Rosemary realised they were no longer a small group of enormous gods, comparatively tiny witches, and a vampire. Many more deities surrounded them – the old gods and newer ones, Brigid and Mabon and Belamus, along with others that she did not recognise.

"Let's sort him out!" the Cailleach cried. She glanced at Rosemary and Athena. "Would you lend a hand? I feel that your magic will be of great use."

"I don't understand why our magic makes any difference at all in the presence of gods," said Rosemary.

Cerridwen turned to them. "Magic is not just about power, it is always more complex. Imagine a meal with no salt or spice."

"Now you're talking Mum's language," said Athena.

Rosemary nodded. "You mean it's some kind of ingredient useful in small doses. I can understand that."

"Like a puzzle or a complicated lock with lots of little parts to unlock," said Athena. "But why us?"

"Time connects all the realms," Cerridwen explained. "And that balance has been destabilised. Your ancestral magic is potent, as is your connection to the physical realms."

"The other realms..." said Athena. "What about the Dreamrealm?"

"That, too, would be a useful ingredient," the Cailleach said, and then laughed her dry cosmic chuckle.

"I wonder if Awa can help too," Athena suggested.

"She said she might, but she can't come here," said Rosemary as she felt her power draining away, going into the pool of energy summoned by the gods.

"She couldn't before," said Athena, "but the realms are destabilised, and so are the protective barriers between them. I managed to get back, didn't I? Maybe Awa can too."

Rosemary nodded. She was weakening, but whatever the gods were doing didn't seem to be working yet. "I'll call to her."

"Save your strength," said Athena, looking worried. She closed her eyes and Rosemary was sure she was using her fae powers as best she could to communicate with the Dreamweaver.

Moments, later, a shimmer appeared in the air and then so did Awa. "What's happening?" she asked in confusion. "I was just in the Dreamrealm and there was some kind of earthquake. Now I'm...wait, I'm really here, aren't I? This is the Underworld!"

"Yippee!" said Veila, somersaulting in the air next to the Dreamweaver. "I've always wondered what it's like down here."

"I'm afraid so," said Rosemary weakly, not sure how much longer she could hold on. Being separated from her physical form was taking its toll and Cerridwen continued to draw on her magic, into the cacophony of power that was being summoned and used on the Oak King.

"But how is this possible?" Awa asked. "Are those...gods?!"

"Yes, they are," said Athena. "I assume the reason you could get here is something to do with the fabric of time unwinding. The realms are colliding. I was able to come here in my physical form. We wouldn't have called you if it wasn't necessary. No idea how we're going to get out, but at this point we all need to lend out power so that there are actually worlds to get back to!"

Awa stood, baffled for a moment, and then quickly adjusted. "How can I help?"

"Send your power towards them," said Athena.

The Dreamweaver focused on the gathered deities nearby, and began sending forth wave after wave of misty purple magic.

Rosemary felt herself fading. Intuitively she knew her physical body was growing weary without its connection to her spirit. Maybe this was the end for her.

Cerridwen turned back from the circle and looked towards her. "My dear, have I taken too much from you?"

"It's okay," said Rosemary, her voice faint. "Just promise...if I die here, promise me that Athena and Burk will get back safely."

"Not going to happen," said Athena.

"No!" Burk protested. "I'll go back and turn you into a vampire if that's what it takes to save your life."

"I feel like this is something I should have a say in," Rosemary interjected, "and maybe a good long think about, too."

"There's no time," Burk retorted. "Send me back to Rosemary's body. I must save her."

Cerridwen shook her head. "Time has already decided your fates, but I can give you some restorative energy. It will keep you going for a little while."

Rosemary gratefully accepted the energy from the goddess, feeling it revive her, though for how long, she wasn't sure. She hated the idea that her fate was decided. It felt so wrong, and so final. "But there's free will," Rosemary muttered, "and chaos. I've met them. Look, they're up there, all chanting together."

"Why *are* they chanting?" Athena asked. "They better be helping too!"

"We must restore the balance," Cerridwen said. "Let us join hands."

Rosemary gulped. The last thing she expected to do was join hands with a goddess. She found herself holding both Athena's and Cerridwen's hands. Awa joined in too. The goddess's was enormous, and Rosemary's hand barely covered a finger. However, she had much more important things to think about at that particular moment than feeling incredibly incy wincy.

The chanting intensified.

The Oak King cried out, and a great burst of sunlight burned through them all.

Burk yelped and fell back. Rosemary let go of the hands she was holding and clutched him. He sizzled in her arms.

"You were going to save me," she said. "You'd better not die on me now."

"The light was brighter than a thousand suns," said Burk, gasping as his skin continued to burn away. "How is it that you're still alive?"

Rosemary looked around. "Athena is cloaked in magic. And I'm not really here. Not in my physical body."

"But you are. I can feel you," said Burk. "You're real..." He was muttering incoherently now. Rosemary felt her own energy fading away.

Forty-One

"No," said Athena, looking down to where Rosemary and Burk lay. "Neither of you are going to die today."

Closing her eyes, she felt herself ascending, soaring back, up, up, up, right to Thorn Manor, which was, of course, in chaos and ruin – back to the room where her mother's physical form lay in the bed that had been pushed safely out of the way of the wreckage of their former house when Athena had magically flung everyone outside.

Athena connected her energy with Rosemary's form, drawing a line of energy between it and her spirit, attempting to pull her mother back. She poured all of her energy into creating a strong channel between Rosemary and her physical form, where she lay with Burk in the Underworld.

A chant rang out from Athena; where the words came from, she had no idea. But she could feel the ancestors guiding her, the ancient magic coursing through her veins, her own familial connection forging a strong bond that spanned all the realms creating an enormous circle linking back to her mother.

Before she knew it, the bond solidified, and Athena slid back into the Underworld.

Coughing and spluttering, she found herself lying next to Rosemary, who was now glowing as her magic rose within her.

Athena could have sworn she heard a baby laugh in pure blissful joy.

Back at Thorn Manor, Neve and Nesta sat on the grass, tears running down their cheeks as they stared at the crumpled house. Their baby, Gwyn, began to glow brighter and brighter. The miracle child, born in the magic of summer, knowingly or not, giggled, sending her own miraculous power towards the Underworld.

In the inky depths of the Underworld, the glow from the distant chanting gods and goddesses shone like an oasis. Cold whispers slithered through the air, coiling around Athena's senses, the sounds echoing like an otherworldly choir.

Suddenly, a figure emerged from the surrounding darkness, her silhouette wreathed in a subtle glowing radiance. Adorned in an ethereal gown of black stone roses that reached up to shroud her face, she moved with a grace that was equal parts powerful and melancholy.

"Elise," Athena breathed, her voice a strained whisper.

The Underworld seemed to tremble under the weight of the divine chorus, the hymn of the gods and goddesses resonating through this forsaken realm. The cryptic ritual they were performing was beyond Athena's comprehension; maybe they needed more power, even that of a fledgeling goddess who Athena used to know.

Elise stared back at Athena, her gaze sharp with fury.

"What are you doing here?" Elise asked, trembling in anger. "I sent you back. You don't belong here!"

A sudden pang shot through Athena, as though an invisible hand was constricting her heart. She reached towards her aching heart. "I'm trying to help."

"No!" Elise shouted. "Go back. You belong to the light."

"Elise," said Athena. "So do you."

Elise scowled at her. "Not anymore. If that fool the Oak King can teach us anything it's that darkness has its place. The light cannot triumph over the darkness!"

"Neither can the darkness," retorted Athena. "Now I understand. That was the prophecy. It wasn't about me at all. It was about you, Elise."

Elise turned away. "I don't care about any ridiculous prophecy. Can't you see that this is where I belong? I belong to the darkness now." The statement wasn't triumphant, it was laced with a bitter acceptance, as though she was admitting defeat to an invisible enemy.

"No," Athena said. "You belong to yourself. You always have. You're not a sidekick. You're not a supporting role. You have your own story, and you get to decide. It's not my job to rescue you, but you can't restore balance to the world by snuffing out all the light. Both are just as necessary."

"I don't even know how to connect to the light anymore,"

Elise confessed, the stone roses of her gown shimmering in deep red luminescence.

"Of course you do," Athena reassured her. "It's part of who you are. You've always been so full of light. So full of hope. You've been my beacon in the darkness."

A heavy silence hung between them, as tangible as the shadows clinging to the corners of the Underworld.

"I'm not yours anymore."

"Maybe you never were," Athena admitted. "But I love you. And you said that you..."

"I do." Elise's words hung in the air, a heavy fog of acknowledgement and loss.

"Marjie said we need hope."

"Marjie..." said Elise, as if only vaguely recalling. Her eyes took on a far-off look, as if she was trying to see through the veil of the past.

Athena clutched her chest as though her heart might burst. "And Fleur..." she added. "Gods she misses you too... so much. Oh, and Neve and Nesta had their baby. She's glowing. It's amazing."

"A miracle," Elise agreed, her voice a hollow whisper.

Athena took a deep breath. "Why are you here?"

"They need me," said Elise, pointing to the gathered gods and goddesses. "They need my help to destroy the Oak King."

Athena's heart sank. "Is that really what has to happen?" she asked, her voice full of uncertainty. "Does that mean we won't have summer anymore?"

"I don't know," said Elise. "But all the gods must join, and I am one of them now."

She didn't say it proudly, and Athena wondered if it was what she really wanted at all. "Do what you have to do."

With a pained expression, Elise stepped into the circle of gods and goddesses. Their chant swelled around the writhing Oak King, their voices harmonising in a spectral melody.

A sudden eruption of light burst out, blinding in its intensity. Athena and Rosemary shielded Burk from the searing brightness.

As the radiance subsided, Elise turned her gaze back towards Athena. "You're right," she conceded. "We need both the darkness and the light."

At her words, a wave of beautiful energy descended, pure and radiant, filled with the melodious sounds of a baby's laughter. This was not a harsh light, but a soothing one, like the first rays of dawn after a long and arduous night.

Athena watched as, with a hesitant hand, Elise reached up towards the light. It seemed to respond to her, drifting towards her and starting to chip away at the stone roses encasing her. As they fell away, they transformed into living blooms. "Both are needed to restore balance."

Athena watched in silent awe as the girl she loved transcended further from her previous mortal existence, evolving into a goddess of not just darkness, but of light as well.

The revelation was as breath-taking as it was overwhelming.

Athena's legs gave way beneath her, and she crumpled to the cold stone floor of the Underworld, her strength finally giving out under the weight of her emotions.

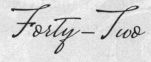

Forty-Two

"Athena!" Rosemary called out as the thunderous chanting grew lounder.

"I'm okay," said Athena. "I don't know about Burk, though."

Rosemary reached for him but didn't dare touch the smouldering body. "He came in so gallantly to try and save me. He helped too...he pulled me out of the endless void. I'm grateful for that. I just kind of wish he never tried..."

"There's not much point in wishing for things you can't have. We've got to make the best of the situation," said Athena sadly.

"You're right," Rosemary conceded. She searched deep inside for something that could help restore her wonderful and devilishly handsome vampire boyfriend's life. His skin had been badly burned by the light. Digging deep inside herself, Rosemary reached out to the earth, drawing from its dark, healing energies. She tapped into the restorative restfulness of the swamps and the soothing, gentle nature of water.

"Please let this work," she murmured as she wove a healing spell of deep, bluish-purple magic around Burk. It shimmered over him and sunk into his skin, and deeper into his very bones.

"Transformation means never being the same," she whispered, hoping he would survive this.

Burk was completely still, but at least he hadn't burst into dust. Rosemary held him, and his eyes opened.

"What have you done?" he asked.

"I don't know," Rosemary admitted. "But I'm hoping I just saved your life."

He grinned at her. "I feel different."

"You've always been a bit different," said Rosemary.

"In my family, I'm the normal one."

Rosemary laughed, just as the ground shook and cracked around them.

An explosion erupted, sending the gods and goddesses flying back.

All was dark as a thick cloud of dust shrouded their vision.

As it began to clear, a subtle glow became visible.

"He's gone!" cried Cerridwen. "The Oak King is no more!"

"Gone? Gone where?" Rosemary looked across to see a crater in the centre of where they'd all stood. "It's not every day you get to see a god destroyed. I thought they were immortal."

"Sometimes the archetypes get corrupted," said Cerridwen. "The Oak King spent too long listening to egotistical human beings. He thought he could do a better job of ruling the world. But it could not be."

"What about summer?" asked Athena. "Does this mean we won't have it again?"

The Morrigan threw back her head and laughed. "Oh, child, summer will come. It always does!" She rolled her eyes.

"Look!" Cailleach gestured to the centre of the crater, where a tiny golden acorn sat.

"This has happened before, hasn't it?" said Athena, narrowing her eyes.

Cerridwen gave her a knowing look. "Why, of course it has. Destruction and rebirth are part of the natural cycles and processes. You humans have the bizarre impression that Myth is something that's never happened, when really, it's something that is always happening, inside and out. It is the very process of the evolution of the universe."

"Though not every year is this dramatic," said Cailleach. "Usually they just have a quick tug-o-war over the seasons and call it quits. I could have done with a nice, restful winter, myself."

"Couldn't we all?!" agreed Rosemary.

"The acorn will grow into an oak. And we also have other gods of the sun, as you know," said Cerridwen. "Do not fear, balance will be restored."

Rosemary looked up to see the three Fates fading into the clouds, the sky darkening into inky blackness. "Do we get to go home now?" she asked Athena.

"About that," said Athena. "I might have slightly destroyed the house."

"What?"

"It's a long story," said Athena. "But I'm sure somebody in Myrtlewood will make us a cup of tea."

"Indeed," said Cerridwen, "tea is exactly what we need! I would invite you all over to my house, but I have a feeling you have something else to attend to back at home."

With that, she threw out her arms. A glowing orb encased Rosemary, Athena, and Burk, while another one covered Awa and Veila.

"Fare thee well," said Cerridwen as she sent them hurtling up through the sky, the two orbs heading in different directions. Rosemary and Athena waved as Awa and Veila disappeared, no doubt back to the Dreamrealm.

Burk seemed to have recovered rather well. In fact, he too was glowing a little bit, or perhaps shimmering.

"Don't tell me he's turned into one of those vampires that sparkle!" Athena whispered, and Rosemary couldn't help but laugh.

Up above them, a light appeared and they found themselves emerging up through it and onto the lawn of Thorn Manor. Rosemary felt an unnerving pulling sensation as if she was being vacuumed up. Her amorphous sense of self was sucked into her physical body, reminding her distinctly of what a glass of water must feel like while being drunk. She spluttered and coughed and blinked into the bright daylight like a new-born rebelling against exposure to the world for the first time.

To Rosemary's surprise, they were surrounded by most of the town, plus a gaggle of druids, fae, the magical authorities, and the Bloodstone Society. This last group puzzled Rosemary and made her slightly anxious, until Elamina explained that they'd helped.

She stared agog at Thorn Manor, which no longer seemed to exist. There was merely wreckage in its place.

"After all that..." Rosemary collapsed on the lawn, overcome by waves of grief for her beautiful family home.

"There, there," said Marjie, who ever resourceful, somehow had produced tea. "Drink up," she advised. "You'll need your strength."

Rosemary sat up and gave Marjie a sort of half-hug. They sat on the lawn together with Neve, Nesta and baby Gwyn, Papa Jack, Dain, Liam, Sherry, and all of their other friends, having a slightly mournful tea party.

Just then, the sky clouded over and snowflakes began to fall.

Athena shivered. "At least winter's coming back."

"Right it is!" said Agatha, emerging from the house, or what remained of the wreckage of it.

"Were you in there the whole time?" Rosemary asked.

"You were!" said Agatha. "We only just dragged you out to the lawn moments ago. Then a sinkhole opened up, Athena and Burk appeared, and you seemed to come back to yourself."

"It was all very bizarre," said Nesta, clutching her glowing baby, who giggled and cooed despite being far too young to do so – if one is to believe developmental psychologists, at any rate.

Rosemary sighed, guzzling her tea.

"I suppose we'll have to find somewhere else to live," said Athena.

Agatha gave her a knowing look.

"Wait a minute," Athena said, looking at Burk. "You're out here in the sunlight."

Burk, who'd been rather quiet, nodded.

"And you're sparkling," said Rosemary. "I told you not to do that."

277

"I wasn't the one who used magic on me," said Burk. "Apparently, I'm now infused with some of your power...I can be here." He held out his hand as if looking at it for the first time. "I wonder if it'll wear off."

"Transformation," said Rosemary, "never leaves us quite the same, does it?"

There was a creaking sound from the house and a shimmer ran across the ground, sparkling in gold light and bringing with it a glorious wave of hope, warming Rosemary's heart and lifting some of the exhaustion from her soul.

It reminded her of the first time she'd returned to Thorn Manor, almost a year earlier. The dilapidated wreck of a house had stirred to life and restored itself right before her unbelieving eyes, and now that very same magic had stirred again.

The shimmer intensified and so did the creaking. As they all watched in astonishment, Thorn Manor reconstructed itself in a cloud of magical dust.

As it cleared, the house was back, but somehow larger, more impressive than before, and with extra vines on the outside.

"Marvellous!" Rosemary cried.

"Interesting," said Athena. "Is that an extra wing?"

"Ah, perfect!" said Marjie. "I was quite hoping for my own wing."

The three of them looked at each other and then burst into laughter.

"Let's go inside," said Rosemary, "before we all catch a chill."

"Now that is the most sensible thing you've said all year," said Agatha.

They all headed inside for some of Papa Jack's famous restorative hot chocolate.

Epilogue

Perched upon the thatched roof of her cottage, Cerridwen looked out over the edge of existence, her gaze lost in the infinite abyss. The cottage, a quaint little edifice with walls of stone and a chimneystack belching ethereal smoke, was comfortably nestled within the vast expanse of the Underworld.

Cerridwen's ageless, hazel eyes, imbued with wisdom, magic, and a deep understanding of time, took in the cosmic panorama. Her silver hair, a manifestation of the countless epochs she'd experienced, tumbled around her in wild curls, catching the soft light that always prevailed here. She was swathed in an emerald cloak, its fabric shimmering with latent enchantment.

To her left, the Morrigan was as striking and inscrutable as ever. Her raven hair and piercing gaze gave her an aura of unpredictability that was both unnerving and oddly comforting. The Morrigan, ever the life of the party, was shaking a cocktail mixer with an enthusiasm that defied their eerie surroundings.

On Cerridwen's other side, the Cailleach was a figure of silent gravity. Her gaze was as sharp as a winter's morning, her skin creased with the stories of millennia. Her robe, patterned with symbols of ancient knowledge, was as blue and cold as a glacial stream.

"You know," began the Morrigan, pouring the effervescent contents of the mixer into three glasses with a flourish, "this apocalypse was quite unlike the last."

Cerridwen smiled, accepting the proffered cocktail. "Indeed, Morrigan. The ingenuity of mortals never ceases to amaze me. Rosemary and her young one, Athena, showed remarkable courage."

"Ah, the witch and her progeny," the Cailleach mused, her frosty eyes softening as she sipped her drink. "Their resourcefulness is a testament to the human spirit. And Myrtlewood...That town carries more magic in its bones than most realms."

The Morrigan, her crimson lips curling into a smirk, added, "I quite liked their Yule festivities. There's something about mortal celebrations, their joy in the face of darkness. It's...infectious."

Cerridwen took a sip of her cocktail, its taste a vibrant symphony of flavours that mingled the sweet with the tart, just as life so often did. She pondered Morrigan's words, her mind wandering through the labyrinth of time.

"Endings and beginnings," she mused aloud, her voice like the gentle rustle of leaves on an ancient tree. "They are but two sides of the same coin, aren't they? Each end heralds a new beginning, and each beginning inevitably culminates in an end."

The Cailleach nodded, her gaze focused on the swirling cocktail in her hand. "Indeed. It is the nature of all things, including

281

us. We are born from the stories told about us, we grow and change with each retelling, and eventually, we fade when the tales cease. But we are never truly gone, are we?"

"No, we are not," Cerridwen agreed, her eyes twinkling with the wisdom of ages. "We are the threads in the great tapestry of mythology, ever-woven and ever-unravelling. Just as winter gives way to spring, death to rebirth, silence to sound, we are part of an unending cycle of transformation and evolution."

Morrigan chuckled, a sound akin to the rustle of raven wings. "And what a ride it is! From the grandeur of creation myths to the quaint charm of mortal tales. From the dramatic end-of-the-world scenarios to the quiet, magic-filled lives of people like Rosemary and Athena. We've been through it all, haven't we?"

Cerridwen could not help but smile at her friend's words. "Indeed, we have. And through it all, we've changed and grown just as the stories have. As the world spins on its axis, as the stars wheel in the sky, we continue to evolve, ever adapting to the rhythm of existence."

She raised her glass towards the infinite void, her companions following suit. "To endings and beginnings, to the cycle of transformation, to the evolution of stories, and to us."

Their glasses clinked together, a crystalline symphony that echoed through the Underworld, a testament to their shared history and the promise of countless stories yet to unfold.

Cerridwen nodded, her gaze returning to the void. "Yes, it is. And now, with Yule behind us, we might find some quiet. A moment of respite to gather our thoughts, and reflect."

But the Morrigan's smirk widened into a grin. "Or we might

not," she retorted, clinking her glass against theirs. "Peace is so terribly dull, don't you think? I'm ready for the next adventure."

With that, the trio lapsed into a comfortable silence, each lost in her thoughts.

Cerridwen took a moment to let the profundity of their toast settle. The Underworld seemed to hum in agreement, a chorus of echoes that whispered promises of the adventures to come. But, as was often the case when dealing with entities as old and powerful as themselves, profundity could quickly give way to frivolity.

As the echoes of Morrigan's words faded into the void, the three goddesses exchanged glances of anticipation, their laughter replaced by thrilling anticipation. Another chapter in their unending story was about to begin.

A personal message from Iris

Hello my lovelies! Thank you so much for joining me on this wonderful journey through Myrtlewood. This is not the end! Well, it's the end of this book, and the end of the first series as I initially was inspired to write one book for each seasonal festival, but there are plenty more Myrtlewood adventures to come! In fact, I have another one on the way – a new spinoff series packed full of many of your favourite characters: Myrtlewood Crones.

I'm sure there will be more Rosemary and Athena focused books coming in future, too, but while I dream them up, I was inspired to write the Myrtlewood Crones series to honour the amazing matriarchs in my family and the wickedly wonderful crones in my grove and witchy community. I've had a lot of fun so far with this series and I'm sure if you loved Myrtlewood, you'll love this one too! I'm even giving you a sneak peek of the Myrtlewood Crones: The Crone of Midnight Embers. Turn the page to read the first two chapters.

Thank you again for your support. Writing this series has completely changed my life and I'm in the outrageously brilliant position now where I can write full-time and bring you even more magic! Whether you've read my books in Kindle Unlimited, bought the ebook, paperbacks or hardbacks, or been part of my review team, you've contributed to making all of this possible. Thank you from the bottom of my heart. Please do continue to leave ratings and reviews because that always helps writers!

Many blessings,

Iris xx

P.S. You can also subscribe to my Patreon account for new chapters and other writing before it's published as well as real magical content like meditations and spells, and access to my Myrtlewood Discord community. Subscribing supports my writing and other creative work!

For more information, see: www.patreon.com/IrisBeaglehole

Delia

꧁

Delia groaned, rolling over and squinting at the morning light as if it was deliberately trying to cause her personal offence. At first it was only exhaustion, but as she turned her head, the hangover quaked inside her skull with a searing pain. She covered her head and rolled over onto her front, tangling the sheets.

That's when the worst part hit her. "What have I done?"

The entire West End would be talking about her. Her ears were burning; actually, her entire head was burning, due to the physical consequences of drinking one too many smoky whiskey sours after "the event" which may have included an act or two of righteous revenge.

The familiar sound of the approaching Death Star blared out. It was the ringtone Gilly had chosen as a joke after Delia's company had put on that one-woman Star Wars show. Delia felt a pang in her chest. She hadn't seen her daughter, Gillian, for a while. So not only was her head throbbing with pain, her chest heavy with embarrassment, she was also missing her grown-up child with the silly sense of humour.

She wasn't going to answer the phone, not at all. But she did glance at it, just to make sure she wasn't not-answering something important.

Kitty's name flashed up on the screen.

Delia sighed and pressed the green button. "Is it as bad as I think it is?" Delia asked her best friend in the world, Kitty Hatton.

"Oh, Deals! You were a star," Kitty crooned.

"Don't lie."

"I'm serious. The whole town will be talking about you. I bet it'll even make it into the London papers."

Delia groaned again; it was becoming her theme song.

"Don't worry, love," Kitty said reassuringly. "It won't be long until you've processed your emotional hangover."

"And the regular hangover that I seem to have as well."

"Oh yes. It was rather nice whiskey, wasn't it?" said Kitty.

"Thank you for helping me drown my sorrows," Delia said.

"Anytime, darling. You know it will all be worth it. When you think about that awful prick."

"A worthless, pathetic little man," Delia muttered.

"Exactly," said Kitty, "and the look on his face. When you emptied his possessions onto the floor, including his mistress's undergarments, poured his special vanilla vodka all over it, and set it on fire! It was genius."

Delia sighed. "It wasn't the affairs that made me do it."

286

"Of course not, love," said Kitty. "It was far worse than that."

"Actually, the affairs were a welcome distraction," Delia admitted. "When you're married to someone like that for so long you begin to pray he'll leave you alone."

Kitty chortled. "Still, it was embarrassing for him. He likes to think he's an upstanding member of society."

"An upstanding little prick," Delia grumbled. "How dare he force me out of my own business?"

"It was very wrong of him," Kitty said, consoling her. "But what are you going to do now?"

"Hide under the biggest rock I can find," said Delia. "I'm sixty-three years old and far too old for hangovers and shame. What am I supposed to do?"

"Go back into acting," said Kitty. "You were brilliant in theatre."

Delia pushed a painful memory out of her mind before it had time to surface. "I don't have the energy for it."

"Start another business then?"

"Even the thought makes me tired. If I never have to look at another costing spreadsheet again, it'll be too soon."

"Well, take early retirement and sue that bastard for all he's worth."

"I suppose I'll have to," said Delia. "He's taken everything else from me."

"Oh, now, now," said Kitty. "That's not true, you still have your brilliant wits and your brilliant daughter and all your wonderful experience. Maybe Jerry did you a favour. This divorce sets you free. Think of it as a fresh start."

Delia couldn't suppress the wave of bitter anger, bursting

forth from her chest. A beam of sunlight caught her eye, bringing more hangover pain with it. She glared across the room at the curtain that never closed properly in her small temporary rented flat.

All of a sudden flames burst forth.

"Blimey biscuits!" she cried out, dropping the phone. She leapt up from the bed, bracing herself against the crashing boulders that insisted on tormenting her skull. She tore the curtain down and stomped on it, coughing as she waved her hand through the smoke to clear it and opened the window to stop the alarm being set off.

"Delia, Delia!" a small voice cried out.

Delia picked up the phone again. "Sorry," she said to Kitty. "Minor disaster. I think my curtain just spontaneously combusted. What do you think that's about?"

"Faulty wiring," said Kitty matter-of-factly.

"I don't think there's any wiring in the curtain," Delia muttered. "Maybe it was the sunlight. It's quite bright, you know."

"It's winter," said Kitty. "I don't know. Perhaps you have a pyromaniacal ghost. Call in a professional. See what they say."

Delia couldn't help feeling that Kitty was deflecting. "Did you do something? Were you trying to distract me from my woes by setting booby traps around the apartment?"

"Of course not, darling," said Kitty. "Anyway, I'd better go. I have brunch with Roger later." Delia made a cooing noise. "How is Roger?"

"Just as romantic as always, dear. So typical, he's probably going to bring me some plastic flowers again. And a bottle of cheap bubbly."

Delia couldn't help but chuckle; her best friend had been dating quite an unusual character indeed. It was almost as if he didn't understand normal human customs.

"I'll call you later," Kitty said briskly, and hung up the phone.

Delia rolled onto her back, staring at the ceiling.

"This is my life now, is it?" she muttered, before glancing around the room at the only-partially-curtained window, the small cramped-but-modern flat.

It had been the first property that was tolerable that she'd found in a tight rental market, after Jerry's betrayal. At the time, anything would do. Delia had just needed somewhere to stay until the divorce settlement came through.

But now, Delia couldn't stand it for one moment longer.

She pulled on the first items of clothing she could find in her wardrobe, which happened to be the same plain black turtleneck and grey knitted cape with black jeans that she almost always wore. She quickly washed her face, applied her scarlet lipstick, and attacked her mostly grey hair with a brush.

"Strange," she muttered.

Amid the grey and silver and sparse strands of her natural black hair, a distinctive red streak stood out, curling from her roots down past her left shoulder.

"I don't remember getting that drunk that I'd let Kitty dye my hair."

She squinted at herself in the mirror. Despite the hangover which seemed to now be fading fast, she didn't actually look too bad. While her face had just as many wrinkles as it had the day before, there was a new clarity in her complexion, and the dark circles she'd anticipated were hardly there at all.

"One hot crone," she muttered to herself, "ready to kick some ass." And that was absolutely true, and the ass in question Jerry.

Marjie

"Flaming teapots!" Marjie muttered, waving a tea towel over the pot. She glared at the flame, which seemed to shrivel and pop out of existence under her gaze before fizzling out. She risked a glance around the shop, but it was a quiet morning. The early customers had cleared out, which probably meant the fire was spontaneous.

Marjie's tea shop always radiated comfort. Today it smelled of cinnamon and vanilla. Her custom brews and baking filled the shop with a tapestry of spices and herbs. Her latest concoction, a new experimental syrup, was bubbling on the stove, a perplexing blend of rosemary, sage, and dried juniper berries.

She'd been stirring it idly moments before, and had then checked the clock, surprised she'd missed her own morning teatime. Marjie had drifted around the kitchen, half daydreaming, only to be shocked to her senses by a flame, erupting red and lively, dancing atop her new teapot.

291

It startled her because the flame hadn't the decency to be caused by something practical. It had appeared with a whimsical spontaneity. Something magical was stirring, something fiery.

"But why?" she muttered to herself.

Marjie had never been particularly good with fire, herself. Her magical specialty was...well, tea and cake, mostly, and party decorations. She had never considered herself to be a particularly powerful witch, though recently she'd felt more of a boost in her own energy.

She narrowed her eyes at the red teapot. She'd only put it on the bench moments ago, ready to brew herself a fresh pot of English breakfast tea. Now, she wondered whether the innocent looking object was cursed.

No, that wasn't it.

She let her mind relax and tuned into her own intuition, which was definitely her other magical speciality.

This feels...ancient and powerful...It can't be...

Marjie opened her eyes but the feeling of an ancient awakening lingered, and Marjie couldn't help but shiver.

She looked around again, wishing there was someone to talk to about all this, but Rosemary and Athena were busy preparing for a dangerous winter solstice mission and her dear friend Papa Jack was looking after Rosemary's chocolate shop as he often did. She made a note to call in later and bring him his favourite thyme and parmesan scones. But right now, she needed to talk to an expert.

Marjie reached for the phone, her hands still smelling of sage and juniper.

There was only one person knowledgeable enough to indulge her worries: Agatha Twigg, historian and curmudgeon extraordinaire.

"Agatha, it's Marjie," she said into the receiver. "You remember that dream I told you about, the one with the fire and Delia?"

A pause, followed by a gruff affirmation on the other end. Marjie knew that Agatha did remember. She had the memory of an owl. She remembered everything, a fact that made her particularly handy in their shared concern of tracking the ebb and flow of mystical events.

Finally, Agatha grumbled, "What's a crone got to do to enjoy a quiet morning?"

"Agatha, this is serious. I believe something's afoot," Marjie confessed. "My teapot just set itself on fire."

Another pause. An exhaled puff that Marjie could practically hear rolling its eyes. "Tea's supposed to be hot, Marjie."

"Not flaming, Agatha!" retorted Marjie, though she couldn't help but chuckle. Agatha's brand of dry wit was a comforting constant.

Marjie was thankful for the unusually quiet morning. No one would overhear as they speculated, in hushed tones, on the meaning of this sign.

Marjie described the flame, the unexpected thrill of its appearance, the echo of the dream she'd had. Could it be that her intuition was right? The ancient powers that were often dismissed as merely legend were real, and they were finally awakening.

"I told you I've felt different lately," said Marjie.

"Of course you do," Agatha said dismissively. "Your whole life was upturned at Samhain."

"Not just that. It's my magic. Don't tell me you aren't feeling something too."

Agatha grunted noncommittally, an affirmation in disguise. "So what?" she said. "Don't tell me you're suggesting we pay her a visit?"

Marjie took a sharp inhale of breath. Of course, there was one person who knew far more than Agatha about ancient magic such as this, but the one they often referred to without naming her always brought a tingle of fear to Marjie's spine.

The forest witch did not like company.

That only made Marjie want to befriend her even more, though all her attempts so far had failed.

"It's worth a try," said Marjie. "What kind of biscuits should I try to offer her this time?"

Agatha's eyeroll was almost audible as she scoffed.

"What?" said Marjie. "Surely there's some kind of treat that might help to win her over, if only we can figure out what it is."

Agatha chuckled. "Pack the ginger snaps." With a final snort, she hung up.

Marjie stared at the phone, a bitter and tangy taste of anticipation on her tongue. The fire was a sign, a stir in the fabric of their tranquil lives. Something was coming and Marjie was about due for an adventure.

To read more: Order the Crone of Midnight Embers!

P.S. You can also subscribe to my Patreon account for new chapters and other writing before it's published as well as real magical content like meditations and spells, and access to my Myrtlewood Discord community. Subscribing supports my writing and other creative work!

For more information, see: www.patreon.com/IrisBeaglehole

About the Author

Iris Beaglehole

Iris Beaglehole is many peculiar things, a writer, researcher, analyst, druid, witch, parent, and would-be astrologer. She loves tea, cats, herbs, and writing quirky characters.

facebook.com/IrisBeaglehole

x.com/IrisBeaglehole

instagram.com/irisbeaglehole